Additional Praise for *Darling?*

"Delightful . . . Schmidt brilliantly combines comic scenes with moving reminiscences. . . . This collection has so many shining moments—of humor, of heartbreak, of grace—that the reader may find himself wondering: why aren't more stories this good?"
—*Publishers Weekly* (starred review)

"*Darling?* is a luminous, fiercely intelligent collection, filled with a ravenous honesty and sung with a music entirely its own. Richly complex and inventive, these stories are well crafted and exuberant as they turn inside-out all matters of heart and soul. They are also enormously fun to read."   —Fred Leebron, author of *Six Figures* and *Out West*

"Fresh and cracklingly funny takes on modern womanhood."
—*Kirkus Reviews*

"[Schmidt] depicts the frustrations of ordinary relationships with elegance and charm."   —*The Hartford Courant*

"Stunning stories . . . masterfully told. Schmidt's wit is brilliant, her themes provocative, her female characters terribly flawed and wonderfully sympathetic. It's tough to write about love and have anything new to say, but Schmidt does just that."   —GoodBooksLately.com

"Stories like fireflies in the late summer night: exquisite, mysterious, and delightful. Heidi Jon Schmidt has the innocent, imagistic eye of a Katherine Mansfield."   —Tom Paine, author of *Scar Vegas*

"In spite of their missteps and misgivings, Heidi Jon Schmidt's characters continue to search for love and understanding. These stories, like the human condition they expose, are poignant, profound, and very, very funny."   —Hester Kaplan, author of *Kinship Theory* and *The Edge of Marriage*

D0108968

Darling?

STORIES

HEIDI JON SCHMIDT

PICADOR USA

NEW YORK

www.picadorusa.com

Picador® is a U.S. registered trademark and is used by St. Martin's Press
under license from Pan Books Limited.

For information on Picador USA Reading Group Guides, as well as order-
ing, please contact the Trade Marketing department at St. Martin's Press.
Phone: 1-800-221-7945 extension 763
Fax: 212-677-7456
E-mail: trademarketing@stmartins.com

Book design by Michelle McMillian

Frontispiece art courtesy of Corbis Inc.

"Songbirds" was first published in *Epoch*, Winter 2000; "The Funeral Party"
was first published in *Epoch,* Summer 2001; "Wild Rice" was first published
in *Provincetown Arts,* Summer 2001; "Blood Poison" was first published in
Epoch, Fall 2001.

Lines on p. 34 from *Collected Poems in English and French* by Samuel
Beckett. Copyright © 1972 by Samuel Beckett. Used by permission of
Grove/Atlantic.

Library of Congress Cataloging-in-Publication Data

Schmidt, Heidi Jon.
        Darling? / Heidi Jon Schmidt.—1st Picador USA pbk. ed.
            p. cm.
        ISBN 0-312-28178-1 (hc)
        ISBN 0-312-30556-7 (pbk)
        1. United States—Social life and customs—20th century—Fiction.
    I. Title.
    PS3569.C51554 D3IM 2001
    813'.54—dc21   2001031952

First Picador USA Paperback Edition: October 2002

10 9 8 7 6 5 4 3 2 1

This book was written for Marisa Rose.

CONTENTS

Songbirds

We wanted to fly Swissair—Switzerland being neutral, the gods would never dash an airliner full of nice well-tailored Swiss people back to earth in flames. But the connection to Venice wouldn't work and we had to go Lufthansa. Garrett was reading *The Decline of the West*, looking up only to order more scotch from the stewardess, who glanced at me with pity, I thought, for my having got stuck beside him. We don't seem married: he's twenty years older and his general fury shows in his face, while I look helpful and trustworthy, his amanuensis maybe, or his nurse. I had on a black jersey suit, bought for the trip; his corduroys were worn translucent and his elbows came through his sweater. What does it matter to him what the living see? A celestial jury will consider what he's reading and spare him, for the first leg of the flight at least.

As we lined up to debark in Frankfurt, the stewardess flicked a curtain shut between us: I went out one side while Garrett and those behind him were directed to the other. I waited at the foot of the ramp until even the pilot was off, and the sign announcing Flight 172 from Boston flipped to read Flight 433 for Hong Kong, but Garrett never came.

I tried the Venice gate, but no luck and no wonder: he didn't know the time or number of the connecting flight, and who knew if he'd remember the destination? He can get lost in a supermarket—why had I ever let go of his hand? Over the public address system a cruel voice snapped out the departures. *There*, I thought, *you wished him away: Germany will oblige you.* I had him paged, but hearing his name in the heavy accent knew he'd never recognize it, so I ran from gate to gate, up and down the escalators and along the endless conveyor belt between terminals, reaching the Venice gate for the third time to find him leaning beside the metal detector, reading the chapter on "Faustian Physics and the Dogma of Force." When he saw me, he sighed and let the book fall to his side—"I almost gave up," he said. "I didn't know what to do." They'd sent him to a lower floor and he'd gone through one terminal and then another until he stumbled into the right spot. Tears stung my eyes at the thought of him lost and frightened, all alone. I lay my head on his shoulder, kissed his unshaven cheek, looked into his eyes that found only fault with me.

He had been seized, after six years of marriage, with the conviction that I was the wrong woman—he loved me, of course, but every time I took off my clothes he felt a dreadful disappointment. He wouldn't have brought it up, but somehow the night before the trip I'd started complaining that he never tells me anything really important, anything that resides in his deepest heart, that it made me feel lonely, as if I hardly knew him.

"Well, if you really want to know . . . ," he began, and went on at some length, ending by insisting that this was a sacred instinct— awful, yes—but wasn't life *mostly* awful, after all?

"*A sacred instinct!*" I roared. "You said you were a rationalist! I *married* a rationalist! A sacred instinct, I have never heard anything so ridiculous." And on I went, shrieking and sobbing, dripping contempt, begging, suggesting he suffered from some ocular or neurological problem and ought to get help from a professional. All of which only inflamed him, until he declared that of all the women he'd slept with (and the one time he'd tried to count he'd had to give up at three hundred) I was the *least* attractive.

"Worse than the dwarf?"

"Well, the dwarf . . ."

"Worse than the woman who peed in her shoes?"

His eyes narrowed, and he looked ready to slit my throat for the honor of the woman who peed in her shoes, and I started crying again and vowed to become a nudist and stick my revolting self under his nose every day for the rest of his life, though in fact I instantly hid myself like a Muslim and began hanging my head so as not to inflict my ugliness on any innocent passersby. When you marry you take a share in someone else's nightmares; this was something I hadn't known.

Exhausted, disgusted, Garrett sat down to comfort me. There was nothing to worry about, he said, he'd always be loyal. I wanted a child, he would see that I got one. His formal locutions, the Calvinist rectitude I'd always loved, began to unnerve me. Was he taking me to Italy then to find a father for my child? I've never seen a working marriage, how would I know what one looks like? I fastened my seat belt: We were circling down over the fourteenth century, a gilded fantasia of pink marble domes reflected in an Adriatic shimmer, the city encompassing east and west, ancient and modern, exquisite beauties, and tortures . . .

"Venezia," Garrett said. "It takes your breath away."

It's the closest airport to my sister Etta (generally spoken of as *poor Etta*), whose husband works in a box factory near Mestre, and whom one must visit when traveling—else, all alone and away from her family, how would she survive? During the visit one raves on about the food, the wine, the art, the romance . . . lest Etta, who lives among a profusion of in-laws in an industrial valley, fail to realize how lucky she is. (No need to link poor Etta with lucky Etta—one pities or envies her as the occasion requires.) Our parents imagine her in Amalfi—they haven't spoken since their divorce, so neither knows what the other is thinking, and now they always agree. I don't tell them this, as it would drive them mad—like looking in the mirror and seeing the person you most despise. I do hint that Etta's is not *la dolce vita,* but this is taken as malicious and has made me the hapless recipient of bushels of Italian tourist brochures, coffee-table books on Tuscany and Bellagio, a case of Chianti, and gallons of extra virgin olive oil, all meant to help me recognize Etta's great good fortune.

I called her from a pay phone on the airport quay.

"Pronto." She clings to the American accent as if it's her last possession; she will not roll an *r.* She refuses, even by Italy, to be carried away. This is my doing: our parents being transfixed by their own drama, I raised her, and her faults reflect my own. I was emotionally ungainly, throwing myself into things and at people—at my high school graduation, for instance, I leapt into the arms of a beloved teacher and knocked him off the podium. It was embarrassing, and Etta had to study me very carefully to avoid becoming like me. She's made a great success of it—she's perfectly cool and still, a pale flower alone in its vase.

"Etta! *Buongiorno!"*

"Buongiorno?"

"It's me, silly," I said, feeling this was unwelcome news.

"Oh, hi," she said. "You sounded Italian . . . Where are you?"

"Venezia!" Did it come as a surprise? The trip had been planned for weeks, and I'd called her from Frankfurt, too.

"We can't pick you up," she said. "Gino can't get off work." And she'd given up her driver's license long ago—the butcher and bakery

are a block away, and Gino takes her to the *mercato* on Saturdays—
she has no need to drive. So I'd have to come by bus—was that so
far beneath me? It was very suspicious, my flying into Venice when
everyone else saves fifty dollars by getting a cheap charter to Milan
and taking the train. Who did I think I was? Just as Etta is envied
and pitied, I am envied and despised. I seem to be succeeding and
they hate me, while Etta ekes along, suffering but beloved—each one
gets something; it's all fair in the end. I'd driven myself nearly mad
in the mall before we left, trying to find a gift she'd think neither
ostentatious nor stingy, settling on a flowery skirt without noticing it
was the image of one she'd borrowed from me years ago and never
returned. The card might have read, "Here, take, so you won't have
to steal."

Because she was, in essence, a thief. This I mulled bitterly as the
water taxi churned through the lagoon, cocooned in a thick fog; it
felt like succumbing to a dream. A tuft of marsh grass would emerge,
followed by the barber pole mooring that marked each island estate,
then a dock thrust out of pure fog: once a woman in a silk scarf and
sunglasses materialized and stepped regally into the boat. Etta never
wanted anything but what I had—she followed me to college, studied
art like me, moved to Boston where I found her a job in a friend's
gallery (they didn't take her seriously, and paid a pitiable wage), an
apartment (roaches, sad neighborhood, landlady insane), and a boyfriend (another hand-me-down) . . . No, I never gave what she deserved. Meanwhile Garrett bought a painting of mine, then another,
then I was going over to help hang them, then . . . Etta went back to
my mother's, got work as a temp. When I visited she touched my
clothing as if calculating how to get it for herself, and then I walked
into the kitchen and found her copying a drawing of mine line for
line as if she intended to divine my central mystery and make off with
that, too.

I became ruthless. Study music, I told her, and she took up the flute, though she knew that if music were worth anything I would have played. Then I married Garrett without one thought for what might become of her. The night before the wedding I found her reading *A Spinster's Life,* a bestseller from 1940 that had latterly found a niche under the back leg of my bureau. "It seems like something I need to prepare for," she told me. The next week my mother called to say she was taking Etta on a cruise: "I've got to do *something* with her," she said. To Etta she spoke of dancing under the stars and dining at the captain's table as if they would be sipping champagne on a transatlantic steamer instead of going around in Caribbean circles while practicing the merengue with a bunch of retirees.

Gino was the cabin steward; he pulled a rose out of someone's bon voyage bouquet and gave it to Etta before the ship left New York. "Italian men," Mother sighed, reporting back to me. "*They* know what romance is. They never forget how to act toward a woman." And she called to mind a time, on her honeymoon, when a croupier leaned in so his lips just brushed her neck as he slid her chips onto 15 red; the winning number. She's a child, an innocent child—it looks absurd, a grown woman like Etta taking advice from her.

"Don't fall for somebody just because you can't understand what he's saying!" I said, and Etta cast (in the mirror; she was dressing for her trip to visit Gino's parents in Villa Padesi) a contemptuous glance at me—what made me so prim? Had I forgotten that mathematician who blinked like an owl as I declared my adoration, then scratched his head violently with both hands and refused my dinner invitation by explaining that he ate only from the basement vending machines? And what about the dance/philosophy major who wanted to give body to Wittgenstein and refused to acknowledge me in daylight? (This: he crept into my room at night and touched me with such

natural urgency it seemed we were growing into each other like vines.)
Not to mention my lesbian phase . . .

All right, I said. I freely admit it; love is—*I am*—absurd. But this
wasn't love, it was marriage! And marriage, I insisted, is pragmatic,
if unconsciously so. Think of Garrett's general raggedness, his hired
assassin look: marrying him was like buying a pit bull in terms of
keeping the relatives at bay. And a Calvinist pit bull—as long as my
behavior was appropriate he never so much as snarled—it was almost
like having parents. When he proposed, I'd asked how well he could
keep me (traditionally a father's duty and I'd long since taken these
over), and he naturally drove me straight to his attorney, who set out
the family accounts. Yes, yes, of course I loved him and we had all
the mystery of sex between us, but *pragmatism made the marriage!*
What could she say for Gino in the department of utility?

She set down her little palette of rouge and looked at me aghast.
"I love him," she said, with some anxious belligerence. Of course—
he would take her away from us, what more attractive quality is there?
And here I—*I*, pursuer of mangy owls and lonesome cowgirls and
God only knew what else—arrived with a lecture on practicality!

My mother passed by, letting the word *Italia* escape from her
mouth like some garish paper bird. A child, with visions of sugar-
plums dancing . . . in fact she herself hoped to marry again, a feat that
would be much easier with Etta flown off on a magic prosciutto than
sulkily researching spinsterhood in a corner of the living room.

"Gucci, Armani, Versace . . ." she repeated the day Etta returned,
as if these were the names of Etta's lovers instead of the labels on
Gino's gifts. (All available at any airport duty-free shop, noticed a
certain shrew.)

"Ignorance and mystery are *not* the same," I decreed, from my
lofty, married perch. "You love him, then visit him, live with him,

even, but don't rush into anything. You have all the time in the world." Though I'd never seen her willing to do anything for love before; if it only happened once every thirty years she might be right to grab the chance.

"A husband and wife—they change each other, bend each other in strange ways, finally they're alone with each other, alone in the world. Or worse, Etta—alone in Italy!" Here I stood, at the confluence of a great subject and an impressionable mind: I was moved to a grandiloquence unusual even for myself.

"This is not love, it's infatuation," I explained. "It's like—it *is*, something out of a dream, one of those dreams where everything feels so wonderful you never want to wake up . . . but you *do* wake up, you *will* wake up, Etta, and . . ."

"I'm pregnant," she said.

"My God! What are you going to do about it?"

"*Have a baby*, Francine," she said. "That's what I'm going to do about it. And we're getting married," she added, nearly stamping her foot the way she used to when she was tiny and I was trying to get her shirt on over her head. "And I'm going to Italy to live with him. And I'm *happy* about it."

"This is not *Masterpiece Theatre,* I hate to tell you," I said, but was drowned out by my mother's effusion: "I always knew *my* children would live wonderful, exotic lives!"

The Stazione Centrale: buses pulled into their spaces on a broad tarmac, scattering pigeons and passengers alike. I went to the ticket line while Garrett stayed with the bags.

"Due biglietti a Villa Padesi." There, had anyone seen it, how competent I was? The maps, the schedules, the phrase books, and presto, here were two tickets, the lire back in the billfold. *"E . . . scusi . . .*

scusi?" I paged through Berlitz. "When does the—? *Quando parte il prossimo autobus a Villa Padesi?*"

"There is a strike at Villa Padesi," the vendor said, unwilling to humor my Italian any longer.

"But—?" I held up the tickets. He shrugged. Hardly his fault, *he* was working, selling people (a species for which Venetians feel only contempt) just what they asked for. "Refunds in the supervisor's office." And he gestured magisterially in the direction of the longest line in the room.

As I came back to Garrett, an old woman was pressing two coins into his hand.

"Alms," he explained, looking pained, and—reminded we had money enough—said, "Let's just take a cab."

"Oh, why not a coach and four?" I said. "Why not fly the Concorde? Etta despises me already, for God's sake." No, there was a train that went nearly as close, though it stopped half an hour in Mestre. Time enough, I thought, for Garrett to take everything back, tell me he lived by the light of my beauty and his sacred instinct was only a hallucination.

"Garrett, we have to talk," I said as soon as we left the station, though I know men fear the words *We have to talk* more than any other sentence on earth. And my voice was just dripping with estrogen—even I found it repellent.

"There's nothing to talk about," he said. "It's terrible, yes, but talking won't make it any less so. We'll get used to it, that's all." He wasn't born into this era: if indeed there's some lost continent submerged beneath conscious life, he believes that's where it should stay. He fell asleep, with his mouth open, while I looked out at the flat landscape, the factories and green canals . . . *Italia*, indeed.

No one sees anything but through his own prism. I'd painted Etta's portrait for a wedding gift, from a photograph she'd sent home—I thought it captured something regal about her, but it made her cry. "It's wonderful," she said. "You do it so easily; you're such a good artist, Francine. It's just . . . I can't bear it, that I look that way."

Different, that is, from me. Cowardly—not, as I saw her, aloof. She'd crept along behind me all this time, full of jealousy and veneration, too loyal to properly hate me, too angry to do anything else, ready to defend me from my most pernicious enemy, though as it happened that person was herself.

"Isn't it wonderful Etta's so *happy*?" Mother kept saying.

"Happy?" To me she seemed lost, a disembodied voice on the transatlantic phone, repeating her few grains of news—Franco's Christmas pageant, Giorgio's first steps.

"My God, she lives in Italy! Who wouldn't be happy?"

"It's hard for her there," said my father, "though she's *very happy*. He's a nice fellow, even-tempered. . . . They don't have a lot to talk about, but I guess everyone looks for something different from marriage. . . ." (His voice was swelling here as usual when he feels he's teaching me something.) "She needs to get to know some people, find some outlet beside the kids."

"What became of the flute?"

"Oh, she doesn't have time for music. But I was thinking you could get her started as an artist, introduce her to some of your people . . . no end of picturesque scenes over there . . . main thing is she's happy, that's all."

I called her up: "I'm glad to hear you're so happy!"

"Who said *that*?" she asked, in an astringent tone I hadn't heard her use in years. "The last time I talked to Ma I couldn't stop crying, and she said I don't know how lucky I am to live here." She sighed. "She's right, I suppose."

"Why would you suppose that?" I asked, laughing—it felt like our old conversations, where the parents were objects of hilarity and we'd sing a phrase from the radio in the middle of a sentence to underscore a point.

But now her voice went cold: "I know it wouldn't be *your* choice, Francine, but I don't always have to feel just what you do, you know. I'm *happy* here, whether you thought I would be or not."

All of which is to say I had to take the train. A sister who refuses to help her poor (but happy) sibling get a foothold as an artist (a job that can hardly be very difficult if I'm doing it, after all) must be ever conscious of the magic of Italy, and willing if necessary to travel by mule. By the time we arrived in Villa Padesi it was late afternoon, and we shouldered our packs and stepped into the street only to see a horde of Vespas coming at us like winged chain saws. We jumped back, Garrett glaring at me as if he couldn't believe all the trouble marrying me had got him into. I set off doggedly down the narrow street; he can't read a map, he has no choice but to follow.

It was hardly a town, really, just a random postwar sprawl creeping outward into the farmlands through a valley laced over by power lines. At the main crossroad a tobacconist faced a newsstand where huge headlines proclaimed NICO SERA E MORTE! LA NAZIONE LAMENTA. "Who's Nico Sera?" Garrett asked, but I'd never heard of him. "He must have been important here." I heard his name pass like a foreboding among the old men at the *caffè* tables next door. It was October—immense rosemaries bushed out between the iron fences along Via Ponte de Soto, and persimmons glowed in the trees. Women leaning from their windows, airing bed linens, watched us with frank suspicion. We might have been the first tourists Villa Padesi had ever seen.

Every yard was fenced, though, against the threat of intruders. The Basso compound, Gino's parents' house and the block of stuccoed flats for the three brothers, was enclosed by a high brick wall. Inside it was quiet except for the cooing in the dovecote and the *scritch* of a hoe, though I couldn't see through the gate who was working. I rang the bell and after a long time Etta came out with the baby on her hip. Her dark dress blew back against her bones, and she brushed her hair out of her face and looked at me hard, to decide whether I was friend or foe.

"I thought you'd be here an hour ago," she said.

"There's a strike . . . ," I explained, but she didn't accept it—after all, we have the money; if we'd really wanted to see her we could have taken a cab. "I've got to pick Franco up at school, right now or the sisters . . . Would you mind—?" and she handed me the baby, who started to wail immediately as she stalked away down the road.

"We should have stayed in Venice. We could have slept there and come here to visit just as easily," Garrett said.

"Are you kidding? She'd be furious. She's been cooking for us for a week."

"How do we get out of here?" he asked as the gate latch clicked behind us, with the baby still crying, reaching for Etta over my shoulder.

"Bus, I guess," I said, feeling pretty well trapped myself. When my parents visit they hardly leave the compound. "I go to see *Etta*," my mother said, when I asked if she'd seen the Giottos in Padua, fifteen minutes away.

"A pretty sister," Gino said that evening, toasting me. Latin flattery, of course; he was the exact Italian my mother imagined, his magnificent hair springing from a magnificent head, a head full of good humor and hospitable impulses, including a lordly consideration for women and a Talmudic knowledge of cuisine. Beyond that he was inscrutable, and I wondered whether, if Freud had been born here a few hundred miles south of Vienna, we'd study our souls as we do or reflect only on the olive and the grape. I was grateful to be called pretty, though, whatever the reason, and looked over to see if Garrett had taken it in.

"To Italy," he was saying, raising his glass high, even gladder of the compliment than I.

Franco came to the kitchen door, a small serious child with his father's face and his mother's resigned expression—he flung his arms out and announced: *"Entrata la pasta!"* and Etta came behind, flushed and smiling, carrying a huge steaming bowl.

"Con funghi," Gino said. *"Bellissima!"*

"I picked them!" Franco said, taking a mushroom off the top for himself and twisting his finger at his cheek as he ate. *"Buono!"* he said.

I supposed that if Etta intended to poison me she wouldn't feed her kids from the same bowl. She'd tried to be warm, thanking me for the skirt, though it had a ruffle and I could see she'd never wear anything like that now. My own coolness I'd hoped to cover with confessions, telling her all about Garrett's and my troubles, while she looked embarrassed and changed the subject to tomato sauce, of which she had put up forty jars with and without oregano. Now her mood had acidified: she bustled in and out of the kitchen on mysterious but apparently very important errands, looking away from us so we grew nervous and guilty. What had we done? What were we supposed to do? Finally something dropped or slammed in the kitchen, and she yelled, "Gino, *where* is the pasta fork?"

"I don't know," Gino called with humor, as if the question were metaphysical.

"Well, it's got to be somewhere," she responded angrily.

Gino picked up his fork and mine and began to serve. "Imagine," he said, "there was a time before pasta forks . . ."

"It *goes* in the drawer next to the stove," she replied, coming to sit down, and we began piling up compliments like sandbags against a flood: How beautiful was the house, the dinner, how charming the children . . . And the flowers—Etta was so creative, she could make something beautiful out of whatever fell to hand! A dahlia on a dry, gnarled stem, with two fat buds like eyeballs on either side, lolled out of a vase on the mantel; her old music stand cast its scrolled shadow into the corner; and the dinner—the pasta, roast chicken stuffed with whole lemons, fresh rough bread and green olive oil—surely anyone who ate would be changed . . .

"This cookbook, *you* sent it," Gino said to me, "It is our . . . Bible! Etta, she cook like she's lived all her life in Italy."

She fed Giorgio a spoonful of pasta *in brodo.* "Which is lucky," she said finally, "because otherwise they'd *really* despise me."

Franco had rooted through the toy box to find a doll with the red pout and bouffant hair of a Hollywood starlet, and the body—the uncircumsized penis, that is—of a little boy.

"Etta, what *is* that?"

"A baby transvestite!" Garrett said with a wicked gleam.

"It's their favorite toy," Etta said sheepishly, and Giorgio reached out of his high chair and grabbed it by the hair, with Franco snatching it back so the *brodo* went over and he slipped in it and hit his head on the tile floor. Etta jumped up, crying, "For heaven's sake, Franco, let the baby have it. You're old enough to share. Look what comes when you don't!" And threw her napkin at Gino: "And you, you couldn't watch them even though you *see* I've got my hands full. . . ."

Gino's shrug was almost imperceptible but all of history was in it. Should a man turn his attention from the civilized consideration of the mushroom harvest toward a speculative endeavor such as the divination of the sources of a woman's fury? No. A man resigns himself to the indecipherability of things. He shrugs, he swings the baby up onto his shoulders. Giorgio bubbled over with joy, and Etta turned to me, undeciphered, hands open in some kind of appeal, but burst into tears before she could speak—*why* wouldn't I save her?

"Here, let's take a walk, you and I," I said, wanting to get her life figured out for her, so it wouldn't weigh on me so, and to have her admit that I *had* been a good mother to her, I'd been right all along.

"I've got two kids, I can't just *go out for a walk*," she said.

"Take a walk, no problem," said Gino, but she dismissed it and he shrugged again and turned on RaiUno, national television, where a serious-looking woman in thick glasses was reporting on Bosnia's day.

"The news is really news over here," Garrett said. "In the U.S. it's just more entertainment." In a moment came *Colpo Grosso,* a kind of strip-*Jeopardy* where the players ran up from the audience and, failing to answer a few questions, found themselves dancing in the ludicrous nude. The contestants looked mostly British—thin, blond, and awkward, striking exaggeratedly casual poses in their wish to seem at ease. "It takes the pleasure out of it somehow," Garrett said in perplexity. The ads showed men striding through woodland, though I'd seen nothing wilder yet than the double row of poplars at the edge of town where Etta had been frightened by some Gypsies.

"Prosecco? Grappa?" Gino was asking. He peeled and quartered an apple with a few strokes, handing the wedges around. Etta was clearing the table—"She get tired, that's all," Gino said when she returned to the kitchen. "You got two kids . . . you got everything! But she gets tired."

I followed her into the kitchen, but finding her at the sink went stubborn and couldn't bring myself to help her. She was determined to despise me, let her have a reason.

"He doesn't listen, he doesn't care at all," she said. "Yesterday I told him I didn't think he'd even mind if I died, and you know what he said? He'd rather lose me than the boys."

"Well, he's no diplomat," I laughed, and she turned away. "But, I mean, don't you think he loves you all, his family?"

She shrugged. "I hardly feel like a woman," she said under her breath, and to me: "They hate me; they all do, and the boys, they're *mezzo-Americano,* they'll never amount to anything. In the States we talk about respecting differences and all that; here they're like . . . clans, or something, It's like . . . the people of Vicenza eat cats."

"What?"

"They say, 'Don't go to Vicenza. They eat cats there,' and Vicenza's only twenty miles away! No one from up here would ever go south of Florence, they think all southerners are thieves, and Americans are—well, you can guess. Nothing I do is right, not the way I sneeze, not the way I hang the clothes on the line. They insist Thanksgiving is in honor of Columbus, and when the Gypsies stole my wallet down on Via il Gruppo, Gino's mother just sniffed that it wouldn't have happened if I'd stayed in the house where I belong!"

"Who are your friends?" I asked.

"Oh, I don't know. Christiana and Marbella, I guess, they try to be nice. But they're busy with the church."

"Ah, yes, the church," I said. I'd been wondering.

"They're Scientologists."

"Etta, those people are crazy!"

"I don't know," she balked—not knowing is a point of pride with her. She'd told me how she explained to Franco that some people believed the Bible and some believed Darwin—the great lesson being not about science or faith, but a righteousness inherent in ignorance. And when I said, "But one of them is right," her eyes narrowed and she said she wouldn't presume to judge such a question. "It's a different way, that's all," she said now. "They gave me that *Dianetics* book, but I don't have time to read."

I felt so sleepy I worried about carbon monoxide and went to open the window, but she asked me not to—these fogs came in from Venice, she said, they get into your lungs. Her laundry was strung on lines over our head, to get the heat from the stove—things took days to dry in the winter, but they didn't believe in electric dryers. I thought how my mother had laughed when I asked what Etta and Gino would have to talk about, saying, "Live a little, Francine. Marriages aren't about conversation, you know!"

"*Bianco, come*, how you say, *latte*? Like milk!" Gino was saying, telling Garrett about the mushrooms. He loved his boys, accepted his life and its lack of expectation with a grace you'd never have seen in the States. National health, maybe, or some mineral in the Italian water. The copy of *Where Angels Fear to Tread* I'd sent to Etta years ago was sitting on her bedside table.

"I mean to get to it, really," she said. "I just don't have the time."

She'd hung my portrait of her over the guest-room bed—where she was least likely to see it, I supposed—and as I unpacked I decided she'd been right to be offended. I'd given up on it too soon, left it while her face still fit convention and missed some idiosyncracy I thought she wouldn't like to see. Without this, her beauty was missing, too. Then, catching sight of myself in the mirror, I had to sympathize with Garrett. Everyone knows men are judged by their wives' attractiveness. Who could blame his embarrassment? I, too, wished I were sleek and lithe; I regretted this tuberous feminine mass—had dressed to disguise it, to look more like a man, but it persisted, seal-like under the very chic suit—formless but for the two large, disappointed eyes.

Undressing though, I wondered what lunatic would quibble— seeing it (me, that is: pink and white, breasts swelling, nipples the lightest touch would awaken), I felt a pull of desire myself. What's more erotic than one's own darling self? When I first knew Garrett he'd once asked me to stand at the window so he could see me in the streetlight, and looking into his face I knew the riches womanhood had conferred on me: it was like coming into a great tract of land, with a swift river running through it and rich soil turned up for the heat—who knew what might grow there? I'd always felt a glad conspiracy with any statue of Venus, knowing she'd certainly wink at me if she only had a head.

Now I looked quickly away from myself, afraid that in the next glance I'd see something hideous, too. Garrett's read more than me, lived longer—he's been there in loco parentis since I was twenty-five. No one is better fitted to see all that's wrong with me. And if he was hallucinating, seeing a swan for a sow, what of it? He's my husband; if I'm ugly in his eyes, ugly I might as well be. As for the portrait— I'd tried to do Etta a favor by giving her face an ordinary, recognizable prettiness, the gold standard women trade on every day.

It was thrilling to wake up the next morning and find everything strange—the thick bedsheets smelling of incense in the perfect dark of the shuttered room. A thoughtful cooing came from the dovecote, but I didn't hear the boys, so it must still have been early. Garrett was heavily asleep beside me, so I tortured myself for him, thinking that my face in the mirror had looked like a worn-out shoe, wondering whether he'd rather have Etta than me.

He's going crazy, I told myself. *Don't accompany him.* He stirred and reached for me—for all of it he still wanted to make love all the time, though instead of pleasure I imagined he looked at me with curiosity and revulsion. I jumped up to avoid him, pushed the heavy shutters open to see the early sunlight deep red in the fig trees, on the tiled roofs and the cornfields behind them and the brick factory buildings across the canal.

"Venice today?" he said, stretching, smiling; we were in Italy, what could be wrong?

"Etta'll be hurt," I said.

"It's deadly here," he said angrily. "What are we going to do all day, watch her cook?"

So an hour later I heard myself explaining that we were taking the bus into Venice for the day, we wanted to see the Miracoli. Etta winced. Was I on a first-name basis with the buildings of Venice, then? The people I know now drop names of buildings and paintings as if they were celebrities. Men approach me with lines like "Have you ever been sculpted?" and I've been called "a slave to an antiquated aesthetic where beauty is the only standard," in *Art News*. It all sounds pompous to me, too.

"Come with us," I said. "You can bring Giorgio, and Christiana or Marbella can pick Franco up at school."

"What would they think?" she asked, and I remembered they feared the Venetian air.

"What would they think about you taking your houseguests on a daytrip?"

She shook her head. "No, I'm making osso buco. Gino comes home for lunch."

"It's just one day," I said. "Or, we could go to Padua—we'd be back by lunchtime."

"Padova," Etta corrected, giving the English pronunciation of the Italian spelling. "Osso buco takes hours. . . . I can't. You go, have a good time," she said, meaning: *Abandon me, so that I in my generosity can forgive you.*

Garrett was happy; we were in a vaporetto. The man smoking in its doorway looked urbane as Nabokov, and when he disembarked at the Accademia, we decided with a glance to follow him. We always pick someone like this, in a foreign city—we're sure there must be ancient quarters; lush, exotic places no Baedeker admits to, places we can slip into by following a stranger through a secret door. A few weeks ago I'd have named this and the sexual undertow as our strongest bonds, the things that held us together in ways past our understanding. Now . . . but Nabokov had a quick, long stride we could hardly keep up with, and my heart began to beat as if my life depended on staying close behind him; everything else fell away. He was wearing crepe soles, so for a long time we heard only the canal sloshing against the *fondamenta* and our own footsteps. I imagined Garrett had picked him to father my child; they'd make some transaction by which I'd find myself alone with him, and this idea so pleased me that I was stunned when he turned off, into a small, fountained courtyard, and I realized he was home and our adventure had come to an end. He stopped to suck the last out of his cigarette in front of the arched door, and we had to go on or he'd know we'd been following. Within ten steps, though, the canal dipped underground and the pavement ended at a wall. We walked back to see Nabokov flick his cigarette into the water, put his key to the lock, and, turning, look over his shoulder at us as if he was used to having strangers dog his steps. "Quite marvelous, isn't it?" he said. His English was exact, almost British. So he was Venice's best representative: he came from somewhere else.

We'd thought we were pushing outward, but really we were heading into the center: I looked down an alley and saw the sign for Harry's Bar. And San Marco opened before us, flooded, the herds of off-season tourists keeping to the wooden walkways while above them the gilded stallions pranced, the great figures emerged from the medieval clock to beat the hours, the fairy-tale bridges crossed into the torture cells. *"La Serenissima,"* Garrett said rhapsodically, as if he knew something.

"Shall we go through the palazzo?" he asked, and I thought, he wishes I was some odd lot he'd met on a bus, an Experience, like Venice, or the woman who peed in her shoes. There was no escaping our question: suddenly we were in a ballroom which was painted with hundreds of women, round breasted, rose-nippled—I wanted to touch them myself—but when Garrett looked up at them the sight turned bitter and I remembered I had been cast out of this pantheon. In the next room was a painting of Saint Agatha, proffering her severed breasts like custards on a tray. Garrett took umbrage at a crucifixion—Christ's belly looked soft. "He looks like a woman!" he said in anger. "He was a carpenter, he would have been solid!"

"No one looks his best during crucifixion," I tried to explain, but he wouldn't have it, so I pulled him on to the Miracoli, the only place in that city of unholy fascinations where one could imagine praying. Across the square was a little restaurant, low and dark, with some kind of party roaring—we took the last seats, in a corner so the waitress had to squeeze behind the celebrants to reach us and for a long time we were left alone. We looked past each other, down at the table, up into the rafters. . . . Then the waitress passed a carafe of wine through the party to us. As I poured it our eyes met, by chance; we both looked quickly away.

"Garrett," I said. "I'm sure you don't mean to hurt me. . . ."

"I hate having to hurt you," he agreed angrily, as if it were essential that he hurt me, and unseemly of me to upset him by mentioning it. After a while he added, with contempt, "What happens between us isn't important. *Look beyond yourself. Accept.* Did you read the paper this morning?" No, and I'd thought him a fool to do so, while the train passed over the long causeway into the city, which hovered over its own shimmering reflection in the lagoon. "Well, if you want to know about suffering . . ."

And he began to talk about American foreign policy, in Nicaragua,

Haiti, Macedonia, Iraq—all the complexities, mistakes, and hypocrisies—he's at work all the time, worrying the rage among nations as if the world were a Chinese puzzle he might solve. He talked and talked until the waitress brought him a plate of tiny calamari fried whole: tasting one he lost his train of thought.

"I thought I ordered the pesto," he said after he'd eaten half of them.

"It's so loud, I don't think she could really hear us," I said. The spirit of the party broke over us like a wave, a joyful shock that stood everything on its head so my little tragedy looked entirely amusing all of a sudden. "I mean, that's why one travels, isn't it?" I said, "So as to order the pesto and get the calamari, and have it all to remember."

"That's not why *I* travel," he said grimly, and I thought *No, he travels in the hope of becoming someone like our Nabokov, so sophisticated life can't get a firm grip on him.* And here he found himself with a mouth full of tentacles—of course it was disappointing.

"If people like us didn't love each other, need each other, then we could die like ants under a shoe—so what?"

His face softened, and I remembered that for all he reads, and knows, still he sees me as wise—an endearing thing in a man.

"When you were lost, in Frankfurt—," he said, taking my hands across the table, his face full of feeling.

"You were the one who was lost in Frankfurt!"

"Let's stay the night here," he said. His hands were shaking, it reminded me of our first meetings when I was so young and everything was so wrong between us that loving him seemed a great bold act of idiotic faith and I wanted only to open myself up to him and say "Come, come inside," and when we went out to dinner he couldn't stand up afterward lest the whole world see his erection.

"*Avete camere libre?*" I asked, at the Locanda Garibaldi, "*con un letto matrimoniale?*" The innkeeper burst into Italian—did Garrett see how I slipped into the language?—by instinctive affinity. We were given a small chamber whose window opened onto a balcony, which looked down a shaft from which a fetid, watery odor arose: the canal. When I washed my face the water from the sink ran out and dripped over the edge. I called Etta from the desk phone.

"The strike's still on. I think we'd better stay here tonight," I said.

"But, dinner . . ."

"You know how long that train takes—we'd never get there in time," I said. "And I know Gino can't take time to come get us. So, we'll be back tomorrow and—and we'll take you all out for dinner, how about that?"

"Gino likes to eat at home."

As we went down the hallway Garrett slid his hand around to squeeze my breast like a teenager. He was resigned to me with all my failings—could I not reconcile myself to him? In the room he pulled my sweater over my head and I kissed him as if I were playing his lover in a movie. I wondered if my torment was some kind of penance: hadn't I loved sex mostly out of pleasure in the munificence of my body, the tender amazement it would raise in a man's eyes, the way one little arch of my back could incite . . .

"You're so beautiful," Garrett said, in mourning for the thing that no longer moved him. *He'll destroy me out of curiosity,* I thought—*he wants to know what I look like in pain.* When he touched me I expected his hands to burn me, but I wanted the child and I put the rest out of my mind, knelt on the bed beside him and let my breasts fall into his hands. He seemed bewitched, overcome—he didn't know my actions were satirical, the motions of the dream woman he wanted me to be. In the end he nestled in against me, feeling, I guessed, forgiven, saying "Giudecca tomorrow," so sleepily. I dreamed my milk wouldn't come and I was trying to cut off my nipple with a pair of scissors, so the baby would have something at least to drink.

. . .

"We've started trying . . . for a baby, I mean," I told Etta the next night, thinking that if I could hit on a subject she had feeling for I'd bring some color to her cheeks.

"That's wonderful," she said, without turning from the sink. "I didn't know you wanted children." Then, to herself really, as if she could speak freely since no one ever heard her: "You wanted me to kill mine."

"What?"

A terrible look crossed her face, but then a spark jumped and she turned to look me in the eye. "You *told* me to have an abortion," she said. "You killed my art, you'd have killed my marriage, you told me to kill my baby, and you painted that portrait that looks as if I'm dead already, because you wish I was. You gave me a *cookbook* . . . out of all you have to give."

"I . . . Etta, I . . . ," I said, thinking: *Yes, I wanted to be free of you, I didn't have the strength to drag you any further. At least I'm sick with guilt about it, isn't that enough?* "I didn't want you condemned to an unhappy marriage," I heard myself saying, and was surprised to remember this was true—I wasn't entirely a gorgon. With that a geyser of bile erupted, and I wanted to ask her how she'd liked lying around cozy at home while I banged my head on the doors of the world so she could float through them in my wake. Not to mention my coloring book that she'd filled up every page of thirty years ago, insisting she was entitled to every single thing I owned—

She saved me, snapping, "I don't want to talk about it," and calling angrily for Gino.

Garrett came instead—"He took the kids to Marco's," he said. "Can I do something?"

"No, no, it's just that we're having a special dinner," she said.

"Polenta, and . . . Well, it's a surprise, really—Gino's favorite . . . real Italian . . . We almost never have them, but they were in the market this morning . . . You'll see."

"The suspense, the intrigue!" I said, pushing away from the argument, and she laughed. There, I thought, she's got out the venom, and there's something left, something real. Here we were in the kitchen together like when we young, the only difference being that we weren't lip-synching to the Supremes. She turned on the broiler and handed me the dripping chicory head to tear up for salad. There was the smell of onions in olive oil and Etta sifted the cornmeal over the pot with one hand, stirring with the other in a quiet, consoling rhythm. The boys came back with Gino and pulled me out with them to see the lizards dart along the outside wall.

Then, "Come, come, don't let it cool!" she was calling, and we sat down around a platter heaped with polenta, strewn with . . .

"Songbirds!" Etta said. Charred corpses, sparrows or finches once, scattered as over a battlefield, their little beaks open, feet splayed upward, curled by the flames.

Gino laughed. "Something different, eh? We used to have songbirds all the time when I was a boy. My father caught them and put them in the cage and when we had enough . . ."

"Songbirds!" Garrett said with a smile playing at the corners of his mouth and a quick glance at me—here it was, history on toast. And here were we, appalled and amused together, as always, in absolute communication without saying a word. Gino plucked the last feathers from one of the birds and popped it into his mouth whole.

"Good," he said thoughtfully, chewing. "She's a good cook, Etta."

"A wonderful cook," I agreed, thinking that if only I'd encouraged her painting I'd see this vision on canvas instead of having to eat it.

"Italia!" we toasted.

When in Rome . . . , I thought, though I was not practicing diplomacy but bitter sisterhood: Etta must never get the better of me. Any hesitation would be taken as an insult, so I lifted a bird between fork and spoon, trying not to damage it further. Garrett, who can't back away from a challenge, had taken five, and I heard a skull crack as he bit down.

"Very good, delicious!" said he, who can't bear to drop a lobster into a pot. I bit a bird in two at the belly so as to avoid its little beak—it tasted mostly of ashes.

Gino cocked a brow and moved as if to give Garrett another helping.

"Oh, no, I couldn't, I've had four already."

Gino leaned across the table and counted with his fork. "No, two," he said.

Etta fed Giorgio a spoonful of polenta. "They made me a little nervous, when I first came," she said with some condescension, "but now I really like them. I mean, it's no different than beef, really." She still sounded ready for a fight. Had I imagined I could fall so easily into the flow of Italy, with no understanding of all she had to swallow? Well, then, more songbirds! Wasn't she the gentle sister, the one who deserved all the babies and love? See the tender care she took, twisting off each little foot, adding it to the neat pile at the side of her plate. "I'm surprised 'Nardo had them this time of year," she said.

"They come in from China," Gino said. "No Italian birdies left."

Garrett poured more wine, and I drank it, wondering if I ought to, but really it seemed impossible that I could be nourishing, or poisoning, some new being inside myself, a child who would inherit a legacy of love and rage like the one passed so long ago to Etta and me. I took a little scorched head in my mouth and snapped its neck with ease.

"You didn't need to go to so much trouble just for us, Etta," I said. "We're family."

Darling?

Waiting at Karp's office door, Daisy thought of Freud's admission that women were still a dark continent to him, and so very nearly said "Dr. Livingstone!" when he appeared. She had insisted on a man, someone honest and exact whose tenderness would be hidden, of course, but vast. Seeing Karp she felt she was safe: he was stooped as under some ancient weight, his nervous fingers raked thin hair. . . . He extended a damp hand, and she relaxed: there would be no accidents of magnetism here. Daisy knew how to fall in love, how to let a man fall in love with her, but now that she was married, settled in life, this attribute had become a liability. It was like having an old gun around; you might lock it away in the attic, put it out of your mind, but sooner or later some rage or despair would remind you that just a few steps up the back staircase and into the dark, you'll find the means to blow a big hole in the world.

She had her rages and despairs listed on a notecard, and rattled them off for Karp: Hugh, her husband, was too gloomy. He had refused her a child, and out with the baby had gone the whole marriage. He touched her now as if she were an unexploded bomb. Not that she couldn't manage, she was an excellent manager—all lives are compromised after all, God knew she was lucky, living in an old whaling port where the feel of history (dark, cold, and fear, transmuted by nostalgia and electricity into a sense of mysterious comfort and intrigue) was still resident in the narrow streets so that vacationers yearned for a keepsake of that time. Daisy kept an antique shop. She had been saved from an anxious, threadbare life: she ought to have been grateful. A marriage requires sacrifice. . . .

She glanced over at Karp: he'd slid down in his chair and was absently rubbing his neck, craning it, absorbed in some sensual agony, while she went on in a dull querulous voice—"I'm sorry," she said, "I need to be less dependent, I expect so much. . . ."

"You feel there are people who make do with less love and encouragement than you, and you'd like to be more like them, so you wouldn't be lonely and sad."

"I didn't say lonely and sad."

"Maybe not. Next week then?"

It was a disappointment—nothing had happened. But then, what was he supposed to do, turn into Fred Astaire and dance her up the wall? *One is ridiculous*, she thought, driving the hundred miles home from Boston, and seeing a bumper sticker that read PRACTICE RANDOM ACTS OF KINDNESS AND SENSELESS BEAUTY, considered ramming the car it was affixed to and putting its sentimental occupants out of their bathetic misery. Courage, that's what was needed, courage in the face of the *smallness* of life. Hers had come to this—a shop full of teacups and candlesticks, and a husband who skulked around the edges, hoping to avoid her notice—she spent her days staring into the past, while the present flowed around her, away. She turned up the radio; she needed to hear Mick Jagger.

Her very admirable lack of concupiscence toward Karp lasted for some weeks, but the dreams wore away at her: Hugh's twin, a man with a woman's full breasts, was trying to seduce her. At first she resisted, then let him kiss her though she recovered herself before the erotic waters closed absolutely over, but he returned the next night and the next, until she gave in . . . upon which he evaporated, and she fell through the floor—

"It was a long, narrow room. . . . Like this room, actually," she reported dutifully to Karp. "Like an apartment I was thinking of moving into."

One of his eyebrows lifted a magnificent centimeter: "Thinking of a move? . . ."

Of course, she had been thinking of moving in here, with him. The inner creature was measuring, calculating, deciding where to put up the paintings, which side of the bed she preferred . . . The outer creature blushed to blazing. *She* was the one who would have to walk past him as she left, holding tight to the doorframe lest a rip tide pull her into his arms.

One is entirely absurd.

"Immerse me, my sweet immersible you . . ." She sang all the time now; she was bursting with Morris S. Karp. How had she failed to recognize his beauty? He was all black and white—a sketch by a ferocious master. His speech was quick and full of thought, and he gestured with open hands like a conductor bringing his orchestra along. True, he was strangely recumbent—she had thought the *patient* reclined . . . instead he was spread before her like a banquet—his shoes with their soles flapping, his hips lush as a mermaid's, the thin shirt touching him the way she wished to . . . His neckties were the key to it—each patterned with its own abstract expressionist galaxy, to show he welcomed the asymmetrical, the disharmonious, the peculiar. His air filter hummed in the corner—he was allergic to every germ and seed. Of course! He was a genius of susceptibility: everything affected him, Daisy's thoughts and feelings no less than the motes rising in the stream of sunlight beside the blind.

Men are made of longing; if you keep still long enough their souls will creep out and take a little nourishment from your cupped hand. So Daisy waited, she knew exactly how Karp would want her once he knew she wanted him; she could feel the print of his first kiss on her lips already. But the etiquette of the consulting room was so horribly restraining! No gifts, no savory dishes to set before him, no gorgeous dress, no letting her hand brush his, smiling into his eyes, taking his worries to her heart, laughing at his jokes, funny or otherwise.

He wanted only the odd, awkward fragments that she usually pushed to the edge of her mind. Things she'd been ashamed of began to look like treasures because Karp would want to know them. It was true she was a snoop—she'd never been alone in a room without ransacking the drawers. And it seemed she was cruel by nature; her conversation was made of faux pas. Talking to an orphan she was bound to mention ancestry, people in wheelchairs heard how she loved to run, and once she'd found herself laying out her plans for a happy old age to a man on his deathbed; it was appalling.

So, Karp said, she was searching for the secrets her benighted parents had missed, the wisdoms that might have kept them from harm—she dared not leave a stone unturned. She smiled miserably, a little cry ripped in her throat—those poor parents, two drowning people pulling each other down—they were long dead; there was no point in thinking about it all again—the main thing was to keep from going under herself. Yes, Karp said: She had all she could do to keep her head above water, while others, crippled, adopted, even dying, seemed blessed with the grace that she, with no one to learn from, had angrily, jealously lacked! Of course, she stayed away from humans, busied herself with their things—antiques are things passed down from generation to generation, no? Furnishing her doll's house, he said, keeping the candle in the window in case her mother returned to earth and needed to find her. A sad thing, wasn't it, a dollhouse with no child?

Of course she loved him; he turned the pieces until they fit, remaking her life as a story—as whole. She grew toward him like a root to water, combing the personal ads though she knew he was married—surely he'd find a way to send her a message, tell her she was loved. After he mentioned Yeats in passing she read Yeats every night, though she'd used to think poems were dull—now she'd have taken them intravenously. When she turned over a plate at a flea market she'd rather it read *Karp* than *Limoges*, and the shop now had a Judaica corner next to the nautical tchochkes. Karp being Jewish, she found herself studying the instructions for koshering, on the back of the box of salt: Place a turkey on an inclined drainboard, sprinkle salt outside and in like a light blanket of snow. Might such a process work on herself? She had absorbed Karp's attitudes without realizing she knew them, heard herself using his pronunciations, felt his expressions on her face. When she was thinking *Karp, Karp, if only you would drive your body into mine* (yes, it was all most embarrassing), she might have considered that she'd already sopped up a good portion of his soul.

"Where'd you grow up?" she asked him.

"You'd like to know something about me."

"Yes, I'd like to know where you grew up."

"But why?"

"Because I was wondering where you grew up!" How to seduce a man if you can't know him? What did his father do? Why psychology? How did he fall in love with his wife? With details like this she could have fashioned a romance of and for him, an image of himself so seductive he'd have had to step into it, and fall in love with its creator.

"The therapist isn't supposed to talk about himself," he explained, sounding plaintive, even exhausted. She was wearing away at him, she would have her victory soon. His consulting room with its burlap wallpaper and diagnostic manuals took on the aspect of a seraglio. Daisy spent hours calculating which outfit would seem most artlessly charming. More angora! Many the bunny must be combed, that her sweaters might call out to be touched while the woman inside them went on innocently murmuring her free associations.

"I dreamed there was a door at the back of the office, another room where we could go, with sunlight, and curtains blowing in the breeze. . . ."

"And? . . ."

"Well, you know, we'd be free of the restrictions . . ."

"Restrictions?"

"*You* know. . . ."

"You feel some restriction here, something rigid or unpleasant, but inescapable. . . ."

She paused a long time, touching her cold fingers to a burning cheek.

"Can you say what you're thinking?"

Was he deaf, dumb and blind? "I'm thinking of . . . of . . . seducing you, making love to you, for God's sake!"

"That's fine," he said. "We can analyze that."

Karp, Karp, he was driving her crazy! She awoke in outrage every morning. Would the sun be rising in the west then? Because he *ought* to have loved her—But, no wonder her husband couldn't bear her— she was nothing to look at, her head was too big for her body . . . or rather the shoulders too narrow; the legs short. . . . No, looking again she saw the shoulders were too *wide*. Whatever, it was a question of proportion—she didn't have any. The things she'd been vain of—she was thin as a girl, she never put an extra morsel into her mouth, her features were sharp and clear—faded when he didn't seem to see them. How could he love a woman with such a witchy chin? It was no coincidence her mother had named her for a flower without whorls or fragrance; she had no softness, no mystery about her. Her mother's own name had been Rose.

She was only Daisy, not kosher for Karp. Slicing the roots of the leggy mock-orange in front of the shop she was overcome—Was this all, then, when a thing didn't grow as expected it must necessarily die? She'd dreamed she was pruning her own hands. But, what a dream—Karp would love it—surely he could come to love the dreamer, too. And she popped the bush out of its bed and heaved it into the compost without another thought, looking up to follow the trajectory of a plane overhead: was it flying in his direction?

Then one morning there he was in the *Boston Globe.* It was a brilliant early summer day; Hugh read *How We Die* while Cyrilla (their daughter—Daisy had long since forgotten there'd been some problem about getting her) played bird-baby-in-a-nest, and Daisy was eating a peach, deciding whether she ought to buy a big lot of Fiestaware though she hated the colors—it would sell quickly, which was supposed to be the point—squinting out to see if the tide was high enough for a quick swim, and, of course, looking for Karp, when she found him, in the gossip column. It being the *Globe,* the gossip column did not, of course, stoop to any actual gossip—usually it was a grinding recitation of who was chairing or being chaired at Harvard, but today:

> *Doubleday is promising a major publicity push for* The Contemporary Parent, *psychologist Morris Karp's manual for two-career families, due out next month.*

It was as if a butterfly pin had flown in through the window and fastened her, fluttering, to the wall. A book, with his picture on the jacket and his voice in every sentence, all his beliefs in evidence. A book to hold close to her schoolgirl's heart—she was going to know him, to understand him, and after that it was only a step. . . .

"Karp wrote a book," she said quietly, reminding herself of an explosion she once heard some miles away—just a soft puff, though it killed two people. Hugh didn't look up—he didn't really believe in Karp. He remembered Daisy had been unhappy for some reason a while back, and she went to the city every Wednesday, she spoke of this Karp occasionally, but he loved his wife, depended on her— why on earth would she see a psychiatrist? He cast the notion aside.

He wouldn't have guessed that in her heart of hearts she had taken a little gossip item for an engagement notice—had laid out, in preparation for her appointment, something like a trousseau, right down to the silk panties—four years of Karp and still she had not convinced herself that panties were not germane. Over them the bride wore a linen shift with a tiny blue check, and a spray of forget-me-nots pinned on. She carried *The Poems of Guillaume Apollinaire*:

> *I am sick with hearing the words of bliss*
> *the love I endure is like a syphilis*
> *and the image that possesses you and never leaves your side*
> *in anguish and insomnia keeps you alive*

and a bouquet of her week's essential moments, to be tossed to Karp's present wife from the landing as the bride ascended the celestial stair- way from his couch to his bed. The bride's dream, of ivory *peau-de-soie,* hand-stitched with over ten thousand seed pearls and cascading in gentle, fingertip-length waves, was this: Karp had embraced her and gone away, leaving his body like a forgotten overcoat in her arms.

He would love her now, he would have to. She drove up Route 3 on the wings of limerance—she who had dreaded the highway was happiest now behind the wheel. To drive was to be nearing Karp! It seemed only hours until she'd be kissing his collarbone, the crook of his arm, until they stumbled together out of the thicket of language into a warm sea. Punching the radio buttons in search of a song exorbitant as feeling, she found herself listening instead to a discussion of children's night terrors on some godforsaken talk station. Not that Cyrilla, little sovereign, had ever had a night terror—she kept her own counsel, busied herself all day making a "pilgrim stew" of acorns and inkberries, slept soundly, ate well. It was a disappointment; she didn't much seem to need a mother. Still Daisy couldn't help listening to the talk show, she didn't know why—only as she turned off the highway and saw a handful of sparrows fly overhead like rice did she realize the voice in the radio was that of her betrothed—of course, he would be always beside her now he was on the air!

He left her at the altar. She sat half an hour in the waiting room and finally decided she must have gotten the time wrong, or the day—her stories had wilted: how ordinary they were after all, the little jealousies and disappointments she'd saved up to tell him, ludicrous fears balanced by ludicrous satisfactions—things he'd heard a thousand times before. She heard his step on the stairway and wanted to run away: he'd find her here with her expectations fallen in around her, a child got up in her mother's clothing . . . and she hadn't been reading French poems either but *Self* magazine, which he probably kept in the waiting room just to see who was idiot enough to open it. . . . She pushed it in between two scholarly journals just in time.

"Sorry," he said perfunctorily, as if he wasn't holding the little fishbowl of her life out in front of him, threatening to let it smash. He was carrying a case of Kleenex and opened some for her before settling himself, waiting . . . for what? Her dream was forgotten, and as Karp didn't bring up the book or the interview, she felt she oughtn't to mention them either—maybe they were the kind of things one was supposed to pretend not to know?

"Nothing going on, I guess," she said, sounding disingenuous even to herself.

"No thoughts?" His smile was dubious and kind; who on earth does not spend his life weaving little nests of thought from the odd bits at hand? She had to speak or give herself away—by now she felt she must have trespassed unforgivably, spying, eavesdropping on him.

"Congratulations," she mumbled, fixing on the Arabic letters in the rug as if she might bring herself to such a boil she'd find herself able to read them. "On the book. I saw in the paper." But he'd known for months without telling her; what could he care for her congratulation? What did she know of him at all? Was he immensely strong as it sometimes seemed, or thin and fragile? Handsome? Ugly? Before she'd looked up his birthday she couldn't have guessed his age—now she wondered whether he was kind, really, or cruel. . . . Ah well, she'd figure it out after they were married.

He was beaming. "Thank you, yes—that does bring up something." And he unfolded a sheet of paper from his pocket—an itinerary. "There will be some scheduling problems. . . . Let's see, next week, New York and the Northeast. Well! There, I *can* see you next week, ten A.M.?"

She scribbled it down. "You're going away?"

"Fifteen cities," he said happily. "Not just the major market cities, but the secondary cities, too."

She nodded. "Very nice."

"Portland, Seattle, Dallas—I think Dallas, wait—" He checked through his appointment book and then some papers on the desk.

"Yes, Dallas and Houston, too, actually . . . I guess they just sort of threw Houston in; it's not that big a market, though the major chains are *fairly* well represented. . . ."

Well, hadn't she prayed he'd want to confide in her?

"Not that I know that much about marketing and distribution," he continued, though he seemed to be the very encyclopedia of marketing and distribution. She watched the time tick away, thinking that, after all, it *was* exciting, and this was the way men *got* excited, so she ought to try to be patient. . . . And following this line of thought she lost his thread and a silence fell which she remembered it was her duty to break.

"It's wonderful," she said.

"What is?"

"Well, you know, whatever you were saying . . ."

"Can you say what you're feeling?"

"Are you crazy?" she asked him. "All right, all right then if you don't care about me. All right, you're going away. But surely you don't imagine that I'm going to sit here and describe for your delectation all the sorrow and humiliation of being rejected by you!" She was sobbing, a very minor matter, of course, to a man who buys Kleenex by the case. She plucked up several tissues in a fury and blew her nose with ostentation, remembering for no particular reason that her father had worked in a Kleenex factory when she was small.

"So, you're angry, you feel—"

"Don't you *dare* talk to me like a psychiatrist!" Horrid little man, this leech who made such nice soft sucking noises, she hadn't noticed until her life was nearly drained—

"Wait, wait," he said. "I'm being defensive, I agree." This only opened a floodgate. . . . She wept so she could hardly hear him. "I made a failure of *technique*," he was helpfully explaining.

"Technique?" Just a technical problem, and here she'd thought he was being mean. She looked away toward the window, where a bumblebee was blundering up the screen.

"Technique," Karp said with a pedagogical gleam, "the *way* I approach a problem, or . . ." He saw the bee, too, and his voice strangled in his throat for a second before he said, extremely calmly, "There's a bee. I'm going to have to kill it," and stood up, very carefully lest he throw his back out, taking several ginger steps toward the window and removing one of his shoes. Daisy came awake, and the room, usually so stuffy, full of half-expressed thoughts and feelings, cleared suddenly—she'd never seen him actually do anything before. A keen suspense was developing, something like a bullfight, maybe—she'd always dreamed of visiting Spain.

The first skirmish ended with a premature cry of triumph from Karp, while *el toro* buzzed away, settling disdainfully again within easy reach. Karp lunged at it, but it flew a few feet, heavily, as if it didn't have quite the wing power to sustain its girth, and set about circling a spot on the wallpaper like a sleepy cat. Karp looked baffled, if martial, and wondered aloud whether he ought to call an exterminator.

Would it be intrusive to intervene? Callous just to sit by? Then the bee tried an offensive maneuver, flying straight at Karp, who flinched away, moaning horribly, his hand jumping to the small of his back, and Daisy leapt to her feet; her moment had come.

"I think I could trap him under a cup," she said.

Karp looked up, smiling frankly for once, without that gynecologist's look he got, of a man feeling around in the dark. "Be my guest!"

And for a moment she was able to act as herself, Daisy the able, the swift. She plunked Karp's coffee mug over the bee, slid an envelope under its mouth, and, since the office window was painted shut against pollens and molds, carried it into the waiting room and shook it free out the door while Karp made helpful and appreciative noises from the corner. No telling whether he was keeping back from the bee or from her—by the time she returned to his office he was back in his chair, his face arranged again into a blank screen.

"Let's see," he said, in his most neutral tone, "you were saying—" But the time; he stood up. "Actually we'll have to pick up there next week."

"It's time?" Had she used up her hour by saving his life?

"I'm afraid . . ." He smiled wretchedly, and then, searching for some gesture of farewell—some way to get rid of her—extended his hand.

Which, having taken, she found herself unable to let go. Some eternal seconds passed, she gazing meaningfully at him, he pleadingly at her, until, with her natural officiousness (but he understood so kindly that her parents had needed her to tell them what to do) pulled him to her, held him tight.

It took an age—thirty seconds at least—to realize he was just standing there, unmoved except maybe by embarrassment and irritation. She had captured rather than embraced him.

"I have someone waiting," he said icily, and pulled the inner door open, before he recovered himself, and, in his most careful, hypnotic, lion tamer's tone, stuck his head right between her jaws. "I mean, if this brings something up, by all means feel free to call . . . but . . ."

The bride fled home to her husband with something like a steak knife lodged in her breast. What could she have been thinking of, trying to seduce a god down from Olympus, imagining that Morris Karp would embrace the likes of her? And on the truck in the next lane *cappuccino* was written with two *n*s. Why can't anyone *spell*? Nobody bothers, nobody cares. . . . What if she just smashed into it until the word stove in on itself, folded the offending *n* out of sight? *Consult the dictionary*! she wanted to scream—and she pressed the accelerator. If she could only go fast enough, maybe a cop would come save her, put her in prison, get this weapon out of her hands.

As Daisy turned in the driveway at home Cyrilla burst out onto the steps, naked and golden with Hugh behind her holding a martini and proffering, beseechingly, a little pink dress. The Dow Jones, he said, with deepest, most satisfactory dread, was sharply up: this could only portend a crash. She hadn't been noticing—when had he become a happy man? *And* another murder in Boston, he said, pointing to the television—why would anyone go into that city, what could be worth risking your life that way? It occurred to Daisy that she loved him more than she'd used to. His gloom felt cozy and familiar; he was only pointing out how big and frightening the world was, why she ought to stay by his hearth. She glanced at the reprehensible television—and there was Karp; his face filled the entire frame.

Talking about toddlers, she guessed, though she couldn't hear or understand him while she was drinking him in this way. To look into his face so closely, see the thoughts pass across it, this was as much as she'd ever asked for—all she'd wanted from the awful embrace. There was a space between his front teeth—how had she missed this? What else didn't she know? When his forty-five seconds were over and the bright generic face of the anchorwoman replaced his, the loss hurt her eyes. "Dr. Karp says it's not the *amount* of time you spend with a child, but whether something meaningful takes place *during* that time," the woman chimed. "Dr. Karp says . . ."

Daisy felt exactly how his arms should have fit around her . . . how he would have lifted her out of her dull, petty self into the light . . . to keep apart from him felt completely unnatural, wrong. And decided that for dinner she would make fettuccine Alfredo—she was ravenous suddenly; the foods she used to disdain rose up and de-manded she acknowledge their deliciousness—what madness could have kept her from eating them all these years?

Three days later she was sitting on the stoop with a bag of macaroons when the UPS man came up the walk with *The Contemporary Parent*—the next thing to having Karp's heart and mind in a jar. She tore at the package with her teeth rather than let the man go. She needed someone, someone in a uniform, with her, lest Karp fly out of the book and castigate her for prying into him again.

"Wanna see a picture of my psychologist?"

The UPS man smiled most uncomfortably, but this was hardly the weirdest request he'd ever acceded to. She held the book open for him, squinting sideways at the photo herself in case the sight of it would blind her.

"He looks very nice," the man said, and seeing this fell short, added, "But . . . smug, maybe?"

"Oh, no!" Daisy said, though she saw what he meant. It wasn't Karp, the raw, honest face she loved, the angel as grocer, giving good quality at fair prices—it was Karp in a state of helpless ingratiation. "No, he's mortified, that's just his mortified look," she said. She knew his mortified look pretty well. "I don't think he likes having his picture taken."

He leaned in to look closer, taking the book out of her hands. He smelled of heaven: sweat and cinnamon chewing gum.

". . . nurturing the inner child?" He had turned to the dedication.

"Oh, that's just the way they talk . . . you know." In her dreams he spoke Hebrew, the language written in flames.

He had not dedicated the book to her, and this came as an insufferable blow. Of course, there was that wife and child. But common sense had played no role in her relations with Karp so far and was hardly about to assert itself now. She scanned the acknowledgments, dusting her fingers over the print in case there was a secret message for her in braille, but no, she was one of the few people on earth whose name did not appear. She'd loved him for years now, while he lived his life among others. . . .

"I, I have some other deliveries—"

"Of course, of course, thanks—"

"I mean, he looks like a very nice man," the UPS man continued, backing away.

Daisy nodded, and opening the book thought of the chunk of plutonium discovered by a Brazilian family in an abandoned clinic: they lived in a world of mud and straw, but this stone glowed blue as twilight—obviously sacred. They built it an altar in their kitchen, carried it into the fields, touched it to the forehead of each newborn child . . . The tumors were immense, the youngest, blessed most often, were first to die. Beware of talismans, sacraments—she closed the book and touched her cheek to the jacket. Could this really be all she was to have of Morris Karp?

By Wednesday she'd handled it enough that it didn't seem quite so dangerous and she dared carry it to his office for her act of contrition. She couldn't actually read the book—the words, being his, were too full of meaning, jewels to be lifted to the eyepiece one by one, but she held the book up and waited with heart slamming—when he came in and saw *The Contemporary Parent* instead of her face, he would have to love her, for a minute at least.

An hour passed with no Karp. Why had she ever touched him, tried to tear him out of the spirit world? He'd had no choice but to disappear.

A little man came up the walk, wearing red suspenders and a

pointed beard, carrying the *Selected Paul Tillich*. He pushed open the door and looked at her with suspicion.

"He's late," she explained. "My appointment was at eleven."

"Mine's at twelve," he replied, and nodded at the clock—it was 12:10.

"I've been here all this time," she said. "He hasn't come."

"I've never known that to happen," the elf replied, opening his book with a snap. After all, she was in a psychologist's office—she must be mad.

But, of course: it wasn't Karp who had vanished, it was herself! The gods know about torture: they had not sentenced her merely to lose him but to be erased from his sight. She heard his step on the stair and her heart beat frantically—he'd open the door, look through her, and take the elf into the sanctuary, and she'd have to return to the underworld alone.

But he came down and motioned to her just as always, taking her into the office and going back to speak a moment with the elf. Daisy was abjectly grateful; she vowed never, ever to touch him, never to trouble him with herself again. Karp sat down pleasantly, silently, as if nothing was out of the ordinary . . . perhaps nothing *was* out of the ordinary? One must follow the local custom—if her watch read twelve and Karp said eleven, then eleven it must be. If he'd opened an umbrella she'd have put her head under the faucet rather than point out the sun—there has to be something certain on earth; let it be Karp's way. He smiled politely, as if she'd never saved his life, never held him. . . .

"You don't love me," she choked.

"I don't sexually abuse you."

"You *pigheadedly* refuse to sexually abuse me!" she wept. Yes, she burned like an immolated monk with longing and fury and shame—

and still it was funny—was this fair? Could he really think that lying beside her, touching and being touched, eyes open so each could see his effect on each other, feel the absolute holiness of it—would count as sexual abuse?

"Therapists don't hug their patients!" he said, then added, "Though, I've been doing this a long time and there have been others— I suppose the most unsettling one was a psychotic *man*—so I've had a wide experience, with hugs, and—"

"I'm sorry," she said, but a rebellion welled up. "No, I'm not— look at you! You don't even guess what you're missing, living your life without me!" She turned the surfaces of her hands lightly, eloquently, together; she was paying him to watch her every gesture, let him at least suffer what he missed. "Wouldn't you like to have that feeling again, like when you were twenty?" she asked.

"You're inviting me to regress with you?"

"When you're dying, please remember you never kissed me."

"It's against the law in Massachusetts," he replied, and began to go over his itinerary again while she wondered if kisses were legal in any of the other major market cities, or if secondary markets were more lenient, in order to attract their share of authors. What about a place like Pittsburgh, for instance? Or maybe she should just fling him down and carve *I Adore You* into his chest with one of those sharp gold-nibbed fountain pens so popular with collectors. Never mind, she was going to stop on the way home for a vanilla milkshake and a BLT. She was infinitely greedy, for food, drink, beauty, love. . . . She would storm over the earth, a giantess, swimming the Atlantic in a few proud strokes, taking everything she wanted. . . . She frightened herself, she needed someone to suppress her.

Harvard Doc Says You *Can* Have It All

The *Herald* had a color picture: Karp at home with his daughter on his knee. This was shocking—a burst of reality in the midst of a dream, like the school principal taking her out of class the day her father died. She kissed her finger and touched it to Karp's lips. She had to renounce him, she understood. He was in the public domain now, might as well be in the grave.

As boxes go, she decided, the television is eerier than the coffin. Karp's head talked on *Frontline,* on *Dateline,* on *Nightline,* while she watched like a cat peering into an aquarium. Blown dry, wearing . . . was that rouge? . . . saying "Well, Ted," manfully as if he'd been saying "Well, Ted," all his life, he strode through the interviews, looking like an eager schoolboy who was sure he had the answer, thinking *Call on me, call on me!* His hand shook, and Daisy pressed hers to the glass, matching her fingers to his. If only she could smash the set, reach in and pluck a wriggling Oprah out of his way. The camera closed in, a child lifted a toy out of his hand: he was a giant of empathy, the father every single viewer had been missing. Real tears glittered in his eyes. If a bee had flown into the studio he would have treated it with such generous respect it would have lost its need to sting.

He was everywhere, on every channel—he had materialized out of the world of dreams and to that world he had returned. There was no way to reach him but by telepathy. Daisy went to Amazon.com, and under the name of Laurel Shipman, of Tyringham, Massachusetts, gave *The Contemporary Parent* five stars: "A must for every man or woman trying to negotiate the complexities of parenting today!! Without this book I don't know where I'd be!"

In fact, the day *The Contemporary Parent* went on the bestseller list, Daisy went on Prozac. There would, of course, be side effects: anxiousness, diminished libido. . . . Karp had said this in his most neutral voice, in *no* way implying her libido was outsized. *This is my body and my blood*, she thought dully as she shook her pill out into her hand. It changed nothing, she lived at the empty black center of herself, getting Cyrilla to preschool, opening the shop, and spending the day in the corner behind the big armoire, hiding from the customers and ordering soft sweaters in the mail. The longing for Karp was always there, now distant, now right beside her—like a mosquito, faint but incessant, unwilling to light, so that she was doomed to flail at it until . . . until she had smashed every damned teacup, every vestige of the past. The UPS man always came at four, with her new sweaters and sometimes a confidence—they were becoming close, they had all that driving in common, and he was grateful to get advice from someone with such a famous shrink. Her fingers trembled, wishing to trace the lines of his tattoo.

Then the tour was over, Karp was home. It was November, the garish fall colors were deepened into rich reds and golds that glowed against the gray sky—by the time she turned into his driveway it was pouring. His door was locked, so she sheltered under the eave, watching the rain sweep across the lawn. A cleaning lady lugged a vacuum into the manse across the street. After a long time Karp came out, unshaven, looking perplexed and angry and frightened all at once—as her mother had, when she was having a spell.

"How long have you been here?" he asked.

"Forty minutes," she said, checking her watch—no, more like an hour.

He peered into her face as if he was ticking through his diagnoses, and she pulled a leaf out of her hair. "Why didn't you ring the bell?"

"I did."

"I'd have heard it," he said decisively. He had given up on her, seen her finally for the madwoman she must certainly be. "I was just upstairs." Why had she stood in the rain, let herself get so bedraggled, why—?

"Maybe it's broken?" she began, though she knew better than to argue—you have to take the person's hand, soothe her (or in this case him)—through these terrors.

"I'm sorry," she said. "I must not have pushed it right. But it doesn't matter. Here we are after all." She smiled and so did he— there, she'd found the key, they'd turned the corner.

But as they sat down his cell phone rang, and he rummaged for it in his briefcase, holding up a finger—it was his publicist; he had to take the call. She tried to dry her hair with a Kleenex, listening as Karp told him to develop a Web site: www.morriskarp.com. By the time he finished the explanation, his beeper was shrieking and he had to go back to the phone—

"No, I can't film until three-thirty," he said, although it was almost that already. "Yes, yes, I'll be ready then." And to her, aside, "You won't mind if there's a camera crew in the waiting room when you go?"

"No," she said, "no, it's okay."

"So—" He smiled; he sank down in the chair. "How are you?"

"I—I—"

"Can you say what you're feeling?"

She swallowed: "I, I guess . . . ," she began, despising the edge of tears in her voice. "I'm afraid, I . . . you seem different. . . ." and heard a murmur, perhaps of understanding—maybe everything was all right and she was hearing his affirmation through the haze.

"I mean, I do understand," she said. "This is a test-tube love— meant as an inoculation against a more destructive strain . . . but . . ." But some people die of inoculations! He murmured again. And then again, though she'd said nothing. She looked up.

His eyes were closed, perhaps meditatively.

"Dr. Karp?" No answer. She cleared her throat. "Dr. Karp?" The response was an elephantine snore.

A wave of tenderness broke over her; the grand proscenium on which she had been giving voice to her passion shrank away, and she found herself in a badly lit room with a dear, nervous, allergic man who was doing his best to love her in accordance with the statutes of the Commonwealth of Massachusetts. Now he gave out with something like a roar, and she laughed aloud. The spell was broken—there was no going about the usual business—they were alone together finally with not a ghost in the room. She loved him, she had wanted his wishes to come true, and now he'd got the book, the publicist, the interview—he'd worked all night, night after night—and he finally felt safe and warm enough to fall asleep *here* with *her*. She ought to be flattered! If she went to him now and stroked his hair, kissed him, he might awaken not just from the quick nap but from the terrible slumber that had kept him from loving her all this time.

"Darling?" This was distinctly a warning shot but it did not awaken him, and in one reckless instant she stood, crossed the rug that lay between them, and fell on her knees at his feet.

But she was not, it turned out, so much a rapist as to kiss a supine psychologist full on the lips in midsnore. She had a spider's impulse to wrap him up and store him safely away—he would satisfy all her hungers for a time—but instead she touched his ankle, very quickly, expecting to receive a shock as from an electric fence.

"Wake up, angel."

"What?" he started, looking up at her in alarm.

"You fell asleep," she said.

"No, no." He shook his head, rubbed his eyes, tried uncomfortably to pull back an inch or two.

"It's okay, I understand."

"I wasn't asleep," he explained to his poor deluded patient, stretching.

"You were *snoring*!"

He smiled. "I wish I could say that only happens when I'm asleep," he said.

"You *snore* when you're *awake*?" She sat back. It may come as a blow, to find you've been playing Carmen in full dress opposite a wakeful snorer. She crept backwards surreptitiously, like a sheepish retriever.

"Not exactly awake, maybe" he explained, with his beautiful hands outstretched. "In a deeper state of consciousness than actual waking, but—"

"*Asleep*! You were asleep!" *Dr. Karp, let us call a spade a spade!* But to Karp there was no such thing as a spade—the conscious world was only a loose assortment of atoms in whose swirls he discerned now one constellation, now another.

"In something of a trance, a state *like* sleep . . . the state of deep listening . . ."

She skootched away another inch or two.

"And I was up most of the night!" he concluded. "A manic psychosis, these things can take hours." Had he been the doctor, or the patient? Was he crazy? He'd insisted she wished he were crazy, so he would seem more like her mother.

"So you fell asleep," she said. "There's no shame in it." But as they argued the stage loomed up again with all the actors in their masks—it was horrible, she started to bawl. "You wrote the book, you solved the emergency, you convinced the publicist, you rescheduled the camera crew, you exhorted me to open my heart, and then you *fell asleep*! I understand you can't touch me, it's against the law, and there's this, this . . . wife . . . so, okay, it's one thing not to *do* it, but not to *feel* it, not to let it take root in your heart, is mean, it's stingy, it's *cheap* somehow—it's just wrong! You stand apart from me, you don't enter into me, you treat me like—like an unexploded bomb!"

"I—" The buzzer rang, and he looked at his watch. "I can't..." He closed his eyes, seeking divine strength? Praying she would disappear? How could she ever know?

"You torture me," he said.

"*I* torture *you*!!" But... probably he was right. Here he was locked in a tiny room with a madwoman whose eyes were glued to the inch of pale skin between his sock and his pant leg, who thought of nothing except kissing his thighs, urging him to surrender himself to her, who was always calculating the width of his hips the better to imagine their thrust—just the thought probably put his back into spasms—how much longer until supper, until he could fall asleep beside his wife?

"I'm sorry," she said, "I'm so sorry, I..."

She pulled open the door and tried to compose herself before passing the cameramen, who were sprawled over the waiting room chairs eating sandwiches like bears raiding a campsite. Turning down the walk, past the innocuous, nonallergenic shrubs, she heard Karp greet them with great warm energy—he was refreshed from his nap, grateful to have escaped her, narrowly, once again—far easier to meet the press, face the nation. And she would have to drive home shaking and sobbing, raging at gluttonous fat drivers, puritanical thin drivers, boorish Republicans and pious Democrats, thinking "I'll tell you which parts of *no* I don't understand!"—feeling less like a human woman than a hive of infuriated bees.

And arrive home to her serene family, Hugh eating a bowl of ice cream and reading a biography of Vlad the Impaler, Cyrilla already asleep. Daisy stood in the hallway outside her door, listening to her quiet breath with envy. Why couldn't the mother possess a bit of the child's composure? What had happened to the very decisive and well-organized woman who had gone to consult a psychologist with her little list of troubles folded carefully in her purse? Wasn't he supposed to rid her of her failings? Instead he had turned her into a beast, ravenous, craving, ready to marry him or murder him or both, whatever would mash them most completely together. She went to the window—she was feeling oceanic—but the darkness was hard as enamel, and she saw only the reflection of the woman Morris Karp had introduced her to: wild-eyed, untended, hair flying off in corkscrews; heart breaking, blood racing . . . she spilled over in all directions; her every thought surprised her. There was more of her than there used to be.

And suddenly Cyrilla was screaming. Daisy went in to find her sitting up, still asleep, speaking in frantic gibberish as if she were arguing with a border guard in hell. "Wake up, Cyllie," she said, but as she tried to embrace her, the child flailed as if Daisy herself were the monster. She started to sing "Lavender's Blue," hearing a strength, a sustaining note, in her voice, where once had been all grief and yearning. Cyrilla woke and pitched into her arms, and Daisy laid her back on the pillow, brushed the damp curls from her face, kissed her as if kisses would keep her safe from harm. "Mama, you're better than a star," Cyrilla said.

"Nearer, anyway," said Hugh, who'd come to stand behind her. Had she dreamed she could abandon him? She was a wife, a mother, her bones ached with the past, but she was here.

How she loved that ache! She could trust it, could return to it over and over, a million times a day. She would always be longing; Karp would always be there. As he opened the door the next week she felt a wave of relief sweep all her suspicions away. He had not followed her parents into the void, he was here in the doorway, he smiled, coughed a little, weakly, from the damp. She blushed with happiness, looked down at her feet, and admitted she'd written the review— worked on his behalf in spite of everything.

"Laurel?" he inquired.

"It's a complex flower, nothing like a Daisy. It thrives in the cold." She snapped out her answers, though something troubled her—yes, the bushes along his walk—they were mountain laurel.

"And Tyringham?"

"Oh, I just pulled it out of a hat, I've only been there once—with a man I was dating years ago; it's not much of a town, a few houses, an old cemetery."

"It's a place where you once walked in a graveyard—"

"—with a man I loved," she said sharply, proudly. Let no one suggest that Daisy Kempton would abandon a passion simply because it was unrequited and absurd.

"Yes." Their eyes met, maybe for the first time, and she looked away, feeling (could it be?) shy. It was a forlorn happiness, to be here together, two peculiar souls warming themselves at the same metaphor.

"Jung said a man has to live out his complexes," she told him, lest he think they were striking a truce. She would not give up—she'd pursue him into his next life, and if she came back as a duck and he a june bug . . . well, the gods have their ways.

"Unlike Jung, I don't sleep with my patients," said the upstanding Karp.

"Freud couldn't be bothered to sleep with his own wife."

His sigh was very nearly a laugh.

"I've developed a—a certain tenderness—toward the UPS man," she said, feeling, of all things, guilty, though surely he'd be relieved. "I had—you know—a dream. . . ." It was a pleasure just to recall it, to feel the familiar longing begin to shape itself around the next hope. "He brought me a package, and . . ."

But the lines in Karp's forehead went so deep suddenly she thought of writing music on them: "So, you attempt to dilute your feelings toward me, and the efficacy of the therapy as well."

A reprimand—could it be? How they irritated each other! Yes, they were growing old together, Karp and she.

A Girl Like You

"I'm here to pick up the prescription for Elspeth Forrest?"

Lane sounded adult and offhand—as if she were fully qualified for life, not at all furtive or peculiar. The pharmacist was young, his face and neck were all pocked, his Adam's apple jumped ridiculously—who would be intimidated by such a person? She turned a mild gaze toward the cosmetics as if she were thinking of trying a new shade of nail polish if he'd just hand over the insulin and let her get on with her day. He tapped the name into his computer, running his finger along the screen to stall a minute, finally saying: "And you are—?"

"Lane Dancie, her daughter." Worthy of a business card.

"Oh, okay," he said, sounding relieved, turning to the refrigerator to take out the bag, double-checking the label. "Yup, Elspeth Forrest," he said. "Insulin in suspension, one hundred units per . . . sterile hypodermic needles . . ." And finally, reluctantly, "How old are you?"

"Thirteen," she said, defiant—she was almost eleven, but people often guessed older. Her face was wary and shrewd, her voice heavy with authority—she did not seem like a little girl. At school she let everyone cheat from her papers—she had all the right answers—but it won her no friends. That morning, the last day of school, Sylvie and Arlita had let her jump rope with them. She'd been so preoccupied with thinking how she'd say casually to Mama, "When I was skipping rope with my friends this morning . . ." (as if such happened every day) that she'd been clumsier even than usual and fallen, scraping knees *and* elbows, and Arlita had glared at Sylvie, who had invited her in, and Sylvie knelt beside her and examining her arm asked suddenly, "Is this a tan, or is it *dirt?*" then dropped the arm as if it was all pointless, there was no use being nice to Lane Dancie no matter how sorry you felt for her—she was a lost cause.

Of course it was dirt—a mottled stain along her arms, up her neck—why hadn't she seen it? She licked her thumb and rubbed at her wrist until a patch came up, then crossed her arms tight over each other—if the pharmacist found her out, he would give up on her, too.

"I can't give you these," he said, but it wasn't the automatic refusal she'd expected—he seemed hurt that she'd taken him for an easy mark. "Even if they were for you you'd have to have an adult."

"She's my mother," she said, rolling her eyes. "What do you think, I want it to get high?"

"This much insulin could kill a person your size!"

"Doug lets me," she said. He had, once, after Mama called and begged him—she hated the insulin, hated leaving their apartment, even using the telephone. She quavered, she didn't have strength for these things—Lanie was the strong one. So Doug the regular pharmacist had let her carry the insulin back, just the one time, he was very clear. And handsome, and confident—hearing his name the boy drew back. Lanie had life on her side for once; it would be easier for him to believe her, give in to her, than ferret out the lie.

"No," he said, suddenly, with an effort. "No."

Tears sprang up as if he'd slapped her. She was late already, and to be late without the insulin . . . Mama would be furious, she'd cry that she had no one to count on, she was alone in all the world, she asked only one little thing of Lanie and even that much Lanie couldn't do. Then she'd get dressed in one of the suits she bought when she was job hunting and sweep down St. George Street looking so commanding people would step out of her way, pick up the prescription, and collapse in angry sobs at home. Or worse, she'd refuse to go and slip into sugar lethargy so Lane had to call the ambulance again.

"Doug *lets* me," she repeated angrily. She felt like a lost child among the high bright aisles. She wouldn't cry though, in front of him or anyone—a pharmacist, was anything duller? She mastered herself with an iron effort, drawing herself up to dismiss him before he dismissed her, when he gave in just as surprisingly as he had balked a second before.

"Okay," he said, sullen. Silence had accomplished this—she of all people should have known that into a silence all fears are drawn. He looked left and right, but there was only an old woman combing the shelves for some ancient powder or liniment. "Okay, this one time."

She laid the bills on the counter—was he impressed she should carry so much?—thanked him stiffly, and left with the drug, the precious ingredient that must be added to Mama to keep her safe and calm. She had pulled it off, she was Lanie the magnificent, and all the way up Highland Avenue she imagined herself in the eye of a camera, starring in one happy scene after another: Lanie's report is returned with an A; Lanie skips rope with her friends; Lanie breezes home clutching her books to her heart, stopping in the pharmacy, crossing at the light, waving to the bus driver who smiles paternally down over her . . . These were scenes her mother could live on, and she could invent them endlessly, it was like having a magical power.

The arms remained crossed, to keep the bad thoughts—of Sylvie and Arlita, and clumsiness, and dirtiness, from wrecking the picture. Seeing Mr. Lathrop in the courtyard, Lanie decided to go around through the alley: he had smiled at her once, in the elevator, where most people gazed over her head as if they were blind to everything beneath their chins. She'd been bringing Casper down for his walk, and he'd said, "I used to have an English setter. They're a nice breed—eager, affectionate—just right for a girl like you." *A girl like you*? How would he know what she was like, when she herself couldn't say? But she'd felt something glowing inside her, something that said: Look, look at me. "A . . . fifth grader? Unless I miss my guess . . . and I'll say a good student, too, quiet, but independent, loves her doggie there" (she realized she had been stroking Casper's head as these words fell, like blessings, on hers) "and . . . the Spice Girls, and . . . chocolate chip cookies?" Here they reached the lobby, but as he turned for the laundry room, he said, "And, she blushes!" as if this were the proof of her perfection. Since then she had, of course, avoided him; she lived on this memory, and if she discovered he'd forgotten her, she might not be able to bear it.

He saw her, though, before she could get away. "There she is and just when I need her," he said. "What do you think?" He held out two packs of seedlings. "Should I put them all together higgledy-piggledy like this?"

He was planting flowers in the forlorn square of grass in front of the building—the *courtyard*, the super called it, the building being named Hampton Court, which had provoked gales of laughter from Mama when they first moved in. Why not the Landfill Arms? she'd asked, and when she took Lanie to school the first time she spoke the words *Hampton Court* with a hint of careless snobbery, the way you might say *The Dakota,* and flashed Lanie a secret smile. She was going to finish up her degree, find a job, and then who knew? Uncle Buddy was going to help her, and he *knew* people, the kind who can speak a word in your favor and change your whole life. Lanie would see: in a few months their Hampton Court period would be over and the day they shook her father off would count as the happiest day of their lives.

And she'd bustled around making the apartment pretty. Her husband was gone and with him all her troubles, and everything must be fresh and bright for the new life. The diabetes that had seemed a crippling burden shrank to a minor annoyance and she swiped the needle into her thigh each morning with a giddy machismo. "God never gives anyone more than he can bear," she said. She had started going to church again—she believed in everything; her husband had carried all the world's ills away with him. One evening she'd danced the Charleston to the ticker-tape maracas on *Wall Street Week*. "The sky's the limit, my blossom!" she said, and to Lanie's amazement she—who had sworn she would never, ever marry again, never have to do with a man—began planning a wedding for Lanie, in St. Patrick's Cathedral, with tall white candles and bridesmaids in red velvet and a wreath of roses on her head.

That image, of all of them, remained, though it was three years now since they moved to Hampton Court, and any idea of a job had long since been abandoned—to lose the Medicaid without a really good salary and insurance—it wasn't worth it. No, *she* would never let *her* daughter become one of those creatures who wore her latchkey around her neck; she intended to be there for Lanie. And there she was waiting, at three o'clock—she was avid, greedy to hear every minute of Lanie's day.

Late as she was, though, Lanie stopped to look into the flowers—they floated over their stems with a crazy brilliance, rose pink, butter yellow, tangerine. Poor Mr. Lathrop—planting a garden in this parched spot was the kind of thing he'd do, cheerful but doomed. He was gaunt and gray-cheeked, with an expression of morose intensity, his eyes popping out slightly as if no matter where he looked he was always staring at the same sad thing, and he seemed to be always alone, but his walk was quick and fluid and somehow hopeful; whenever Lanie saw him she imagined he was on his way to someplace exciting. Once he had gotten into the elevator carrying a Chinese dinner in one hand and a bunch of red tulips in the other, but it wasn't for guests, he said—he just liked to do everything right once in a while.

"Ummm," she said, drawing it out, relishing the attention. "I like them all together."

"Higgledy-piggledy it is then," he said, and she laughed, because she could see he hoped she would, and he started singing and dancing a high silly step, throwing his arms and legs out so wildly she felt embarrassed for him.

"Oh, the higgledy-piggledies give her the giggledies," he sang. "When the higgledy-piggledies give her the giggledies, I do the jiggledy, piggledy ho!"

It was something you might do for a three-year-old, but he was trying to please her, so she kept laughing.

"Will they grow?" she couldn't help but ask.

"Some flowers do better in poor soil," he told her. "Portulacas, nasturtiums . . . the less they have, the more they bloom. You can eat the nasturtiums, they're peppery—want to try one?"

This seemed like taking candy from a stranger, and she shook her head but could hardly croak out the *no*—wouldn't it be madness when someone was kind to you, to turn him away? He folded the flower and pushed it into her half-open mouth with a finger. It felt like velvet and tasted like perfume, but she chewed and swallowed it and smiled at him, thinking she might absorb something of him this way.

"Here," he said, picking three more—"Take some home. They're good in a salad, too."

. . .

Mama was sitting on her bed, holding a finger-stick blood-sample kit and crying.

"Where *were* you?" she asked. She had that awful, familiar expression; the smallest thing could send her spiraling down—she was frightened, heartbroken, suspicious, and she needed to account for these feelings, to find some way to explain them. When she was mad even Casper felt it—now he lay with his chin on the rug, looking balefully up at Lanie as if he blamed her, too.

"At the pharmacy."

"For forty-five minutes?"

"I stayed after school to jump rope with Arlita and Sylvie. . . . We lost track of the time. I'm sorry."

"No you're not, you're *not* sorry!" Mama said. "You don't care— you're having a good time with your friends and you don't care, that's all. And I'm here all alone, and I can't, I can't . . ." She held the lancet poised over her finger but couldn't bring herself to stab it.

"Here, let me," Lanie said. "I'm good at this, Ma, remember?" She took the hand tight so Mama couldn't squirm away, and pricked it, caught the welling drop, folded the poor finger gently back into the hand. Why it had to be, that someone who so feared the needle should have diabetes . . . The Greeks would have thought it a punishment, and Mama let out a wild sob as if Lanie were Nemesis herself.

"It's way up, Ma," she said, going for the insulin.

"I try so hard, Lanie," Mama said. This was the cruellest thing— she seemed to think Lane had the power to cure her, that if only she was good enough Lanie would take the curse away. Thank God for the needle gun—they'd got it with the Medicaid. It went so fast, at first Mama said it was painless, though after a few months she'd seemed to feel the shots again even worse than before.

"Arm or leg?" Lanie asked.

"Leg," her mother said, resigning herself. Lanie grabbed her thigh hard to squeeze out the feeling, pressed the gun to the skin, pulled the trigger. Nothing ever sounded so fast, so certain as that needle. She didn't suppose she would mind it as Ma did—she was not going to mind things, she was going to live a bold life. When she went for a shot at school the nurses always said how brave she was. And when the others mocked her she turned her face away—they were young, that was all, they didn't know who they were talking to. Let them laugh—Uncle Bud knew people at NBC, he was going to get her a screen test for the soaps. The image of herself, dirty, her ear sticking out through her lank hair, pushed itself into her mind, but she slammed the door on it. They would soon be enlightened, her classmates, the people who should have been her friends—she would be leaving the likes of them behind.

The ordeal over, Mama relaxed a little, though she was still wary. "I *did* go out," she said, defending herself against the unspoken complaint. "I got you something . . . but now I suppose you had a snack on the way home."

There, set out on the table with a glass of milk, was a cupcake with an inch of sugar frosting piped out to look like pink and yellow roses. The note beside the plate read, "For the rose of my heart. Happy Summer Vacation." Sweets. Mama wanted Lanie to have everything, and she knew the exact shape of everything—the outline of the void in her own life.

"It's beautiful," Lanie said, with just the right feeling, she thought. The cake was no better than the nasturtium though; it was all sugar and no taste, and the thought of Mama going through all her careful rituals, showering, making up her face, checking the mirror a hundred times all for the sake of a trip across the street to buy a cupcake, and then waiting, waiting for Lane to come home and see . . . It stuck in her throat, but she ate every bite.

"Beautiful like my beautiful girl," her mother said, smoothing Lanie's hair and kissing the top of her head before she sank woozily into the couch. "Would you bring me a little glass of wine, honey? I think it might help my head."

"Is it okay?" Lanie asked, because it wasn't—wine was no better than cake—the sugar burned up her veins like acid, made her head ache so that light had to be filtered, noise muffled, all of life muted, recast in pastel. Lanie had the nasturtiums in her pocket; she wanted both to show them off and to keep them a secret—they were so bright she felt they might hurt Mama's eyes.

"Of course it's okay," Mama said, irritated again. Lanie was so officious, full of rules like a horrible little nurses' aide, she knew. A little wine, what harm could it do? Lanie poured as little as she dared.

"Would you like to have Arlita over sometime—?" Mama asked suddenly. "Maybe to spend the night?"

This, from someone who fled into her room when she so much as heard footsteps in the hall, was a heroic offer. She wanted to make amends—she so desperately wanted to be a good mother. She'd have done anything for Lanie if only she could.

"Oh, Arlita's going to camp," Lane said lightly. "But, thank you, it's a great idea. Maybe in August after she gets back." She took Casper's leash down from its hook, and he jumped up and charged toward her, paws on her shoulders to lick her face, nearly knocking her down. Mama smiled tenderly at the picture before her, and the knot in Lanie's chest loosened: the planets were back in their proper orbits, the summer was stretching ahead, anything was possible, anything at all.

She waited until Mama was in bed—seven-thirty—to run the bath, so she wouldn't have to explain anything. She usually took showers and not many of those—Mama washed so often Lane had *bathing* filed under *madness* in her mind. Once she was immersed, though, she wanted to stay there forever. Telling a story of herself like the stories of fashion models ("for breakfast she has only strawberries and the purest spring water . . . such delicate beauty must be nourished by perfect comfort and soothing ritual") until it verged into the story of a young goddess ("washed in the waters of the Aegean, she returned to the island of Cythera where the spirits fed her a salad of flowers to restore her strength before her pilgrimage to Delphi was to begin . . ."), she lay back and felt herself dissolving—all that wrought-up tenseness that Mama hated in her seemed to melt away. She had to scrub fiercely, but when it was done there she was, glowing pale as the statue of a goddess, and there seemed something so tender and poignant in her body that Zeus would surely flash down from the heavens and carry her away.

By the time she was dressed again it was eight-thirty, but what is eight-thirty on the longest night of the year, when you are pale as a goddess and Uncle Bud is going to get you a job at NBC? "Come on, Casper," she whispered. "Let's go down and see the flowers." She could feel him shivering with excitement as she clipped the leash on— it reminded her never to be so eager—it would be awful if people knew how much one wanted them.

Mr. Lathrop was in the lobby waiting for the elevator.

"Just the person I'd been hoping to see!" he said. "I was going up to the roof—want to come?" And without waiting for an answer he stepped in and pushed the button for the twelfth floor.

"Penthouse, James," he said to the air, and up they went. "To your left," he said, holding the door for Lanie and Casper, "around the corner, and voilà!"

The sign on the door read EMERGENCY EXIT, ALARM WILL SOUND, but he threw it open and ushered them gallantly through. At the top of the passage the light was brilliant, and when they stepped into it, he swept his arm out as if the view of the city shimmering in the confluence of rivers were his own invention and he was operating the stately ships and the sails that flicked between them by remote control.

"Is it—?" Was it real? Because how could it be? People said there was a view from the north side, but Lanie hadn't realized this meant one side of the building looked out on a different world. She let Casper off the leash, and he ran lightly, doggily around the chimneys, sniffing in the corners, rolling on a piece of AstroTurf set up like a putting green as if it were a real green lawn. There were beach chairs set up, one with a folding umbrella attached and a rubber tree planted nearby in a barrel, and a shuffleboard chalked on the asphalt with a plastic paperweight for a puck.

"No one's here tonight," Mr. Lathrop said, "but it can get pretty lively."

Could it be, that he had taken her to a kind of secret place where all the quiet, exhausted tenants of this building, who hardly acknowledged each other inside, suddenly came out in their T-shirts and Bermuda shorts to socialize and bask in the sun? She started toward the edge to look down, but she had to step back—it seemed as if some irresistible force would pull her over.

"It's safe," Mr. Lathrop said, and set his hand on her shoulder. "See, it's the same brick wall as the rest of the building. It's no different than looking out your bedroom window. It only feels different, that's all. Look, it comes up to your waist—you're not going to fall." Seeing her scrubbed arms outstretched she thought *yes,* maybe she did dare to look out from here.

Casper came around the chimney with a tennis ball in his mouth, which he dropped expectantly at Mr. Lathrop's feet. "He's so obedient!" Mr. Lathrop said, which was hardly the truth, and Lanie wondered if Casper was imitating the dogs on TV. He raced after the ball when Mr. Lathrop threw it and was back in a flash, stepping like a parade horse though his dignity was compromised by the sight of his tail madly wagging.

"Go, tiger!" Mr. Lathrop said to him, skipping the ball along the asphalt. "Do you see over there?" he asked Lanie. "Those trees?" She followed his pointing arm to a surprising green thicket there in the midst of the tenements and avenues.

"That's where I grew up," he told her. "The whole island used to look like that—can you imagine there were farms here?"

She could not. She could hardly believe Staten Island hadn't been paved over since the day the world was made, or that Mr. Lathrop had ever been a boy. She felt nearly the same vertigo, looking up at him, as she had looking down from the rooftop a minute before.

"I used to shoot ducks over there," he said. "Rex was a wonderful hunting dog. Casper would be, too—it's hard on these outdoor dogs, living in the city. There were deer in there, too." His voice had grown distant and sad; he was confiding—amazingly—in *her*!

"That's where I first kissed my wife, in fact." The word—*wife*—stabbed her.

"You wouldn't have guessed that, I suppose," he said when she didn't answer. "I don't seem the type?" he asked. "Who'd marry me?"

"Oh, no!" Lanie said. "That's not what I meant!" She forgot that she hadn't spoken. She wanted to ask where this wife was, but she imagined that, like Mama, she had grown to despise him and pushed him out of her life.

"I'm *not* the type, that's all," he said. "Some people are meant to be alone."

"You seem like a very nice person to me," Lanie said, cursing herself for the banality—if only she could find the words to comfort him, to draw the thorn out of his paw . . . Well, it would be magic, he would belong to her.

"It must be nearly your bedtime," he said then, looking very busy and serious suddenly, accepting the ball from Casper without even patting him and turning back toward the steps, though it couldn't have been much past nine. So after all that, he still thought of her as a child!

The center of gravity had changed; it was located in Mr. Lathrop's apartment, number 301. Lanie said nothing to Mama, who was always afraid someone would steal Lanie's love from her. How could a mother fear such a thing? But she did, and her fear made it seem possible, so that Lanie feared it herself sometimes, too. She kept him a secret, never spoke his name aloud, which meant there was no way to contain him: he got loose in her mind like ether, and when she woke up in the morning she felt like he'd been with her all night, and when she knew she might see him her heart battered itself against her ribs like a frenzied animal in a cage.

The next day it was Casper's turn for the bath—he looked extremely skeptical at first, but she whispered to him that he would love it, and while she was lathering him he began to revel, rolling in the water and shaking himself until she wrapped him in a towel and lugged him out in her arms like a monstrous baby. He smelled like fresh laundry, and when she set him down, he raced around the room and jumped back and forth over the coffee table like a circus dog, and Mama laughed in the old way and Lanie felt like the girl in the camera eye whose life was all energy and accomplishment, no secret cravings, no fears. Taking him out to walk she pushed the button for the up elevator by mistake, and in a minute he was yanking her up the stairs to the roof.

"Ah, here you are!" Mr. Lathrop said, really glad to see her she thought, cautioning herself against such ideas. "Is it your birthday?" he asked.

"No."

"Oh, what a shame!" he said. "And I've gone and gotten you a present . . ."

It was a paper box with two gilt crickets mounted on springs inside, which began to chirp as the lid was opened and fell silent as soon as it closed.

"It's the best thing on Mott Street," he said, peering into her face. "What do you think?"

He'd been in the midst of the city, where people streamed around you and everything was bright and quick and fascinating, and he'd been thinking of her.

"I *love* it," she said, unable to lift her eyes—if she stared at it hard enough, she would understand the secret message she was sure must be there. They weren't alone today—there was a breeze and Mr. and Mrs. Chartov, who usually huddled in the back of the elevator, whispering together as if they were still afraid of the KGB, were taking advantage of it, she asleep with her skirts pulled up to sun her heavy, pale legs, while he read a spy novel with a dagger on the cover. Henry Ramos was playing *boules* on the AstroTurf with another man Lanie didn't know, while Florence Sklar, the very flirtatious and very old lady who lived across the hall from them, weeded an herb garden she had planted in a barrel, wearing carmine lipstick and a panama hat.

Lanie went to the edge to look out over the place where Mr. Lathrop had proposed to his wife. "Did you live on a farm?" she asked him, wanting that falling sensation she'd had when he confided in her the night before, expecting him to change the subject, but he began to give such a long, full answer that it seemed he must have been thinking it out all day. His father had been a chemist, and died young, and then . . .

"Did she die, too, your mother?" Lanie asked.

"No," he said, looking off over the water. "No . . ." But he sounded as if he wasn't sure. "She just didn't know what to do, without him. She wasn't . . . strong."

I'm strong, Lanie thought. She remembered how she made the boy fill the prescription, how she steadied Mama along by balancing insulin and sugar, exercise and sleep, always keeping a little snack and a happy story on hand. Mr. Lathrop (call him Hank, he said, and she did, but in her thoughts he was always *mister*) could rest his head on her shoulder, he would be safe with her.

Casper found the tennis ball again and dropped it at Mr. Lathrop's feet, looking up at him with a yearning Lanie hadn't seen before, that made her think absently that dogs care more for men—certainly Casper had loved her father best of all. Mr. Lathrop took the ball and skipped across the roof like a stone on a lake, his attention fixed inward the whole time. He wasn't handsome; a thick vein pulsed in his temple, and one eye was overcast somehow—it was a hurt to be kissed away. And his shoulders were broad, sheltering. She knew about love—she had watched the couples in the park, the way they couldn't keep apart from each other. If she dared to touch him . . . But she did not. She knew about sex, too—the man puts his penis in your vagina. It seemed a cold thing, but she would bear it gratefully for the sake of love.

When she wanted to prove he really existed she could open the cricket box and hear them chirp—by mid-July the lid no longer closed tightly, and if she left it in the east window, they'd wake her when the sun cleared the Federal Building in the morning. That meant, Hank said, it was light that activated them . . . a chemical reaction. He really was Hank now, and she was Lane—he younger, she more adult; they knew each other's paths and where to cross them— they saw each other every day. He knew so much—all about chemicals, medicines, the way things work—she absorbed it all as if life were an enormous contraption she needed his knowledge to steer. After lunch, as soon as she'd done her mother's blood levels, she'd run to the library and grab a mystery for Mama and something for herself, anything to hold up in front of her so Mama wouldn't see the new expressions—every kind of longing and satisfaction—that were shaping her face. She looked in every mirror she passed—she was beginning to see something she liked there, a listening spirit that a man might come to love. Whenever she saw her reflection now she wondered what he had seen in her, what he meant when he said "a girl like you."

She kept the books under the roof stairway so she could act as if she'd been at the library all afternoon, a ruse Mama either believed or accepted, it hardly mattered which. Once Lane forgot a whole batch and owed three dollars by the time she returned them—she didn't have it, of course, and the nice librarian wasn't there, and some snippy substitute refused to let her take any more books. The blood sprang to her cheeks as if she'd been slapped, and she turned away vowing never to enter that building again, and in the midst of thinking "You'll be seeing me on NBC any day, bitch," she realized the summer was passing with no word from Uncle Bud, and her mother was as silent about him as about her father now—it would be poison to mention him—so she thought, instead, "I'm going to marry Hank Lathrop, and you'll still be nobody."

Though why the library volunteer would be jealous of such a thing she could not be sure—but she felt it to the bottom of herself—it would be the proudest victory, to have won his love. And he didn't work, he must have money, he could take care of them—Mama, too— he would keep them safe, she would keep him warm.

She had won him, she believed she had. She hoarded his confidences, kept them close to her heart, took them out when she was alone to hold them to the light and marvel, that he had given these things to her. He told her more and more and more. She could feel his story beginning to circle around both of them, binding them tight to each other. When he hugged Casper, burying his face in the dog's neck, he must be wishing to hold her. Yes, she was coming into that rarest and most precious of possessions—a man's heart. And all because she knew the secret of adults, that they are no less frightened than children and if you care for them properly they will love you in return.

Casper was like a child, too, panting and wagging his tail in a frenzy, bounding to fetch the ball a hundred times in a row. If they were engrossed in their conversation and forgot to throw it again right away he'd race in circles around the AstroTurf and try to retrieve Mr. Ramos's *boules*.

"No, *no*, Casper!" she called, laughing, and he bounded over to her and licked her face and nearly bowled her over. "No!" she said, laughing, scratching his ears, and Hank gave him a biscuit from his shirt pocket and threw the ball. And looking away toward the spot where he'd kissed his wife said that it was right after they were married that Rex had to be put down.

"That's life, I guess," he said, "one loss after another. When I met Sarah . . . It was the first time since my dad died that I felt—I felt—" He wove his fingers together, and she said she knew. "Twelve years ago . . . I thought when we were this age we'd be looking back at our life. . . ."

Twelve years! Then, this was a sadness from before Lane was born, a sadness the entire span of her life had not eased. She laid her hand on his shoulder and felt it tense—it was the same as with her mother; pain drew the being into a fist around it, you couldn't open the hand again no matter how you tried. "What happened?" she asked him, lobbing the ball softly into the corner just to get Casper out of the way.

"I guess—I guess she didn't want me anymore," he said, and his lip trembled, and Casper brought the ball back with his tail wagging so hard it looked like he'd tip himself over, and Hank took it from him and packed it between his hands like a snowball. "No, there was no mystery, she didn't want me. . . ." And he hurled the ball away as if he meant to be rid of it forever.

It bounced beside the chimney and sailed over the wall, bright and still against the sky for a moment before it fell out of sight, with Casper behind it, gone in one ecstatic bound.

"That's how it is sometimes, with men and women," Hank was saying, looking down at the floor as if to keep from any distraction. She couldn't interrupt him—what would she say? She couldn't believe it herself, that she had just seen Casper leap away into the sky. "I thought, I thought—but I was wrong." He looked up, finally, looking to her for an answer.

"He went over the edge," she said, still staring at the spot she'd last seen him as if a celestial version of Casper might come trotting back through the air.

"He—what?" Hank shook his head, getting the past out of it.

"Casper, he—the ball bounced and he went after it."

"No, honey, he can't . . . ," he said, and her heart quieted—he was so reasonable, he would explain now how it couldn't have happened, there were laws of gravity and velocity that prevented such a thing . . . or how there was an awning down there where Casper would have landed softly like a dog in a movie, or how he could fix a broken dog . . . But watching his face she saw his calculations prove out the wrong way. He went to look over the wall, then took her by both arms and turned her toward the stairs.

"I'll take you home," he said. "Then I'll go down and see what I can do."

. . .

"He died happy, Lanie," her mother said. "He was doing what he loved best, with the girl he loved most, he probably didn't even feel anything. You said you didn't hear him cry. It's better this way, I'm sure of it, darling—he lived a good life, and died in an instant, what more could you ask?"

She had a mother's tutelary manner but Lane knew what she was saying: that Lane was all she had in the world and if she gave in to grief they'd both be lost.

"I suppose it's true," she said, trying to see it this way, thinking how he'd lain on the carpet all that time hardly lifting his head, and then from the first time Hank threw the ball for him he was alive again and watching, watching, afraid to miss a single chance. He had leapt over the wall as if now that he had Hank, he felt he could fly. "His last moment was a happy one," she said.

"See?" Mama said. "Think how lucky he was, that you loved him so, all his life long." And she took Lane's hand and smiled tenderly. You could see how pretty she had been—that her kind face had once been the definition of beauty. "Try to be happy for him, honey," she said. "He's gone up to heaven, with God."

Life wasn't real to Mama anymore—she couldn't see the pain in its loss. Lane was grateful for mourning—the thought of Casper dying out of pure exuberance, as he had, made her throat close with grief, which was much better than the staring without seeing, living blind.

Hank had never called her, or knocked on her door—this would have been impossible, taboo—but when she carried the trash to the incinerator in the morning she found him standing in the hall, waiting for her, with a bag of chocolate chip cookies.

"Thank you," she said. "It was so nice of you to think of me. . . ." She took a bite but couldn't swallow.

"I know it was my fault," he said, and his voice was terrible, his face in the dim light was worse. "I'm sorry," he said, "I'm so sorry you can't know—to hurt *you*, who I—" There it was, what she had prayed for—he loved her. She'd have made any sacrifice—the penis in the vagina, or some kind of pain. Indians pierced their skin and ran leather cords through, to prove themselves. Her thoughts had been full of blood, but it was supposed to be her own.

"I buried him in the woods—the woods I showed you?" he said. "Do you want—?"

It was raining—a steady, cold rain that had beaten the portulaca blossoms into soggy tissue along the walkway. They turned down Union Avenue together, leaving Hampton Court behind them as if this were the most ordinary thing on earth instead of a jailbreak, a flight into Lane's dreams. It was hard to keep up with his stride, but her heart felt steady as a piston—as long as she stood beside him she was not to be daunted, she could climb any height. If Casper was the price the gods demanded . . . Here everything swung wild, she couldn't think, so she only walked, beside Hank Lathrop, away from Hampton Court.

"I used to know every tree in here," Hank said, turning up from the bus stop into the woods. The air seemed green, as if the color were leaching out of the leaves. Lane was soaked through and only wished for more.

"The whole hillside was wooded, it wasn't just this patch. See, they couldn't build here, it's too rocky, too steep." There were beer cans and Styrofoam hamburger boxes all over, and in a clearing was a slashed armchair with the stuffing spilling out. Behind it the grave was marked with a forked branch, covered with fallen leaves.

"Did he—? Do you think—?" She wanted him to say Casper hadn't suffered, but she couldn't ask for fear of the wrong answer. No matter though, Hank had heard none of it.

"I was about your age when Dad died," he said. "I couldn't look, at the wake—I ran away—I—"

She was thinking about how soft Casper had been—when he was a puppy, when she was young, Mama used to beat eggs into his food for his coat. He was so small and so breathlessly avid he used to flip over backwards every time she patted him. There he had been all this time—it was like having a child, the tenderest part of herself, to care for, and at the same time he had seemed to keep watch over her. Things would happen to her now that he wouldn't know . . . She imagined writing him a letter somehow . . .

"I'm so sorry," Hank said. He made a strangled sound, a kind of sob, like ice breaking in his chest. "Lane, I don't know how to make it up to you. . . ."

"You didn't mean to," she said. "And he died happy, think of that. He died doing what he loved to do best." The empty phrases were heavy on her tongue, and she looked into the ground for fear she'd give herself away and hurt his feelings.

"He loved you," she said. It was so familiar, this act of reassurance, she took his hand almost without thinking. So much had happened, all the rules were gone. She pulled him toward her, and when he didn't move she yanked harder as if he were just another obstacle she needed to budge. She held him tight against her, imagining she could pull him around her against the cold and misery. For a long time he stood still, then his arms came up around her, not with love or even lust, only exhaustion. He gave a small cry and slumped against her so she staggered back under his weight and had to push at him to keep them both from falling.

"It's pouring," he said. Perhaps he'd just noticed. He strode back to Hampton Court with such long steps it seemed like he was hoping to lose her. Going up in the elevator he hardly looked at her, and when he got off at the third floor he gave a funny, limp little wave

that seemed both apologetic and defiant—it wasn't his fault everything was so bleak, he'd done what he could, he'd planted some
flowers.

Mama was in bed, sound asleep—but the hypodermic gun was
beside the bed, with only one used insulin vial in the wastebasket, so
probably she was okay. Lanie stood at the window, looking down at
the pavement where Casper had died. She supposed she ought to cry,
but she didn't really feel sad anymore—only curious, possessed of a
cold strangeness that set her outside everything, even herself. The
sight of her pale, scrubbed arms made her sick, reminding her of her
childish dreams of love and glory—how pathetic. Asleep, her mother
looked even more vulnerable than usual—how could anyone be so
weak? Lane's contempt for her felt exactly like courage. She took up
the hypodermic gun, thinking how easy it would be, to use it—and
the boy had said one dose could kill her. Then her mother could see
firsthand, what it's like when the thing you love best dies without
pain, and goes up to heaven with God.

Wild Rice

"I can pay you a thousand dollars for the week."

Phyllis Giustameer sounded as dry and calculating as a spider, and she made me this offer as if she could already taste me. She was the director of the Cranberry Coast Writers' Conference, which had, she assured me, an international reputation. And she was asking me (little me!) to teach the short-story class, the plum so many Major Authors were just dying to bite into . . . all this *and* a thousand dollars for the week!

"It sounds wonderful," I said. I hate to dash any pleasure, even a spider's, even when I'm the fly. And a thousand dollars for one week of teaching—teaching creative writing, which everyone knows is the easiest thing in the world—*is* a lot of money. It's antisocial, unde-mocratic to look the wrong way at a thousand dollars, even if your husband, like mine, is an investment banker. I might need comfort, or purpose, or laughter, but I did not need a thousand dollars, not at all. Still, saying no felt wrong, sinful even, as if I'd be denying the old, hungry, socialistic self and admitting that I was now a member of the group whose heads, in the event of a revolution, would be found on pikes instead of shoulders.

Though as far as I could tell, every potential revolutionary was presently under a beach umbrella, reapplying sunscreen and luxuriating in a bestseller: on the bay side, at least, no one was reading *Das Kapital*.

"I'm honored. Thank you for thinking of me. But . . ."

But what? But I'm too lazy to drive up the cape in the summer traffic every day for a week? Too timid to face a classroom full of people who think I know something? That I may seem healthy but I'm a closet quadriplegic? No, as usual everything true was either unspeakable or absurd. I thought of saying I was busy—this being such a universal excuse that everyone accepts it, even though often enough "I'm busy" means "I need to spend hours staring." No one has ever been less busy than I am. I gave up my teaching job when I married Scott, and since I lost the baby I mostly just sit. I try to look like I'm reading, or making notes, but really I'm immersed all day in a sea of bitterness and disappointment, and every once in a while I'm able to come up and gasp a quick breath in the sunlight before I go under again.

"A thousand dollars," Phyllis repeated. "There's not many can match that." No, it would be better to give in and teach the class. Not to need a thousand dollars is a terrible thing.

"It *is* a lot of money," I said, and I could hear her relax, even feel it.

"Then we're agreed," she said, "I'll see you in July."

The week before I started she called again. The class was only half filled, and it simply wouldn't pay to go on with it, she was so sorry but we'd have to cancel—unless, of course . . . Well, if I could do it for five hundred dollars—five hundred was nothing to sneeze at, and the load would be lighter, of course. The poetry teacher had been willing . . .

"Oh, dear," I said, seeing the escape hatch open. "Oh, no, please don't worry. It's much better to cancel, I'm sure . . ."

"Of course, they're coming from as far away as Kansas and Louisiana," said Phyllis. "I'd hate to disappoint them."

"They won't be disappointed! They'll be relieved! Now they can go to the beach! They'll save money and they won't have to sit through some boring class."

"They've paid their deposits," she said stiffly. "They've already sent in two hundred dollars apiece."

"You could send it back?"

"All right," she snapped. "A thousand it is, and we'll expect you on Sunday."

I had accidentally driven a hard bargain. Scott laughed when I told him—he won't take me to buy a car because I worry about the salesmen, having to act that way to make a living, and I get so intent on showing them I *really do* believe what they're saying, that I'm sure they're right that this sedan with all its options is as powerful as the jungle beast it's named after, that there have been instances when I've talked a price *up*. I sat down on the step and thought—look at that, I've made a thousand dollars, all by myself.

On Sunday evening, August 3, I drove down to Swansea—a town of great maples, long stone walls, and austere colonial buildings faithfully restored. Our quarters—the old county courthouse—was a tall building with high, narrow windows, leaning slightly in the shadow of an enormous linden tree, painted a dour shade of gray. A good place for a witch trial, and the tree would make an excellent gallows. Inside the courthouse a narrow pew-lined aisle led to the bench, where a tray of plastic champagne glasses was set out—this was our introductory meeting, just, as Phyllis had said, to break the ice and put everyone at ease.

She was bustling purposelessly around our classroom—the former jury room, piled to the ceiling now with properties from an amateur theater company—feathered hats and silk kimonos, papier-mâché boulders, an antique radio, a life-size plastic horse. A pair of thrones with velvet cushions stood on a platform behind the table. The windows were painted over to suggest stained glass—they shut out the clear, golden evening entirely.

"Here's our teacher!" Phyllis said, coming toward me with a directorial smile that revealed a fortune in gold teeth, wearing a knit suit thirty years out of fashion, in the same shade of lavender as her hair. "The students have paid their deposits," she told me. "Marge here will collect the balance tonight."

Marge was a person of absolute utility, brick shaped, with a helmet of dark hair and eyes like stones. She had both hands tight on her cash box as if I might snatch it away. Her glance was enough to elicit a check from each student who arrived, except Melanie, the youngest, who was studying creative writing, Phyllis told me, in order to develop a second source of income, since she was pregnant and her husband, a welder, was out of work.

"Would it be all right if I brought the rest on Thursday?" Melanie asked.

"We like to get things settled up front," Marge said.

"Could I postdate the check?"

Marge was silent.

"All right, dear," Phyllis said kindly, "three hundred, dated August seventh. That will be fine."

The others looked at Melanie with something like envy. Not one of them could afford to be here. They'd driven across the state or the country, camped in the local guest houses, and arrived with sharp pencils and thick notebooks like supplicants who hear a voice in a dream, fall to their knees, and crawl through the deserts toward God. Some had a few pages of manuscript, others were, as one put it, "virgin territory"—fertile, if as yet untilled. Yes, they were all women, aware they possessed something powerful beyond measure, something others (men) desperately need, still unable to guess what that essential thing might be. No man on earth perceives in himself forty rich acres and is willing like a woman to plow the crop under every year. But where would you find a table of men, each glowing with the natural expectation that he'll excel in a discipline of which he knows not one thing?

"First, a brief orientation," said Phyllis brightly. "This is the Old County Courthouse—the oldest courthouse in continuous use in this country. We are currently awaiting National Historic Status, which would require that the roof be returned to the original slate. Slate, as you know, is expensive . . ."

These workshops, my "Aspects of the Short Story," and the afternoon "Poetry of Instinct" had been developed to provide cash for the renovations. Phyllis, a collector of early American antiques, was treasurer of the Swansea Historical Society. Her husband was in advertising and knew what people will pay for: if you promise a woman you will develop her ineffable inner substance into a source of income and pride, she'll be good for a thousand at least. Thus the Cranberry Coast Writers' Conference was born. Once Phyllis got talking about the building she forgot creative writing entirely, and it wasn't until fifteen minutes later, when, speaking of the cost of replacing the old furnace, she stole a glance at the cash box, and she remembered why the rest of us were there.

"Well," she said, "that's something about the courthouse, now let's go around and everybody can introduce herself."

The door opened and a small, enormously fat woman entered,

dressed in a yellow polka-dot shift and very pretty in spite of her immensity, with rosy cheeks and a fringe of black curls escaping under her straw hat. "I'm sorry," she said. "I had to take a cab—I'm afraid to drive at night. Back home in Louisiana, I live right in the middle of town and I just walk."

She settled happily onto a chair that seemed ill-designed to hold her, and during the moment of collective suspense while we all awaited its collapse, introduced herself as Lucy DesRochers of East Sourwood, Louisiana. "I know I can write," she said. "They've always told me I was a natural writer, back home. Since my divorce I've been teaching kindergarten, but I want to develop a writing business so I can work out of my home. My pastor thinks I have a real talent for words, that I should be writing children's books. But I need to know the markets. Back home in Louisiana, we aren't savvy on these things." She spoke in a confiding, girlish drawl as if everyone she'd ever met had loved her, wanted to protect her. I did, too.

"Writing for children is pretty far out of my field . . ." I said.

"Marketing," Phyllis interrupted, "is marketing. I'm sure some of your marketing knowledge is applicable to the children's markets."

"I don't really have a lot of marketing knowledge," I said with a laugh. I'd refused to have blurbs on my book because I find the whole blurb thing so revolting, only to be left enduring the appalled silence of people who looked as it with its blank jacket as if it were a poor deformed baby. A similar silence fell now—I'd admitted an ignorance so shocking it could not possibly be true.

Joy, a Professor of Culture Studies in Arkansas, was also interested in marketing, particularly for serious fiction. She hit the word *serious* in a way that alarmed me, and I wished she wasn't sitting beside Lucy, because this made her look even thinner and more pallid than she was—her hair, her complexion, and her clothing were colorless as oatmeal and one felt she might have been given her name as a rebuke.

"I know there's a novel in me," she said. "I just need to get it out on the page."

There was a novel in Linda, too—a medical thriller about a gang of rogue surgeons who slip knockout drops into people's drinks and steal their kidneys for resale on the organ black market. "I'd have written it down," she said, "but I've got scheduling problems. I work nights, and I take care of my husband during the day. It's his back—I mean that's what we thought, but it turned out to be ALS and he needs to have me there. Not that it's so bad, there's a lot worse things—you don't have any pain with ALS, your mind doesn't go, only your muscles, until you can't, you know, swallow . . ."

"So. You're interested in the medical fiction market," Phyllis interrupted, and turned to Mattie, who said proudly that she was sixty-five. There was no novel in Mattie—there was a guide for the middle-aged divorcée.

"It's really a series of short stories—chapters, I mean," she said, holding the manuscript out in both hands as if she loved its weight. I scanned the contents: "Adultery: It's Not Just in the Bible" and "Life on $65.00 a Week" caught my eye.

"I'm hoping for mass market," she said. "My youngest goes to college this year."

And finally Melanie, the only one who wanted to write stories: with a baby you don't get much time to yourself, so she needed something she could work on during an afternoon nap.

"It looks like it's going to be a *terrific* class," Phyllis said, "so let's hear from our teacher." She read out my resume—most impressive— I could hardly wait to meet the illustrious author. ". . . someone who can really give us the lowdown on what we need to stay on the cutting edge of the literary business today," she said decisively, and five notebooks opened, five pens were poised. Drinks and cheese, she'd said— I'd expected a cocktail party. I had nothing prepared.

"They say fiction writing can't be taught," I began, feeling a terrible cold draft from Phyllis's direction. "And, of course, that's true. Still, to be able to sit down with other writers, to think and talk about each other's work" (though, I remembered, they hardly had any work yet, but in a few days, when those novels started to blossom . . .), "to consider the author's deepest intention and see how he or she—er, she, has brought it to life, where she's succeeded, where she might do better . . ." and I was off. I'd forgotten how much I knew, and cared, in fact I'd forgotten who I was: I'd come to think of myself as the person whose baby grew in on itself and had to be surgically removed. Now here I was quoting Melville: "Why do you try to enlarge your mind? Subtilize it!"; demonstrating how Flaubert tapped his sentences out on his writing table; trying to illuminate the larger meaning of "write what you know."

Thinking, what if they don't know anything? But the bulk of their collective knowledge would be immense; they'd seen as much birth, death, character, and fate as Sophocles. Whatever it was that had constricted Joy until she spoke in a monotone and seemed to have nothing left in her *except* a novel must be worthy of a novel itself, and Linda, who could happily describe the uplifting aspects of watching one's husband die of a degenerative neuromuscular disease, must have just the kind of maverick authority a narrator needs to grab a reader and point out the things he's overlooked all his life. I got excited, thinking I'd draw all their talents out of them and they'd be amazed with themselves.

"No ideas but in things," I said. "That's William Carlos Williams. Can you see what he means? If you were describing this room what detail would you choose first? And why?"

They pulled back from the table as if they were trying to hide behind each other. After a long silence Melanie peeped, "The thrones, maybe?"

"Okay!" I said. "And why?"

Marge, looking fed up with the blather, turned to me and asked, sharply: "You *will* discuss marketing?"

The pencils went still; their hungry faces turned to me. I calculated: they'd paid five hundred dollars apiece for this class, money that could still be refunded if they asked for it now. Then they could buy shoes with it, or books, or put it toward medical care or their children's education.

I took a deep breath.

"There is no market for literary fiction," I said, incurring two incredulous and five uncomprehending stares; it was like saying there was no God. "And even if there was 'a market,' even if *anyone* had a prayer of making money from short stories, the only way to do it would be to follow your natural instincts, your own idiosyncracy—then throw yourself on the mercy of the marketplace and hope for a piece of incredible luck—that you've told a story people are interested in right now." Behind the swinging door in the kitchenette, I heard a swell of whispering and a clattering of plates. Champagne, I thought, would help wash this news down.

"Well, surely you can give them some names and addresses, dear," said Phyllis. "I mean, we clearly said *marketing* in the brochure." How had Phyllis and I become a *we* all of a sudden? "After all, *you've* been published . . ." she said.

"So you have to admit it can happen," said Lucy brightly.

"Because it *did* happen, to you," Melanie added, gesturing toward the copy of my book that Phyllis had been holding up for them. Her voice was so sweet and full of hope and admiration that there seemed no choice but to fulfill her dreams.

I felt obligated to tell them that I wasn't exactly feeding my family with the proceeds from my stories—in fact the publisher no sooner bought the book than they started acting as if they'd done it out of generosity, and by now I was inclined to agree. Reading a story is like taking a drop of rubbing alcohol on your tongue—at first it seems like nothing but when it starts to work it curdles every cell. All the longings, the prayers unanswered that drive us through our lives, the ironies we slip on so hilariously—isn't it just better to put them out of one's mind? Novels have long skeins of character in great sweeps of history; in movies lovemaking looks as beautiful as it feels; in poems one smooth stone might equal redemption and paintings have color at the very least, a sculpture can give you a pang of desire just like a man . . . No, a story is a grim thing . . . to publish one is a kindness, to publish a whole book full is pure philanthropy.

But my students hoped to gather up the scraps and shards of their lives and fit them together into something beautiful and whole, to reclaim their sufferings as art. They had no language for this ambition, so they talked about fame—and, of course, money, the need of which they knew sorely well. The most immediate source of it was the cash box now resting under Marge's vigilant hands. Surely Phyllis didn't want to take the bread out of these women's mouths just to put a slate roof on the courthouse? I glanced at her, thinking she'd understand and in a minute there'd be refunds all around, but her whole being was involved in a frown.

The kitchen door swung open, and two very gentle, worried-looking ladies emerged on tiptoe with a tray of Oreos and Fig Newtons, and several gallons of Coke. "Now," said one, "what can we pour you, Diet or Classic?"

Coca-Cola—Phyllis told me aside—supplied the soda for free. The champagne glasses I'd seen were props for the theater company. For us there was Coke, cookies donated by Nabisco, and a dietetic cheese. Raising her voice, she asked "How much did *Yankee* pay you for the story you published there? I'll bet that was several hundred right there." Everyone gathered around me. Yes, I said, but *Yankee* is one of six or seven magazines that pay at all, and even those . . .

"Now, I'm sure a hardheaded businesswoman like yourself can give us more suggestions than *that*," said Phyllis, as if I must be saving all the really good opportunities for myself.

"No, really," I said.

"I just love your *shirt*," Melanie said, rubbing the fabric between her fingers as if the stuff might confer magical powers, and they gathered around me, examining my clothes, my hair, as if *I* was the thing they'd come to study. The shirt was from the thrift shop, of course—having money is embarrassing enough without going around spending it, too.

Lucy, seeming in a trance, said, "I think I could make myself a shirt like this," and turned over a button to see how it was attached, asking, "Does *Yankee* pay on acceptance, or publication?"

"Just one thing," Phyllis said, taking me aside again. "Lettie's husband has Alzheimer's, so he usually comes in with her during the day—she'll be here to make your lunch, you know. He's very quiet, he won't cause you any trouble. I just didn't want you to be alarmed."

His name was Arthur, and when I arrived the next morning I found him slumped in the larger of the two thrones. The day was scorching, but the windows were painted obdurately shut.

"No one else has complained," Phyllis said, seeming to imply that for the sake of a thousand dollars most people would be willing to stop breathing for a week, and to feel that in addition to greed and obstinacy I was now displaying an unfortunate tendency toward invalidism. I told her I was worried about Arthur, who obligingly lifted his huge, ashen head for a moment, then let it fall back to his chest.

"Well, if you'd like to take up a collection, I'd be happy to go pick up a fan," Phyllis said, but Lettie emerged from the kitchen with an ancient one she'd found among the props. Her step was light as if she feared her slightest movement would disturb us, and she spoke quietly, to herself all the time—narrating a gentle, ironic version of each moment the way someone else might knit something to pull up around her shoulders on a cold night.

"Yes, a breeze," she said, plugging the fan in. "A breeze is better . . ." and enumerating the odd lots as she passed them: "silk peonies, of course, a garden gate, Arthur, a bushel of Mylar snowflakes, and—oh!—a mirror, a mirror, how unkind!" She turned away from it and went back to the kitchen, while Melanie, who had been watching me watch her, smiled sadly as if she knew just what I was thinking.

Ten minutes had passed, three hours and fifty minutes to go. Ordinarily I would talk about the students' manuscripts, but neither Linda nor Joy had submitted one and Mattie's book was several hundred pages of advice about how to stay cheerful and pleasant while recognizing that your husband of twenty years is having an affair and that you are tilting, loveless and penniless, into old age.

Lucy's piece appeared to be a eulogy for her father, and Melanie's began: "It was a perfect, cloudless day, and our oars cut into the river like knives going through deep-green butter." Best to find a modest goal: I decided that by the time they were finished with my class on the short story, they would all know what a short story was.

I drew a diagram of a conventional plot on the blackboard. Already I heard the women making lunch in the kitchen—what could it be, that they would start so early?

"The conflict," I said, "is the thread the reader follows through the story. Usually it's tiny—the kind of thing that makes you curious in your own life, like a piece of gossip that you try to understand. It's an irritant, a grain of sand—you'll turn it into a pearl." They all, even Arthur, watched me like a field of sunflowers following the day. I was their teacher, I would give them something that felt simple as warmth and helped them grow.

It made me sad. I'd copied the plot diagram out of a literature textbook; I know nothing about plots at all. My own stories were written out of longing and disappointment: life, which had been advertised to me as a clear path from one happy event to the next, had turned out to be a series of bewilderments through which one stumbled blindly, doing one's best to avoid embarrassment, acting properly jubilant or sorrowful in spite of one's own rage and confusion, and generally pretending one had some idea how to carry on. I'd started writing down events and conversations to study them and maybe learn to get some of it right. This became a habit, then hardened into a superstition, so finally I'd feel my life was draining away from me if I didn't get it down on a page. Then, out of love madness—feelings that would have driven someone else to murder—I started going back and back over everything, making it into stories with the idea that a man I yearned for would read them and realize he ought to have loved me.

I don't suppose he ever saw the book, but publishing it did change things. I became someone who'd accomplished something—the most frightening, confusing, and embarrassing position yet. I started to teach writing at the community college, was asked to address the trustees—Scott, my husband, was one of them. He married me and convinced me to give up teaching . . . but here I was, speaking with merry authority—in short, impersonating a person, pretending to have no share in the common desperation.

As I talked I was aware of a certain suspense radiating from the kitchen. Bursts of low, intense talk were punctuated by sudden frenzies of chopping; cabinet doors opened, water ran, then came a sudden "Oh!" and Lettie rushed through the room, saying in her anxious undertone: "I forgot! How could I forget?" She returned fifteen minutes later with a package of melba toast, which came out at lunchtime beside a platter of cold cuts so fleshily sliced they were difficult to look at and impossible to eat. Whatever had been chopped, washed, or discussed did not appear, and I wondered if I'd only imagined the travail behind the swinging door. I ate a Fig Newton, listening to Linda's stories of the faith remedies her husband had tried: "I mean, I wouldn't wish it on any of you," she said, "but I believe God always has a reason"—everyone but Joy nodded gravely—"and for growth in a marriage, ALS is really something . . ."

Inspirational books had been a help. In fact, she wondered if I'd read one she liked, called *Writing from the Deepest Chamber of the Heart.*

"Oh, that's such a wonderful book," Melanie said. "Don't you think so?"

I'd never heard of it.

"That's the thing—there are so many," Melanie sighed. "You *can't* read them all! I mean, I didn't know about that guy you mentioned last night! But Dorothea Solewicz, she's just *awesome.*" The others agreed—they'd all read it and Mattie had a copy in her purse, along with two other manuals of writing advice and a collection of aromatherapy sachets for writers, with scents for lyricism, insight, courage, et cetera.

"Look," Joy said, turning the book over. "Isn't she beautiful? Like Michelle Pfieffer . . ."

That was another thing they wanted from me—an airbrush, a quick liposuction. More exactly, a metamorphosis out of sadness, which repels love, into grace, which would attract it. Dorothea Solewicz did, indeed, look beautiful and was most accomplished, being the author of this book and a book of exercises one can do with one's cat, dividing her time between her ranch in Colorado and the beach house in Malibu, where she lived with her husband—yes, he was an investment banker, too.

"I'm dealing in snake oil," I told Scott when I got home. "They're paying five hundred dollars apiece to Phyllis Giustameer, and they think they're going to feed their families on fiction—it's horrible. I'm preparing them for a profession that doesn't exist!"

"All for the sake of a thousand dollars . . ." he said, in disbelief. He makes a thousand dollars during a hiccup; a sneeze can go into five figures. "Instead of—" He flicked his hand out over the yard toward the water. All this, he'd got it for me. The squash blossoms were fleshing up, swallowtails looped over the tiger lilies in back. The tide was full and someone on one of the boats was playing a saxophone with the slow pulse of crickets as a backbeat; everything spoke of surfeit, contentment. If the baby had lived and grown, I thought, it would have been almost a year old. Oh, I knew what my ladies wanted—to see something form in their own hands, something whole and alive in whose beautiful face their own image would be clear.

"They're paying you for hope, honey," Scott said. "You're in business to give it to them. You don't get very far in the world selling bitter pills."

"What category would a eulogy come under?" Lucy asked the next morning. "I mean, *is* it a short story? Is that what they mean?"

Already that morning I'd achieved one of those feats of strength only the desperate can perform, lifting the window a foot from its sash and propping it with the ice bucket so we could get a little air and a glimpse of the green world—who knew what else might be possible? I addressed a brief prayer to Emily Post and the words came: "Really, Lucy, a eulogy is a category all of its own."

"Well, who would publish that, then?" Lucy asked. "I mean, I couldn't find it in *Writer's Market*, but after the funeral *everyone* said it ought to be printed. . . . Everyone loved my father so. 'His heart was big as all outdoors,' " she said, quoting her opening line.

Melanie caught my eye with a quick, derisive glance, and I looked guiltily away. Linda was drawing a fluffy dog in the margin of her notebook, and Arthur was excavating earwax with a fingernail, but Lucy went on speaking of the events of her childhood as if they were artifacts whose every scratch held a revelation. She had the first attribute of a writer, I thought—she was certain the world would want—would pay—to know whatever she was thinking.

"When you write a eulogy," I said, "you're writing for people who already care about your subject—the people who come to the funeral. If you want to publish it, you have to think how to make people who never met your father take an interest in him, too. Think about it—what do you like to read yourself?"

"Oh, I don't like to read," she said quickly, as if I'd accused her of a secret vice.

"What makes you want to write?"

"Well—reading and writing—they're completely different things!"

"Okay," I said, "Okay, yes . . . but who do you expect will read this piece? Ninety percent of marketing is knowing your audience."

I felt them come alive. "Could you repeat that?" Joy asked. "Ninety percent of marketing is—? I just want to be sure I got it exactly."

"But how do you know your audience?" Linda asked. "I mean, I wish we could meet some editors here. How do you find out what editors want?"

Various answers came from different sides of the table—"Sex!" someone said.

"Legal thrillers," Linda insisted. "I mean, since O. J. When really the most important things happen in hospitals. . . ."

"They want characters who live in New York," Lucy said bitterly. "If you're from Louisiana they couldn't care less."

"They want something revelatory, original," I said.

"Revelatory, original," Arthur seemed to repeat, but the others slumped—they'd just gotten me down to earth and here I bounced back into the ether again.

"Something *interesting*, I mean." I said. "Lucy, it sounds as if your father was a wonderful man, and if you could *show* some of that in your piece, then—"

"It's six pages—I don't want to retype it," she said irritably. "I'm just trying to decide where to send it to."

I had the kind of headache where you feel your brain is being scooped out with a melon baller, and was in perfect sympathy with the fan, which had been methodically heroic, turning back and forth, back and forth, trying to whisk the heavy air into a breeze. Give them snake oil, I thought, make them happy. What does it matter to you?

"Try *The New Yorker*," I snapped. "They like human interest. And *Esquire*, it's all about men."

"What are those addresses?" Lucy asked, her pen poised.

"You'd have to check them in the library," I said. "That's another important aspect of marketing. You want to study the magazines, read a year's worth of back issues, really get to know what they want." I read this in a dentist's office once. Their pens went to work again, and Lucy still looked suspicious, as if I was making it all too hard.

"What's the circulation on those?" she asked me. "I want to start at the top."

Melanie laughed. "She doesn't have the circulation figures for all the national magazines in her head, Lucy," she said. "She's saying we need to learn to write first."

I wanted to hug her. Now she excused herself sheepishly to go to the bathroom again, and as she left, with one hand at rest on her belly and the other pressing the small of her back, Mattie said, "Doesn't she look just radiant?" Yes, that child inside her was like a battery that kept recharging her in spite of her troubles. The thought came down on me like a strap, reminding me how, when I asked the doctor if my baby had been a boy or a girl, he'd said it was like a large black olive; it had no human traits.

It was impossible though not to love Melanie; she listened so carefully, distilling the wisdom out of my speeches, asking earnest questions, like a religious novice, determined that if she really gave herself up to it she'd write something inspiring, rise above earthly toil and pain. It was youth, I supposed; there was so much time left for her, of course her life would change.

We'd come to know each other a little, to see the truth of each other's lives in the manuscripts; and the more we did, the more careful we were to speak of "the narrator," never to dream an author might be as venal, as self-deluded, as her characters. We'd have died if Joy thought we recognized her in the chilled, motionless woman who occupied the haunted mansion in the book of which she'd now written three pages. Joy thought everything was a text and gave no credence to reality, but the others had so much experience between them that they hardly believed in fiction. They wrote as a way of passing their lives through their fingers one more time, peering in to search out what had really happened, or perhaps to reinvent what had happened, or just to have one last glimpse of a lost love. So sometimes we just threw fiction to the winds, and raged at a "narrator's" husband, grieved for the dead father of the "main character."

As each woman read her pages aloud (the Xerox fee being prohibitive), the story underneath began to leak. Melanie's green butter story had turned out to be about her first marriage: on their honeymoon her husband stood up in their canoe and threw his arms out to embrace her, saying, "I'm in heaven with an angel!" And lost his footing, fell overboard, and drowned. After Mattie's divorce, her adoptive son had gotten her natural daughter pregnant; they'd had to put her grandchild up for adoption. Linda's twelve-year-old brother had thrown a snowball at a car whose driver, a neighbor, swerved, hit a lightpole, and was paralyzed from the waist down. Her family (father a postman; mother, like Linda, a nurse) was driven out of their town—the father slipped into alcoholism afterward and died young, and the year in detention had schooled the brother in crime so that some time later he murdered a convenience store clerk and went to prison for good. "So it's odd, it's *fair* in a way, that my husband should end in a wheelchair, you know?" she said.

"I don't, I've never quite . . . known . . . what to make of it, I guess." It was Melanie speaking, though it could have been any of them. "Like, he was there, then he was under the water and gone. . . . Was it just . . . random? Was there something I—? . . . I don't know." Mattie reached over to take her hand while I sat ineffectually by, wondering how they managed to bear the weights life had settled on them, and why, in a world full of therapies, they had all come to me.

"Let's concentrate on the first paragraph," I said, thinking I had no aptitude for social work and must do my best to keep the discussion on writing, though this felt abominably cold and my teacherish voice sickened me. "This is a good place to talk about metaphors, how they can enrich or detract from your work. I think you've wanted to show how beautiful the water was, how wonderful everything felt even though death was right there beside you. But when the reader has the picture in his mind, of these two people rowing through rancid butter—"

Melanie flushed, guilty of having clumsily described her husband's death. "How do you think I could do better?" she asked.

"What do you want the reader to know?"

"How, I guess, how innocent we were," she said, her voice breaking. I raced in to suggest several excellent ways of revealing innocence in a pair of characters who think mistakenly that they're just at the start of their lives, but she interrupted: "And how . . . have you ever been on a whale watch? You know how you look down and you can just barely see the whale's outline underwater, and you think it's rising, in a minute it'll break the surface and you'll see it clearly? I dream I can see him that way, sometimes, and all day I feel like he's alive again and I'm going to run into him in the grocery store or something. That's the thing—that he seems to be right there—" And she reached out as if to touch him. "—even though he's been dead five years."

"You know, you could just say all that," I said.

"Really?" And then, bubbling over, "You see, I *know* it's possible. I believe I *can* do it. It *can't* be as hard as you say." *It* being the achievement of redemption through art? Riches and fame? Or were they two strains of the same thing? After all, a story fully told *does* change everything; think of the remedies by placebo, the cures at Lourdes—what do I know of it all except that it's an immense relief to capture even a tiny piece of all the life that flows daily through one's hands. Dorothea Solewicz (they had forced the book on me) believed the physical act of writing was therapeutic, even if the words made no sense, and I myself knew a man who no sooner wrote his dissertation on Dostoyevsky than he became a psychopharmacologist and began dispensing Prozac at $240 an hour (a career trajectory Phyllis might want to keep in mind).

"People have done it," I said, "or there wouldn't be a bestseller list. Of course, first you have to write something."

"Exactly," Melanie said, maternal already toward everyone in the room, as inspiring as a heroine in a war movie. "We *can* do it, I know we can."

Then to herself, hardly audible. "It can't be that he just died."

No, it could not be. I felt fiercely that there *ought* to be a market for eulogies, a magazine widely distributed, printed on acid-free paper so the story of every life could go on. Even my baby, the child without qualities, would have a page.

"People smile and disappear," Arthur said, gleeful as a three-year-old upending a gravy boat. He seemed to be part of the group by now, and like the rest of us was especially fond of Melanie. She was the one who really noticed him: she imagined he was listening and could understand. Once she'd tried to ask his opinion, but he'd only looked at her in sad reproach, as if he assumed it was mockery. Now Lettie came out of the kitchen with her platter and he began to repeat her name softly, like a mantra, the subject of a life's meditation.

Thursday I arrived to find him struggling against her as she tried to sit him down on the throne. "I have to—I have to—I'm late—" he said.

"He's having a bad day," she told me. He was beating his open palms in the air as if fending off aggressive butterflies. Lettie smiled faintly, apologizing. "He's usually very good, but this happens once in a while," she said. They'd been reporters for the same newspaper— I wondered at the light resignation in her voice, how well she seemed to take it that they would both weaken now, losing parts of themselves until they died. I'll be bellowing when my time comes.

I'd promised the class that day would be devoted to the business end.

"We want to know *everything*," said Melanie, who had become their spokeswoman. She was particularly happy and confident—her husband had a job interview in the afternoon. "I mean, from the beginning. Do you write a first draft in longhand? How do you get an agent? What did *you* do, I mean, to get where you are?"

"I haven't exactly gotten anywhere," I said.

"You know what I mean," she said. "How did you get published, famous?" The words *famous* and *writer* have gotten so tightly fused together it's impossible to tear them apart.

"I'm not . . . ," I began, but here they all were with my image so bright in their eyes, and I'd relentlessly thwarted them, going on and on about the difficulty of art while they who knew so much about the world must have wondered what on earth I could mean. Is writing a short story as hard as suctioning out your husband's lungs, or begging your landlord to wait another month for the rent? No, the writing wasn't the problem: the problem was how to make a sale! I'd done that, but here I was refusing to give my secrets away. Suddenly I felt the courageous thing would be not to confess how small, how fearful I was, but to climb up on the pedestal they'd built for me and let them see me staunch and immortal, so they could have the comfort of believing for a moment in someone stronger than themselves.

"Yes," I said, "I always write my first draft in longhand, then as I type it into the computer, I begin the process of revision . . ." I'd never blathered at such dull length in my life, or seen such rapt attention.

"What's it like to sell a story?" Linda asked, and I told them about the first one, how the check appeared in the mailbox and I rushed out to buy champagne. They clapped hands to hearts like children at a story hour.

"Wouldn't it be wonderful?" Melanie said. "Oh, just to think that it could happen to *me*!" Then, feeling a scruple: "All of us, it could happen to all of us, it could! How much—I mean, if you don't mind my asking—how much did you make for it?"

"Five hundred dollars." Which was approximately ten times my average paycheck, for the eight stories I'd sold in the last six years.

"Well, gosh," Melanie said. "So, you only have to sell a couple stories a month."

"Well, there are a lot of writers . . ."

"There goes the gloom and doom again," she teased. "The fact is, it *can* be done."

Something ricocheted against the door frame, rolled across the floor and came to a stop at her feet. Arthur's wedding ring.

"She's *expecting* me!" he said. I wondered if the *she* he referred to was Death. He'd been stamping his feet, writhing as though he were tied, so anxiously that Lettie had to come out from the kitchen every few minutes to reassure him. Melanie picked up the ring and replaced it tenderly on his finger, and he beamed at her as if she'd just agreed to his marriage proposal.

I'd brought my book in, the copy I'd kept revising, and they passed it from hand to hand like a Dead Sea Scroll.

"And someone painted this picture for the cover, after they read the book?" Linda said, smoothing her hand over the jacket. I nodded, and she said, "I can't believe it, I just can't."

Then, opening to some of my corrections: "But, who wrote in it?" As if it were graffiti.

"I did," I said, starting to explain, but it was inconceivable, that I might want to change something already printed. Lucy gently removed its jacket and touched her finger to my name on the spine, opened it, said "Library of Congress" reverentially, and asked "Now, do they want a manuscript to say *copyright* on every page?"

"No," I said, remembering how strange it had felt to have the very charitable publisher take this thing that came straight out of my dreams and slap it into shape like a hamburger patty, put it in a stylish jacket, and send it out into the world alone.

"Where are the blurbs?" Melanie asked, and a wave of suspicion passed among them, immediately overcome by politeness, as if she'd asked if I had a glass eye.

"But there was publicity, right?" Linda said. "The newspapers came?" I'd brought the *Cape Cod Chronicle,* with a big color picture of me headlined LOCAL AUTHOR WINS ACCLAIM—this referring to my sentence in an omnibus review in the *Cleveland Plain Dealer.*

"You look so beautiful," they sighed. "Just think . . ."

Just think . . . my editor, enduring a change of medication, had been wont to call me up and shout "Nobody talks to me like that!" as soon as I answered the phone. The publicist had a baby and forgot to send out review copies. My father, always competitive, *died* on my publication date, so that instead of signing autographs in the local bookstore I found myself arguing with a funeral director over what sort of clothing a body should wear to its cremation.

On the other hand, a woman in Wisconsin had, by some freak accident, bought the book and read it, and was moved by it to send me a pound of wild rice, which I stretched out over most of the next year, cooking it by the half cup when I felt hurt or ashamed, thinking: on this one person, I have had an effect.

"Could I borrow this?" Lucy asked me when the book had gone around the table and fallen into her hands. "I mean, just to read a little overnight?"

"I'd let you, but it's my revising copy," I said. The others had bought them and asked for my autograph. "It's not something I can afford to lose. I'm sorry . . ."

"I'll bring it back," she said, offended. "Look." She shook out a plastic rain bonnet from her purse and wrapped the book up in it. "I'll take good care of it, I will."

"Well, it's very important to me," I said, but I could see I wouldn't get it back without a physical struggle. And the activity in the kitchen could no longer be contained: Lettie burst through the door with the platter.

"This was the best class yet," she said to me. Did they just sit behind the swinging door all morning listening, rattling the silverware so I wouldn't guess?

At home, Scott said to me out of the blue, "It could have been worse, you know."

"What could?"

"It could have been a *small* black olive." And I started to laugh; I thought I'd never stop.

"Lucy won't be coming," Phyllis said when we were all assembled for our last day of class. "She got a little bug and decided to go home."

"Oh, no," Mattie said, "I brought her a book. Look, everybody, I went into Hyannis yesterday and look what I got—five books of essays . . . short stories . . ." She glanced at me, then back at the books, and said "*short* essays," proudly, offering a compromise. "A dollar apiece!" she said. "I got one for each!" Linda got a collection of baseball writing, Joy's was on small business management. For me there was a fresh copy of *Writing from the Deepest Chamber of the Heart*, and Lucy had been destined for *A Bruce Chatwin Reader*.

"A first edition," she said. "That means rare . . . It won't be long before we've all written books like these," she said. "Essays! I mean stories! I mean . . ."

"I hope you're right," Melanie said, "because Bobby didn't get the job." Everyone turned to comfort her, but she insisted she wasn't worried. "Because you know what, I wrote all night—I just couldn't stop!—and here's my story. It's like I'm a new person! I'm just sure this is going to work out now, everything's going to be fine."

"It was a perfect day, the first day of my honeymoon, the beginning of a new life, and the sun was dancing on the water," it began. It had

some music, and the meaning was clear. My heart raced; I'd taught someone something.

"This is so much better," I said, beginning to list all the improvements, but she burst out joyfully—

"Do you see, do you see, I told you I could do it!"

"Yes, you did." I could say anything; I'd never see them again. Perhaps Lucy had taken my teachings deepest to heart, and decided to steal what she couldn't earn.

"You told me you could and you were right," I said. "You were."

"And now, thanks to your advice, I know just how to sell it," she said.

"It was *such* a wonderful class," Linda said, full of feeling, and they all joined her until I blushed. For five hundred dollars they'd bought something they could have got from a paperback edition of *Anna Karenina*: the sense that ordinary, daily events are worthy of rapt attention. They'd fallen in love with me because I sat at the head of their table—how wonderful it would be if, for just a few minutes a day, I could be the person they thought they saw. I'd typed up a reading list and they took their copies as if they were prescriptions: read these; become like me.

"It's possible, it is," Linda said. "If you trust in the Lord . . ."

"Well, a higher power," Melanie corrected, glancing at me, their pet heretic, with anxious expectation. Would I allow them to be agnostics, or must they go all the way to atheism? It was noon, though, the kitchen door was about to open; I'd be saved by a platter of ham and cheese.

Before it could reach us, Phyllis burst in with a camera and a long envelope, which she ceremoniously handed to me.

"Thank you," I said, embarrassed, reaching for my purse.

"Open it, open it," she insisted, louder the more I demurred. Finally she grabbed it back from me, pulled the check out, and read it with heavy emphasis: *"A thousand dollars."* The class leaned in to see the magic sum. Melanie smiled knowingly—would I admit there was money in writing now?

"Let's everyone gather around for a picture," Phyllis said. "You just stay there, and class, gather in behind her. Lettie, you come out, too, we'd like to kind of fill up the frame here." This was diplomacy—the fact was that Arthur would be smack in the middle unless someone stood in front of him. I wanted to tell Phyllis this was proper, that when you're writing death is always with you in the room . . . But if there was one thing I'd learned that week it was to hold my damnable tongue.

"Joy and Lettie, closer," Phyllis said. "I want to thank every one of you for your generous support of the County Courthouse Restoration Fund. Hold the check a little higher, Patsy. That's better. Now a big, big smile."

She must have focused right in on it—you can read the sum even in the little picture on the brochure. It's odd she used it, since my face pretty much says "Don't hit me," and since I wasn't invited to teach there again. But at least Lettie and Joy are blocking the view of Arthur, and they're all of them beaming out at the world with confidence and pride. Yes, life is a leaky vessel, but they can see the good ship *Art* in the distance, coming to bear them away.

Fishman's Fascination

Why should it be the morning of the wedding that the news came down from the Mormon genealogists? Liane spread the chart out, over the dresses laid on her bed, and traced with a finger the line back, through her mother, her grandmother . . . back eight generations and there they were: Abraham and Rachel, Solomon and Sarah . . . So, it was true: her mother the lugubrious Catholic had been Jewish all along! Keeping her finger on the chart, as if to hold those names still there until she found a witness, Liane looked up and caught her own amazed face in the mirror. Yes, there *was* something in it, something she'd never been able to place. . . . She, Liane Thistlemore, who had never been anyone, really, was suddenly—a Jew! She felt a puff of destiny inflate her; she lifted, just slightly, off the ground.

It was too much—like finding a passport to a place she only knew from dreams. And then, of course, it was nothing. She was still the same woman she'd been before the mail came: hectic, blushing, fumbling for polite conversation while her inner voice produced only spiteful ironies; waiting and watching (checking the mail, the answering machine, every face on the street), alert for the flash that would charge her perfectly satisfactory life with astonishment, with revelation.

She thought of the poster from her childhood Sunday School classroom: an insipid Jesus surrounded by rosy children and fleecy lambs. That was Christianity and it could not contain her. Then had come the cataclysmic coincidence of Rebecca Mizner's bas mitzvah and their seventh-grade study of Anne Frank. Rebecca Mizner, that little plump-kneed girl who wailed about her impetigo, while her mother sprayed Lysol on anything Liane touched while visiting . . . Rebecca, at the sacred center of a great rite of passage, while Liane, who *lived* in a holy rapture, had to mark her own coming of age by learning to insert a Tampax? It would not do. She'd sat fuming amid the congregation of Temple Beth-El while Rebecca stared at the floor and mumbled her portion. "Ch," Liane had tried, in the back of her throat, *"challah; l'chaim." Oh, Rebecca, stand aside!* Rebecca's older brother, Gabe, was just back from Israel, his massed curls bouncing on his shoulders, his face full of curiosity. His eyes met Liane's; he smiled. The premonition of physical love dawned over her, and in its glow all the strands intertwined: she would live with high moral intensity, make a metaphysical pilgrimage into a foreign realm, suffer for a great cause instead of her usual suffering for no good reason at all. No other story had been fierce enough, bloody enough, ripe enough with symbol and ritual, for the always yearning, newly throbbing creature she had been—she must have the story of the Jews for her own.

Thus had the Old Testament got filed under the mattress with *The Story of O*. And then, like all evidence of secret longing, forgotten: distilled and diluted to suffuse her thoughts all these years. Religion seemed to her now a kind of nostalgia, a picturesque ruin that proved that once—long ago—people used to be certain about something. And the Jews—she bore them (*us*, rather, she reminded herself) a grudge; they were so cozy together, declaring themselves apart while insisting on being included, seeing swastikas at the bottom of every teacup, going on about the *Jewish* tradition of charity, the *Jewish* tradition of study, as if such things were unheard of beyond the pale. (Dangerously close to the truth, this, which made it doubly infuriating.) At the word, the thought—*Jewish*—a breath of envy, excitement, and disdain passed over her, too light to be noticed before it was gone.

"Derek," she called, to her husband the descendant of Myles Standish. (How they laughed at his mother's pride in this—had ever a family suffered a sheep as black as Myles Standish? And even if Myles Standish *had* been, instead of a Brutal Warrior–cum–Religious Nut, a Great Benevolent Thinker such as, say, Maimonides—could one inherit some distant ancestor's honor, like a sauceboat, or some strain of disease? Silly idea!) Silly to feel, as Liane definitely did, that fortune had whispered an endearment in her ear.

"Derek, guess what? I'm a Jew!"

He came out with his face half covered in shaving lather. "Very nice," he said, squinting at the chart. "It looks like you are about . . . hmm, one sixty-fourth Jewish. I congratulate you."

"No," she said, "look here—it's all in the women. On my *mother's* side."

He smiled. When he was uncertain about something he treated it with polite condescension until it went away. *Wasps*, she thought, *are discomfitted by perplexity. Jews live for it.*

"The *Jews*," she said, "would consider me a Jew."

"Well, felicitations." He retreated rather nervously.

"You mean *Mazel tov!*" she said, sticking out her tongue.

She refolded the chart. She had to get Cecily to the baby-sitter, and dress—and what *did* one wear, to an evening wedding, a Jewish wedding, a wedding in the city? It must be nice to have a religion, a culture, a class . . . something that was woven into you, that *couldn't* change. As it was she never knew what to put on. Her dresses looked hopelessly Waspy, all silk and flowers, utterly wrong. *Shmattes,* they were—the Jews would only laugh: what could it be, this fairy simplicity, but a pose? *They* (we, she said to herself, *we*) would be confident, certain, quick. *They* would wear . . . but what?

If she were really a Jew, of course, she'd have known. She'd have been dressed long since, and be out solving world problems by now. "I'm a person of the book," she said unconvincingly. Blood has nothing to do with it, what matters is what comes down to you hand to hand. She held up dress after dress in the mirror, feeling the anxiety of the chameleon: if she didn't assume precisely the colors of the background, would the others have her for lunch?

But when she was dressed (a linen sheath, dove gray, and pearls from Derek's mother—she'd go as a young birch and leave the questions of human parentage aside), and swept Cecily up for a last kiss, she held her daughter's gaze for a second, sending a spark across to blaze up there: *Look what I've passed to you, my girl. Anything is possible,* she thought, anything. It's there in plain sight, you have only to turn your head a little, and *voilà!* She'd buy *The Gifts of the Jews,* she'd absorb it like . . . like . . . a communion wafer. No, it was hopeless, her feet touched back to earth and she hurried off click, click, click on her heels.

Walking down Bayside Avenue toward the Silverbergs' she felt almost distinguished. Her hips were disguised under the sheath; she looked very nearly thin. And Derek strode beside her, lean and sharp-faced like a fox or a British spy. In his navy suit jacket he seemed well-nigh Anglican. Ascetic, devoted to scholarship above everything—that was what she'd seen when she fell in love with him, without thinking he might devote himself to scholarship above her.

"Oh!" he said suddenly, "this must be . . . ," and dived into a mo-rass of cantaloupe chiffon, warmly seizing a plump little satin-trussed blond girl before Liane could reach him.

"She *looked* like a bride . . . ," he said, as the giggling maidens readjusted themselves.

"Of course she looked like a bride! It's a Saturday in June, every third woman you see is a bride! This isn't even the right block! Does she look like *Naomi*?" Naomi, the daughter of Derek's old friend Len, had been a dark-eyed child who seemed to be gazing straight past you, back into history, and had grown now into an earnest, thoughtful woman whose clear eyes were turned directly toward the future. She was writing her dissertation on water rights in Gaza, and spared no opportunity to remind her mother the lawyer that very few things were simple enough to be decided in court. The girl Derek had hugged was erupting vesuvially from her bodice and wore an amethyst crucifix around her neck and a diamond stud in her tongue.

"Well—" he hung his head, winsomely sheepish. He hadn't known June was a month of weddings; in fact he didn't definitely know it was June. He trusted Liane to guide him in the daily matters. When they traveled she just said "Turn here," and forgot even to tell him where they were going.

To Israel, dear! They turned up the Silverberg driveway promptly at six and found themselves alone with the caterers. The year's first breath of heat hit Liane like a drug, making everything vivid and strange. The white tents hovered over the lawn, the bouquets of red and pink roses also held spikes of buds like rubbery green chicken hearts, and the striped poles of the *chuppah,* leaning against a tree trunk, looked like a horse's cast-off jousting garment.

"Didn't they say six?" she asked, but of course Derek wouldn't know, and now Len's wife, Barbara, came out and cried, "Guests!" as if they were a couple of rats just up from the sewer, then regained her composure, which was usually absolute (she brooked no uncertainty, the better to assert herself in court), came and kissed them, summoned a twinkling young waiter to pour lemonade, and disappeared back inside, calling a bright warning: "Lenny, guests!" She was wearing black organdy; a mother of the bride dress circa 1963—perhaps her own mother had worn it and handed it down. So, Liane thought, two gaffes in the first five minutes—her sheath that had seemed so perfect felt gauche now that Barbara of the courtroom suits had come as a frump, and apparently one was not supposed to arrive at a Jewish wedding on time.

There were too many nuances; you couldn't get it right. Len and Derek had been thrown together when barred from the same fraternities in college years before, Len being too Jewish and Derek too strange. They'd stood up at each other's weddings, but Derek's first two didn't take, so by the time he and Liane had their three-minute ceremony Len had just sent a card—she hardly knew him. And she was so much younger, had missed the time of fraternities and everything else that defined that generation's lives.

And in the presence of religion she was always wrong. At church with her mother she'd see stonemasons genuflect with perfect simplicity while she was so clumsy the act seemed nearly satirical. The poignancy of it—the kneeling before a painted God on a gilded cross in a church whose spire pointed straight out into the infinite dark—pained her until she had to laugh, to keep from crying. And that was in her own faith! In a synagogue she felt paralyzed, certain that at the next blink she'd be unmasked as an impostor.

Jewish at last, she became *more* awkward. Her head was full of words like *yeshiva* and *tsuris* that she was afraid to pronounce lest their syllables band together against her . . . words that ought to have been hers. She wanted to tell everyone, but how did you make such an announcement, and what could it possibly mean? Only that she was barging in to loot a great tradition for her own ends. She had no legacy of suffering, striving in a hostile world. And what were her accomplishments? Cecily, of course, and she had nice garden and did well at her job—fund-raising for a college already heavily endowed. Did she direct the benefactors to go buy wells for desperate villages instead? No, she was naturally ambitious and tried to bring in more money every year. She did not deserve to be Jewish. She was an ordinary woman making her way through a mundane life—it was utterly unbearable.

"I thought we were late," said a quiet, insinuating woman's voice in Liane's ear—Derek's first wife, Marsha (née Waldman, recently Takemoto), was behind her. Marsha was hardly a close friend, but in the circumstances Liane was glad to see her.

"We were the first ones to get here, and I don't think we'll be forgiven," she said.

Marsha laughed. "Punctuality, Derek's great belief," she said. "He can't help it, you know, it's his upbringing."

A Wasp upbringing, all good posture and mortification of the flesh. Their language! "Care for a dip?"—meaning "Let's throw ourselves into the sea!" Or "Nippy out!"—pronounced with relish as if the phrase itself linked them with millions of equally hearty Wasps every-where, all of them in unison stepping out on their mats, taking a deep breath, and proclaiming, "Nippy out!" She had imagined she'd save Derek from all that, but in fact it had only grown stronger, and recently she'd caught him diving into a freezing lake just so he could say how "invigorating" it was. These Wasps, they turn proudly away from their senses, from anything that can't be described in a jovial phrase. Liane felt a sweet kinship with Marsha, who had suffered the same things.

"Fishman's coming, Len says," Marsha said.

Fishman! Lenny often spoke of Fishman, but neither Derek nor Liane had ever met him, so the natural comedy of his name had taken hold and Liane pictured him as an ungainly, waddling person with a turned-down mouth and wide-set, staring eyes, like the fish-footmen in *Alice in Wonderland*. Though, in fact, he was the legendary Fishman and his name was always spoken in a hush. The thought of meeting him finally seemed wonderfully exciting, all the more so because Liane wasn't sure why. What was he legendary for? A particular warmth or intensity, maybe: a way of looking at you that showed he was honestly interested, or a gift for speaking out his own thoughts and feelings in all their curious depth . . . Liane turned around to look for him, but saw no one unusual. Still, she was left with the restless sense that if she really studied every face in this crowd, she'd find something special in one of them—something she'd waited all her life to see.

It was a quarter of seven, and the service (did they—we—call it a *service?*) was beginning. Marsha, like Barbara, was in black, obviously obeying some secret Jewish dress code, but just as Liane was feeling entirely in the wrong, a woman with gray sausage curls and a dress covered with vivid pink and blue hydrangeas brushed by.

"Is that a *rabbi?*" Marsha asked, as the woman ascended the altar (did we call it an altar?). Marsha was so short she had to go up on tiptoe to talk into Liane's ear. *"My God,"* she said, as if they were slaughtering a lamb up there.

"Mine, too, it turns out!" Liane chirped—but the ceremony had begun, the first *Adonai* was already resounding, and Marsha went on, ruefully, to herself, "or not, in fact, my God at all."

"What do you mean?" asked Liane, knowing she ought to keep quiet but remembering how everyone had talked through Rebecca Mizner's bas mitzvah, while her mother told her with reverence (as her father set an example of silent Congregational decorum) that for the Jews talk was a part of the sacred life.

"I grew up among Unitarians!" Marsha said. "I hardly knew what

Judaism was! I suppose that's why I married Derek; he seemed so familiar. But then Barbara's not exactly Yentl. I mean, she belongs to the ACLU, not the temple! All that wailing and schlepping the Talmud around—"

"*Torah,*" Liane bristled. "The Talmud is sixty-three volumes."

"Whatever," Marsha said. Unitarian indeed! All these years Marsha had done nothing but carp about being Jewish—her allergies, her tormenting mother, her frizzy hair and susceptibility to wine—these and almost every other one of her characteristics were danced out with glee disguised as vexation, for the sake of taunting Liane. Marsha even moaned about her own tendency to complain! (Though she used the word *nudzh,* to point out that she, Marsha, had access to a vigorous and naturally comical language that Liane wasn't allowed to get near.) How *like* Marsha, to join the Unitarians suddenly just when Liane had crept into the pale!

"I mean," Marsha said, nodding toward Barbara, "to *go* Jewish suddenly, when your children are all grown . . . It seems, well, *grasping,* don't you think?" Her dry whisper sounded of a little girl's confidence and a snake's oscillation, both. Had *she* been in touch with the Mormons? And why do the Mormons keep tabs on everyone this way? Up went the *chuppah,* the flower girls scattered their petals. Naomi, who had gone not only Jewish but girlish for the occasion, maneuvered her hooped skirt between the poles and turned her biblical eyes adoringly toward her beloved, one Trevor Tarrington, whose parents, a pair of thin, wan physicians, stood behind him looking entirely desiccated as if the life force had leached out of them and they were likely, at any moment, to disintegrate. And *Adonai, Adonai . . .*

"That is *not* a rabbi," said Marsha. It was true that in the woman's brightly lipsticked mouth the Hebrew took on great deliberate vowels as if for a study of Midwestern pronunciation.

Still, the seven blessings, photocopied in Hebrew and English, fell over her like a tallis—nearly weightless but signifying everything: the centuries of holding the crystal of life up, turning every facet to the light, seeking, studying, understanding. Hearing them, her eyes full of those tears peculiar to weddings—tears wept at the sight of people trying to cram the immensity of hope into the very modest vessel of possibility—Liane thought, *Yes, I know what to value, I belong with the Jews.* Her mother always touched the Mizner's mezuzah in a demonstration of the reverence she felt Liane had lacked, so that Liane (who was given at the time to hiding behind the back hedge, pricking herself with barberry thorns as if pain was the clearest channel toward pleasure), contemplating her own inadequacy against such a great tradition, would go inside and plunk with heavy heart on the creaking plastic cover of the velvet sofa, to hear Mrs. Mizner continue her running count of Rebecca's calories.

But—Liane's mother had *known*, all while she was taking Communion and rhapsodizing about "the Jews," that she *was* one! What, *why?* It was only a few weeks ago that she'd told Liane her grandmother was Jewish, as if it were a fact of no interest at all.

"Really?" Liane had asked, mildly. Her mother tended to concoct: there was the uncle who leapt from the White House balcony during a state dinner, the second cousin who was 'quite certainly' Tennessee Williams's inspiration when he created Blanche Dubois. These unnamed paragons stood as proof that despair and insanity need not be insuperable barriers; an idea as important, in Liane's family, as the proud bond with Myles Standish was in Derek's. When Liane was about to approach some Brahmin for a donation she'd think—*After all*, my people *have been to dinner at the White House*—and it straightened her spine.

"Why didn't you ever tell me?"

"I didn't like to upset Daddy."

"How would it have upset Daddy?"

"How would it upset *Klaus*?" her mother asked, laughing. "His people came from Hamburg, you know."

"In, like, the 1800s."

"Still, you can't be too careful," she'd said lightly, while Liane tried to imagine what it was she couldn't be too careful about. Careful not to go around rudely making Germans feel guilty by being Jewish? Not to let your husband know you, in case he might decide to murder you? Not to let even your own daughter see who you were? No, this must be only a new delusion of grandeur: "My people have been tormented through history and triumphant." Right, Mom.

But strangely enough her mother had been telling the truth.

"It is the tradition among our people to recall our sorrow at the destruction of the Temple . . ."

". . . by *breaking* something," Marsha said in Liane's ear, "at the instant of highest celebration, the union of two souls. Barbaric, wouldn't you say?"

The groom, who looked like a young Bill Clinton, a happy-go-lucky hound dog out to sniff his way around the world, gave a blithe shrug, set his foot down lightly on the glass to check its placement, then, satisfied, stamped down hard. A most gratifying crunch, and he grinned widely.

"In this way," Marsha continued, and it occurred to Liane that she was trying to be friendly, to say *I'm on your side*, "we take destruction unto ourselves, we *become* the destroyers! Mazel tov!"

"Mazel tov!" Liane said, feeling as if something had snapped in her, too—a vial of smelling salts—she wanted to laugh, dance, take part in the thing, whatever it was. Naomi beamed on Trevor's arm; her father, who with his orchestra conductor's mane and pallor looked exactly like Jehovah, regal and mischievous at once, linked his arm in Barbara's, and they came striding up the aisle with Trevor's parents in the rear. A drop slid between Liane's breasts: it was ninety-seven degrees and so still, not a tablecloth corner lifted. The fat roses hung their heads in their immense bouquets. It had happened, whatever happens at a wedding.

"Mazel tov, Mazel tov!"

"How touching," Marsha whispered, "they've imported some real Jews for the occasion."

"Like stocking a pond!" Liane said. They were two lizards on a sunny rock, Marsha and she. "But was it? A genuine rabbi, I mean?"

Marsha raised her eyes to the Unitarian heavens. "Genuine rabbis, my dear, do not reconcile Silverbergs with Tarringtons. Remember when Sharon married Mike O'Connor? Every rabbi she asked turned her down. Even the one from Provincetown, who married Joel and Adam at the Ramrod Room, said he 'didn't do mixed weddings'! Sharon thought he meant he wouldn't marry women to men!"

"Mazel tov," Liane called as the bridal party went by, and saw a cloud shade Barbara's face as if she took it as a gibe. Barbara had a Judaic sore spot, and Liane was always tempted to poke it, maybe to see if it matched her own. The last time they'd been out to dinner, Barbara had exclaimed, "It means the death of the Jews!" loudly just as the waiter arrived, so his spiel about salmon in cracked peppercorns with a ginger-wasabi sauce had sounded like a formal apology.

"I mean, congratulations!" Liane amended, and Barbara's eyes narrowed as if, though Mazel tov was suspicious, this was a real insult. Liane looked away. And glimpsed, suddenly, the profile of . . . Gabe Mizner! Or, a man with the same wild hair, square chin, and broken angled nose. It couldn't be, though, the real Gabe would be younger. And Gabe lived in Jerusalem, but then one felt so much closer to Jerusalem today, and already there'd been the miracle of the genealogical table, and the heat made everything so strange—

And they were all here together for the only time in their lives—

everyone could fall in love as he liked. She followed Gabe's ghost with her eyes as she'd followed the original Gabe at the bas mitzvah reception long ago. There was something in his face . . . the shape of the upper lip, the set of the jaw . . . something fascinating. Because of it she felt a suppressed excitement, as if something shocking and wonderful was about to happen. When he was out of her view for a moment her spirits clouded, until her eye lit on someone else, a woman whose hips spread wide as a double bass under her chiffon skirt. All Liane's work to look slender, and here she found herself mesmerized by amplitude—how typical, how infuriating! This woman soon became more womanly yet, sitting on a step to weep, then abandoned to weeping, rocking her small daughter on her lap while the child gazed out through the embrace brightly as if this were the only window she had on the world. Liane imagined the woman's husband had just died . . . or a divorce maybe, or . . . Whatever, she had never seen such frank public sorrow and this attracted her, too; she had forgotten what a luxury sorrow can be.

As she watched the weeping woman, Gabe's ghost seemed to be watching her. His eyes glittered avidly in a pale face: he looked Russian, she thought, without knowing what that might mean. One knows so little! But at the word *Russia* her mind raced, past daffodils and snowscapes (Dr. Zhivago), dachas in the Crimea where hearts beat all the faster for the fragility of the souls they must sustain (Chekhov), peasants haying (Anna Karenina)—then smashed up against a red wall (Stalin). That was her impression of Russia, and part of her impression of Gabe's ghost, who would be conjuring some equally ill-informed idea of her right now. But when Derek excused himself, Gabe's eyes followed him. He hadn't been watching Liane at all.

Derek was tending in the direction of the only African-American guests, a thin fragile woman with a painfully ingratiating smile and hair straightened, then curled, and—maybe her daughter? She looked as supple as her mother was brittle, with an animal grace Liane envied and would never have mentioned aloud since it was probably a racist notion. The back of her dress dipped far enough below her waist that it was clear she had not confined herself in any ridiculous undergarments—a dancer, Liane thought, or a goddess.

"I'm going over to meet them," Derek said, "they look so alone." But another couple had gotten there first—old leftists, she guessed, still marching along the road to justice and thus clear-eyed, handsome and strong at seventy, and aware of their presence, their effect. He looked so easily authoritative he hardly had to move, but she, in silk blouse and pants the exact blue-gray of Mao's tunic, seemed to move with the breeze. Her thick gray braid fell to her waist—she'd have been a cerebral, modernist dancer, cool as if her body were just an idea—Liane imagined the black woman had been her student, that they'd parted when the younger allowed her senses to overrule her intellect and broke her teacher's heart. By now, though, the older woman would have had second thoughts; the younger second feelings . . .

"What makes them seem particularly alone?" Liane asked. "None of us knows anyone. We're all standing around in twos."

She turned to see the old leftist laugh, too heartily, at something the younger woman said, and break away toward the bar.

"They're probably friends of Barbara's, from the ACLU," he said knowingly. "I'll just go over and say 'Well, I see you're all by yourselves,' " he said.

"They are *not* all by themselves! People are *trampling* each other to reach them," Liane snapped. "If you're bound and determined to go, don't do it to be a good boy." His beneficent instincts flew awry: once some sot on the next bar stool had made an incoherent crack about Israel and Derek had introduced himself as Howard Goldstein and produced an erudite, if grandiloquent, lecture on the history of anti-Semitism.

Or the Irishman they'd met on a train in France, Derek suddenly adopting a thick brogue and sympathizing with the man's assumed craving for a pint of Guinness. "It's the world's great beer!" he'd protested when Liane, seeing the man wince, shook her head. "Yeats, Joyce, Guinness—Ireland's pride!"

He only wanted to dissolve that big white house he'd come from in an alcoholic solution, and join the real people—the ones in the bar. Her heart softened—she'd always said she married him because he made being a Wasp seem so ethnic. Ethnic meaning that cord between a man's heritage and his aspiration where shame and aversion mix with longing and pride, exciting a woman's tenderness and her passion. The mystery of his childhood had entranced her, tempting her to rifle the trunks in his mother's attic, smell the heavy woolens, unfold the disintegrating letters sent back a century ago, from Calcutta or Singapore. The house was filled with Indian tapestry and Chinese porcelain and Indonesian brass, and redolent of sandalwood still. Yes, they ate dinners boiled beyond texture, then thoroughly creamed—they were above food, vain of their stoicism, thrifty and flinty and all the things those ancestors (the Reverend Sewall, Vestina the temperance crusader) who glowered on their walls had passed down. It was very exotic, really—entirely grim and strange.

"Go, go on," she said, remembering that he had (would that she could have seen it) dated Angela Davis after college, brought her home to his assiduously welcoming parents. All was smooth and lovely until his mother forgot herself and directed her guest to clear the table. To be black, always marked off so certain people would hate you and others fawn on you, without knowing you in any way! To have the universal unconscious attached to you so you're dragging the carcass of history behind you even when you're just running in to buy a bottle of milk—no, no! What can it be, to love some group of people, some race or religion? It's no better than hating them!

As if he were reading her thoughts Derek started reminiscing about his childhood vacations . . . Butterworth Lodge, on Lake Setunquet, the lodge, the clambakes, the canoeing parties—

"No Jews in those canoes," said Marsha, looking as if further shell-fish references might endanger her, and gazing at Derek very distantly as if she'd remembered suddenly an ancient feud between them.

"But you're a Unitarian!" Liane teased.

"Not by the standards of Butterworth Lodge!" Marsha sighed. "No, I was really only a Unitarian wannabe."

(*So you admit, you switch religious purely for conversational convenience!* Liane thundered, in her mind.)

"I only looked in at the windows of those houses, crammed with, with . . . Chinese gongs, for God's sake, and embroidered footstools . . . and among them *his mother*" (she and Liane had a common subject in their horror of Derek's mother), "this little white-haired lady no less imperious for her senility, got up in so many layers of lace and satin you thought she might die and just be lost among all the *things*—"

"They were missionaries!" Derek said, taking mock offense. "People *gave* them things, gongs and things—"

"Yes, and you see how their son followed in their footsteps, bringing lost sheep like me into the fold," Marsha went on. "I remember the first time I went for dinner there—no one talked! I mean, no subject was polite enough!"

"We were *Wasps*!" Derek cried. "That's our culture! The Japanese take their shoes off and sit on the floor!"

"So there they sat, saying how nice the weather had been, how leafy the tree was, even how good the dinner was, as if you could taste it! I believe an alarm would have sounded if a clove of garlic so much as entered that house."

"A chime perhaps, certainly not an alarm," Derek said, imitating the tone of voice his mother had shared with Julia Child. "Blandness is a venerable Wasp tradition. I've never heard such bigotry! Let me tell you something—after Marsha and I got married I sat down to read the Old Testament, I thought I ought to get to know my wife's people. Well, one tribe came and asked to join the Israelites, and the Israelites said they'd be welcome if the men were circumcised, so they submitted to circumcision and while they were all doubled over in agony the Israelites swarmed down and slaughtered them! I thought, my God, who are these monsters? I read no further."

"*Very* polite," said Marsha, with an "I told you so" smile.

The harp was zipped into its sack and trundled back down the drive-way. Night was coming—high luminous reaches of blue showed be-yond the maples massed overhead, and across the street the still waters of the bay glowed. Next door a lamp blinked on behind a leaded window. One had the feeling of wealth, that is, of beauty, safety, and abundance. Dinner was served, and onstage a blues band was checking the mikes, which meant Liane would have to beg someone to dance with her, as Derek felt dancing was somehow de-meaning.

"If she were a *real* rabbi," Marsha went on, finding Rabbi Mela-med's place card at their table, "she'd be seated with the *real* Jews. As it is they've got her surrounded by you and Derek, who don't have the radar. . . ."

Or else God *does* have a plan, Liane thought, and I've been called here, seated next to the rabbi, for a reason. Who knew? . . . A semi-rabbi might be more sympathetic toward Liane the instant Jew. But

Liane could hardly lift her eyes from her plate, never mind introduce herself or tell her story. They'd accuse her of lying, shouldering in where she didn't belong; they'd take the wonderful secret away from her. She bolted her chicken brochette while the rabbi spoke of her other job—she was an interior decorator, which might explain the dress—and detailed her exercise regimen, which began with a short run and ended with sixty-one laps at the health club pool. Fortified by the risotto with spring vegetables, Liane imagined backing this woman up against a wall and informing her that rabbis are supposed to be old and bearded and speak in parables, and never, ever, think about interior decoration, and certainly not go on and on about their damnable aerobic fitness as if endorphins were more important than faith.

"Why sixty-one?" she asked instead, hoping to hear it was a number of mystical significance, maybe from cabala—but it had to do with the length of the pool. The phrase *citrus allergy* floated over from Marsha's conversation, light as the lime sorbet.

To whom could she say it? "I'm a Jew, a Jew!" What could it mean, the subterranean pull, all these years, of a religion or culture she hardly knew? The sight of little Rebecca Mizner, exalted suddenly, bearing the Torah down the aisle, the prayers, the cantor, the men in their tallises, her mother saying, in that lugubrious churchy hush with which she had kept her husband's utilitarian attitudes at bay: "Do you see, here the sacred is a natural part of everyday life." Then her mother had her own marriage of twenty years—never mind the four children—annulled. These religions know how to serve up the barbaric necessities, in a fragrant, mysterious sauce. One loves, one ceases to love. One wants a bite of Christ, a sip of his blood . . . or a slice of the baby's penis, just a little one. One sins and wants to atone, fasts and feasts, dreads and longs for the moment when, finally one can set the dearly beloved body aflame.

Feeling herself swept into the current of life, at thirteen, seeing Rebecca Mizner initiated into the fearful mysteries, she had felt so ready to say yes, yes, and let life take her, and there came Gabe Mizner back from the Six Day War. *He'd* been in mortal danger for a *sacred* reason, while Vietnam, a perpetual motion meat grinder, churned on. She'd asked him to dance, finally, and been mortified to see him look at her as a child—he who seemed to represent the entire continent of adulthood: eros, danger, belief. Years later a man, kissing her, called her "my *shiksa*," and she determined to hear love in it, as "You're not my mother, I can fuck you into the next world . . ." which he did for some months, until he began to feel she hadn't properly bathed.

"When you shower with someone you're about to make love to, you don't always wash behind your ears," she'd said, hurt and prim.

"It's not the ears . . ." She just hadn't been clean enough, that was all.

"So, there was a mikvah?" Marsha baited the rabbi, eyes sparkling.

"Well, in Reform Judaism . . ." She looked down at her plate.

Lenny came over and put a hand on Derek's shoulder. "Fishman's been *following* you," he announced.

"Fishman!" Derek said. "Where?"

Len looked toward the bar, the buffet, the dance floor—"I don't know. I just saw him a minute ago." Then he leaned down and whispered dramatically: "He wants to know *all*. I don't think it's too much to say he's obsessed with you!"

"What?" Derek asked in mock-horror, though it was anything but odd. Everyone shared Fishman's fascination—Liane had used to feel it herself. And why? Because Derek *looked* like those ancestors, like a Wasp, his eyes stern, mouth set in righteous fortitude and cold certainty. Who ever sees such a facial expression today? He was counter-charismatic: seeming distant even when he was right beside you, slicing through a crowd as if nothing mattered but his destination (the bar). Liane thought of him as a deacon, who, finding his church insufficiently austere, had become an atheist as a more physical man might have turned to vandalism. Which is to say, she'd made a romance of him, a story based on his ancestry—the way one makes a story out of everyone.

"Len, why is Fishman legendary?" she asked, and his pursed lips trembled with suppressed comedy.

"It's not something you can really put into words," he said. "I was going to introduce you . . ."

"After all these years?" Derek said. "I'm not sure we should break the spell."

"Dance with me!" Liane begged the rabbi's husband.

"Your husband will kill me," he said, glancing in Derek's direction as if literally in fear. Which was correct! If people fall into love and fascination based on the color of eyes or the angle of nose, then they can stand in mortal terror of each other for just the same reasons. She'd had a Jewish doctor once who told her he'd used to cover the emergency room on Christmas. But he'd learned: *"That's when the guns come out."* A shiver had run over him, and he looked at her with eyes that seemed to have glimpsed a specter. Driving away from his office that windy day, she'd had to swerve to avoid a rogue Christmas tree that was barreling toward her like a tinseled tumbleweed. Life is treacherous; is it any wonder people stick with their familiars?

"He won't kill you!" she said. "He may be willing to pay you." And she pulled him toward the dance floor though he looked utterly miserable. Derek jumped up as soon as they left and headed toward the black women, while Gabe's ghost watched from across the lawn.

So, Gabe's ghost must be Fishman! This seemed nearly a miracle. Now she could follow his movements as he followed Derek, as Derek pursued the black women, who . . . well, it would be interesting to know. They were all part of the great human chain of stalkers, each avidly watching the next, intrigued by difference, consoled by similarity, searching, searching for some face, some being that might promise perfect union, absolute satisfaction.

All the musicians were black, and all older, so they carried a mystical authority as if they might not be flawed live people but great blues players from history, become ideals now they were dead. The deep thrum of the bass felt like a man's voice when your ear is to his chest, and the singer in her immensity might have been Mother Nature; she swayed like a windblown tree. The weeping woman was dancing with abandon now, as if she'd shed all her tears and been utterly freed. It was dark, the day's heat dispelled; the waiters with their napkined bottles were no longer needed; there had been enough wine, enough talk, enough of everything, there was need only of music now. Everyone was alone, finally, in his own imagination, free to cast the silvered net of fantasy over whomever he chose. Liane thought of the weeping woman undressed—the frank swelling of her breasts, her thighs, the split red as a fig . . . yes, it was divine, being a woman, a person of the hips—she smiled at the rabbi's horribly nervous husband, draped her arms over his shoulders, and leaned back against the swell of the music, until, to her amazement and his relief, Derek cut in.

"So, are they from the ACLU?" she asked.

"No," he admitted. "They are the cleaning lady and her daughter, a nurse." He gathered her up. "I feel like it's *our* wedding," he said. He loved her, her husband—it always felt strange.

"Every wedding deepens your own somehow," she said. "They remind you what you intended." And what would that be? Only to possess the other, free him, consume him, and become him, that was all.

"I suppose that's so," he said. Something had brightened, softened him—he held tight to her waist and let her carry him away. Over his shoulder she saw Fishman stride over to speak to Len. His curls looked like razor wire, Liane saw with a thrill—exactly like Gabe's. She could feel again what it had been like, at thirteen, to brush against a real soldier. But she remembered, suddenly, that Gabe had *not* been a soldier. He'd been an exchange student, spending his year in Jerusalem, and she a girl who was looking for rapture, religious and erotic at once. How she had worried for Gabe, during the Six Day War—thank heaven it had only been six days!

Marsha had snatched up the rabbi's husband and, attempting some kind of wild hora beside them, turned her heel and fell down.

"It's the citrus," she said thickly, while Derek, lifting her back to her feet, said, "I thought Jews didn't drink," so she grimaced and said, "You never understood," and Derek, settling her in her chair said in puzzlement, "Come to think of it, the Jews I know drink like fish . . . The Jews . . . the Jews . . ." He put his hands to his temples as if trying to put down a sudden headache or receive an extrasensory communication.

"Anyway she's a Unitarian," Liane said spitefully.

And the music took a turn into "Take Me to the River."

"I *love* this song!" Liane cried, and Derek said in the voice of an impartial jury that yes, it was a good song, and she held his hands in the air and danced absolutely against him, while he looked simultaneously ecstatic and appalled. The woman of the hips was dancing alone, aswim in the music, without sorrow or joy. Naomi, who would wake up the next morning to ask herself: *What have I done?* stood smiling up at Trevor, sweet and exhausted, while the singer intoned in her great, up-from-the-earth voice:

"Ladies and Gentlemen, you've been listening to the Twilight Blues Band, and we want to thank you for your wonderful hospitality. I'm a good Southern Baptist and I wish for *all of you* that you may *go* to the river and be washed in the waters of the lord . . ."

A baptism! Mazel tov! And here was Fishman, the embodiment of something she'd been yearning for for years, standing on the lawn in front of the dance platform, to peer up at her husband. She found her voice: "Fishman!"

He looked up at the dancers, but seeing no one he knew, looked higher, expecting a hovering angel maybe? Whether it was the music, or the champagne, or the way the tide had risen silently until now a wave lapped, then another, setting up a slow counterpoint as if a second drummer had just joined in . . . whatever, everything felt Jewish—as if the thread of the sacred was woven through the daily fabric—and Liane wanted to kneel down and say, "Fishman, it's me, and we can get married and go to Israel where even the wars have meaning, and we'll live and die for a reason and . . ."

"Fishman!" she repeated. "Down here!"

His eyes lit; he saw her, asking: "Do I *know* you?"

Blood Poison

"You probably don't believe this is my daughter," my father said to the cabdriver. "You're wondering: Where did a broken-down old guy like him come up with a gal like that?"

It was only an hour since I'd gotten off the train and already my father had explained to two strangers that we weren't having an affair. The first was the bartender at the Oyster Bar, where Pop had pulled out my stool as if New York were his overcoat and he was spreading it over a puddle for me. The bartender looked as if he had long since stopped seeing individual faces or thinking of anything except whatever he himself was obsessed with—money or football or his prostate or maybe some kind of love or ideal. He nodded without listening, dealing out some packets of crackers like cards. The place was full—of men and women who looked busier and more purposeful than I'd ever been—and the chalkboard listed oysters named for all the places I'd have felt more at home: Cotuit, Wellfleet, Chincoteague—low-tide towns where the few people left behind through the winter huddle in the souvenir shop doorways, stamping their feet and swearing under the clouds of their breath.

To the bartender I'd given an apologetic smile, which went, of course, unnoticed. The cab driver, Ahmed Sineduy, license number 0017533, cried "Yes!" with wonderful enthusiasm, as if he had indeed been trying to imagine what would attract me to my father.

"In fact," Pop crowed, "I *created* her!"

I'd convinced him to have a drink at lunch—a mistake, but I wanted one myself. He makes me nervous—I don't know him very well. He and my mother married young, and after I was born he drifted away, taking long and longer visits to his mother in the city until finally we noticed that he was living with her and visiting us. I'd study the New York news every night, first thinking I might see him, later that if I came to understand the city, I'd get a sense of my father, too. Phrases like "truck rollover in the Midtown Tunnel" were invested with incalculable glamour for me, and when people spoke of the Queensboro Bridge or the East River they might as well have been talking about the Great Obelisk of Shalmanezar and the Red Sea.

Twice a year my mother put me on the train to the city so I could spend the weekend with him. In my grandmother's apartment it was still 1945, and I pushed the mother-of-pearl buttons on the radio set, expecting to hear FDR, while Pop made supper and Grammy offered me hoarded bits of chocolate and cake. We tried to act familiar, which meant we couldn't ask the kind of questions that might have helped us figure each other out, and year after year the distance grew. If Pop was doing well in the market he talked a mile a minute, spreading out maps and showing me pictures of the houses—sometimes whole islands—he meant to buy. When he was losing he was silent, and would start out of his trance every few minutes to ask how I was doing in school. As soon as I could I'd escape to the guest room, pull the velvet drapes, and fold myself into the heavy bed linens, where in my fantasies some man as commanding and enveloping as Zeus the swan held me in the tightest grip you can imagine, while all the lights of the city whirled over our heads.

So, yes, I was an overheated child, and so fervid an adolescent I became accustomed to seeing my teachers squirm and look away from me, praying I'd go elsewhere for the extra help next time. By college the pedagogical discomfort was happily transformed, and there was no end to the office hours available for a girl whose palpitating heart was quite nearly visible through her blouse. How I loved school!

With my father I keep my hair shaken down over my eyes like a dog, though I still come twice a year to visit. It pleases him to think of himself as a father, and God has damned me to try and please him. When my mother gave up her quest to draw him back to us and started the divorce, he sobbed like a lost little boy. And now that my grandmother's dead, I'm the only family he has.

This time I was even "on business"—I was flying to Cincinnati in the morning for a job interview—a Visiting Assistant Professor job of the sort that a person like me would be very lucky to have; a job I needed to escape a debilitating love: a professor, of course, my Louis—an authority on Balzac, about whom no one else gives a damn. When I first met him he was railing at some translator's disrespect for an original text, and I remember thinking that he was *really angry*, that a crime against meaning was no less brutal to him than a physical assault. Needless to say I threw myself at him, and at Balzac. I swam through *The Human Comedy* as if it were a river I had to cross to reach him, but when I reached the other shore he was gone. By then I'd studied long enough to see Louis had such feeling for literature because ordinary life seemed so empty to him. And I was the very emissary of the ordinary—eating, bleeding, laughing, et cetera—a constant reminder of how much better Balzac had done than God. Louis began to inflict little cruelties, insults and condescensions, like cigarette burns, wherever he knew I was tender, and

I slowly found myself entirely absorbed in these wounds—with each I became sicker, but it seemed an ailment only Louis's gentle care could cure. In a minute of clarity I realized I'd have to tear myself out of his life by the roots, and taking a job in a distant city looked like the surest way.

The cab zipped uptown, switching lanes and skirting bike messengers and double-parked delivery trucks with an ease I should have found alarming, but I leaned back. I had faith in Ahmed. As long as he was talking to my father I was safe.

"Seventy-nine?" Ahmed asked.

"Fifty-six and a half!" my father replied. His age.

"Fifty-six?" Ahmed hit the brake. We were already somewhere in the Sixties.

"Seventy-ninth Street," I said. "Museum of Natural History." Natural History in springtime; in September, the Met. Once, when I was maybe ten, we tried something different, a piano concert at Lincoln Center. I had a velvet dress, and Pop kept whispering things about the music to me, pointing out the movements in a concerto, praising the pianist's fine technique. He had never said a word about music before, and certainly I'd never heard him speak with rapture—he was trying to impress me, I realized—he wanted my esteem. And I tried—I worked at admiring him the way a doubting priest works at faith.

"But you must see plenty of men out with girls who aren't their daughters," he was saying to Ahmed, thinking perhaps of Louis, who's fifty-three. "It happens all the time."

He made it sound like a horror: something too awful to think about, like a child crushed under a bus or chained in a basement, one of the travesties he absorbs out of the paper, and can't stop talking about, almost as if he'd suffered them himself. He keeps his eye trained on the pain in the news; he can't bear to look at real life.

He quit his job during the divorce; he couldn't stand to give money to people who rejected him. After that he went into business for himself, borrowing office space from acquaintances, empty desks he could use for a few months or a year, in a cubicle on some eighteenth or twenty-fifth or forty-seventh floor where a couple of sour men smoked cigars and followed the ticker tape all day. Visiting, I'd stand at the window, watching the secretaries gather like pigeons on the pavement below, thinking that someday I'd become one of them and work silently all day among people who took no notice of me. Then we'd go home to Grammy, who still called him Skipper, his childhood name. They fought over trifles as if they were married, but she had no notion of money and was happy as long as he didn't waste food or throw away any reusable string. When she died she left him a pantry full of egg crates and plastic containers, but he had already spent her fortune.

In his new flat on Staten Island, he was perfectly content, he told me again and again. Yes, it faced north, but he wasn't one of these people who had to have sunlight, and what a relief just to cook for himself. It wasn't as if he were isolated—he had the *Times* and fifty-two channels. He would have been amazed to realize that the pretty morning news anchor he admired was younger than I was, that if he were to meet her by one of the fabulous accidents he imagined, he, too, would be "out with a girl" right now.

"Have any children yourself?" he asked Ahmed, with his salesman's hearty voice.

"Seventy-nine!" Ahmed declared.

"No English," I mouthed to Pop, twice before he understood.

"Aha!" he said. He cleared his throat. He had that tutelary gleam in his eye—he was going to show me how little distance there is between cultures, how much can be accomplished with a smile, a concerned tone. He thought, quite rightly, that I was an awkward, inward girl, in need of social training. Where did Ahmed come from, he asked—Syria? Lebanon? India, perhaps?

When Ahmed said Karachi, my father turned out to have a few words of Punjabi, and an enthusiastic accent, too.

Ahmed burst into speech.

"Whoa, whoa, you're way beyond me!" Pop said. "Slow down, wa-a-a-y down."

By Seventy-ninth Street Ahmed had taught him some basic insults, and the words for *father* and *daughter*.

"Nice guy," Pop said as the cab fishtailed away from us. "Wish I could have tipped him."

"What did you say to him?" I asked.

"Isn't it a beautiful evening," he told me. "The janitor at the office taught me. He has a wife and three kids back there. . . . He doesn't have much hope of getting them over, but he sends money. . . ."

He sighed so heavily, thinking of this family torn apart, that I was afraid he was going to cry. He's so tall, has such broad shoulders, that when he gets weepy it's like seeing a statue melt. Even now I'll be doing the dishes or walking the dog and I suddenly feel his sadness go through me. I think of him as a little boy, his own father dying— he'll say "when I died," by accident, when he speaks of it—I never know what to do to assuage it, any more than I did when I was ten. One morning back then he told me that my mother didn't want to make love to him anymore. I had only the vaguest idea of what he meant and I sat stupidly over my cinnamon toast searching for something helpful while his lip began to tremble, as if I was his last hope and had failed him.

By now he's so solitary he expects no consolation, and he walked along tightly for a minute, entirely constricted by sadness, and then threw it off with a quick little gesture, like breaking a chain.

"He taught me to say, 'Wow, get the legs on that babe,' too," he laughed, holding the door to the automatic teller open for me. There was hardly room for two people in the booth. I edged into the corner while he fed his card to the machine.

"We'll have to see," he said. "Last week they credited me with sixty dollars by mistake. In fact, I'm overdrawn." He punched in his number: 1014, the date of his marriage to my mother.

"I've got money," I said. I was embarrassed how much—Louis never let me help with the rent, so my salary went straight into the bank.

"No, no, honey," he told me. "I think we'll be fine here. I've *been* making money. I started with five thousand and I was doing great all through March—I was up to twenty-five. Then I lost a few thousand last week, a few more Monday, and Friday another seventeen . . ."

By my math this meant he was broke. I'd guessed it, seeing his posture from the train window as he waited on the platform, and when, over the whole course of lunch, he never spoke of buying any islands at all.

"As long as they didn't catch the error," he said, "we ought to be all right." We heard the rollers inside the machine as they shuffled the bills; then it spat three starched twenties at us through pursed rubber lips.

"The town's ours," said Pop, as if we'd drawn three cherries on a slot machine. His luck was turning, he could feel it. I could hardly keep up with him as he strode back toward the museum.

"Two adults," he said to the cashier, and "Can it really be, you're an adult?" to me, and then, to the cashier again, "She's my daughter. What do you think?"

Her badge read CYNTHIA POST, DOCENT. She had a kind of brisk official grace, and she glanced at me and gave him a perfunctory smile. As I accepted my museum pin from her, I thought that although she might have been unhappy in her life she did not look as if she'd often been confused. She would have spent her whole life here, walking to the museum past her grocery, her florist, her dry cleaner, the school she and her children had attended, the church she had been married in. I regarded her with both condescension and jealousy—I would never belong so squarely to anything. I'd put on a hat that morning because it seems to me that only very confident people wear hats— so that I'd appear to be self-assured—but I felt only foolish and ostentatious, like a child dressed up in her mother's clothes.

My father, of course, looked great. Age has given him the look of dignity, and he takes a professional pleasure in conversation. No one has ever sounded more reasonable, more calm and knowing. If he told you to buy something, you'd buy, or he'd explain it slower, with more stubborn patience, until you did. He solicited Cynthia Post's suggestion of the best exhibit, and as we took the direction she suggested (something interactive in the Rocks and Minerals) her smile was newly warm. Following him down the corridor, one hand on my hat as I tried to keep pace with his stride, I felt for a minute as I used to when I visited: happy and excited just to be in his company, sure that if I could only manage to keep my hand in his he'd pull me around the corner into a new world.

"Did she say the second right, or the third?" he asked me. The hallway ended in three closed doors. Two were locked, so we went through the third and down another long passage toward a sign that read ENTRANCE, which turned out to be one of a pile of ENTRANCE signs stored against another locked door. There was hardly any light and I felt terribly claustrophobic suddenly, as if we were trapped here together forever. After all the years of visiting museums I'm still never comfortable in one—even in a roomful of Renoirs I long for a window, and the Museum of Natural History, the final repository of moon rocks and extinct sparrows and other small, dun-colored things whose significance one would never believe if it weren't written out for you, always seemed to me the loneliest place in the world. To stand here now with my father was to guess what it might feel like in my grave.

Pop took a credit card out of his wallet and slid it down the doorjamb.

"Voilà!" he said, pushing the door open and ushering me through. "I'm way over the limit on that card anyway," he said.

We were in my favorite room—the dioramas of aboriginal life. It was empty except for us and a troupe of black Girl Scouts whose noses were pressed to the glass to see Cro-Magnon man forage and the Vikings set to sea. I peered in over their heads; I love ant colonies, too, and model trains, quattrocento crucifixions—those representations of life where everyone takes part, whether sowing or winnowing, rowing or raising the sail. You never see anyone like me, loitering at the edge of the scene, too fearful to make an effort, wishing only to escape his little glassed-in world.

My father checked his watch. He had done the fatherly thing by bringing me: now what? He turned his attention to the scouts. He's friend to all little girls now, watching them on the street, in the library or the supermarket, befriending them in elevators, smiling down over them with an unbearable nostalgia. Nostalgia for me, I suppose, though like most nostalgia this was not yearning for something lost but for something that had never been; an old wish so deeply etched into memory that finally it was clear as if real. Every one of these children was the child I might have been—a child who flew off the schoolbus into her father's arms and who was gentle and delicate, shy and kind. I had been most disappointing, talking too much, laughing too loudly, though "unnaturally" silent with him. He was still saving elephant jokes for me while I was soldiering my pompous twelve-year-old way through *The Feminine Mystique*, and I could tell from his face, when he walked in to find me reading it in the bathtub, that he was certain it must be filth. He stood there looking down at me with his characteristic puzzled, hurt expression, wondering what could be wrong, how I could have become the way I was. "Does your mother know you're reading that?" he asked finally, but he left before I could answer as if he had to get away from me. Even my body was becoming obscene.

Now he looked down over these little girls in their uniforms and berets as if he might find a new daughter among them. Two of them, whispering together, became gradually aware of him and grew silent.

"Why you staring?" one of them asked, sharp as her own mother, I supposed. The mother who had woven those hundred braids and fastened them with red and yellow beads.

"I was wondering which badges you have there," he told her.

She was maybe seven; pride quickly overwhelmed her suspicion. She lifted her sash and began, in a careful, earnest voice, to describe them, pressing a finger to each embroidered circle: there was one for reading, one for learning to swim, one for refusing drugs. He bent to look more closely, asking how how she had earned them, expressing amazement that such a small girl could have accomplished such difficult tasks. The whole troupe, wary at first, then eager, reconstellated around him.

"Girls?" Their leader fixed a level gaze on them—they had been taught not to take up with strangers, in fact there was a badge for that, too. They turned unwillingly from my father's attention and re-formed their line of pairs, holding hands as they went on toward the Bird Room. The one with the red and yellow beads took a last quick glance over her shoulder at us as she left the room.

"It's terrific," he said, watching them. "They're from Paterson. You know what a sewer Paterson is? But that little girl, she looked me right in the eye when I spoke to her, she—"

He broke off. His eyes were brimming.

"If I could find the right woman," he said, "I'd start all over again, and this time it wouldn't be one child, I'd like to have four or five—or six! or seven! I suppose that surprises you . . . ," he said with some kind of belligerence.

"Not at all," I said. I'd have been surprised if he didn't dream of such things, but it seems his penance for never having completely entered into marriage is that he can't get completely divorced. He never dated anyone after my mother. He told me once that as a young man he had assumed that husband and wife became, sexually, one being, so that if split, both halves must die. Adultery must then be physically appalling: when a colleague of his had casually mentioned a mistress, my father had begun to retch as if he'd heard of a bestial crime.

"I'm so glad we can *talk* to each other!" he said now. We had come to the Hall of Dinosaurs, and I made a show of studying a stegosaurus spine.

"People have such awful relations with their children these days," he went on. "But I feel there's nothing I wouldn't be comfortable telling you."

I was afraid this might be true, and indeed, a minute later he was feeling comfortable enough to tell me about a sore he had on his back, somewhere near the seventh vertebra—no, he hadn't been to the doctor—and here, with his arm twisted and groping in the back of his shirt, he stopped to ponder medical costs and the arrogance of the educated, and to remind me that he had treated his own athlete's foot for years with a simple formula of diluted sulfuric acid. But this thing was painful, and he couldn't see it, that was the real problem.

"It's there, there, a little up," he said, turning his back to me and trying to reach it with his thumb.

"A little *up*," he said again, with irritation, because I was supposed, apparently, to examine it. I looked around in the vain hope that someone might come through, some white rabbit of a scientist carrying a large bone, the kind of man I always dream will save me.

"Up, up, *there*," Pop said, giving a little moan as I touched the sore. "It hurts," he said, in the voice of a child.

"I'll look at it when we get back to the Island," I promised, thinking he'd forget it by then.

The Hall of African Mammals opened before us, long, cool and dark like the nave of a cathedral, its polished marble walls glistening, its chapels dedicated not to saints but to species endangered or extinct. In the center was a stuffed woolly mammoth lifting its trumpeting head. A young waiter in a tuxedo shirt was arranging café tables around it.

"Hello!" my father called to him, across the room. "Is this a private party?"

No, it was a regular thing on Fridays, came the answer, though not until five.

It was a quarter past four. Could my father prevail upon him—? He'd been bringing me here since I was six—

The waiter interrupted him—sit anywhere, he said. It was easier to pour a couple of early drinks than listen to the story. He brought us two gin-and-tonics and a cup of Goldfish crackers and left us alone.

As I lifted my drink my father looked me up and down quickly, startled, as if he had just realized again that he was out with a woman. I was glad the waiter had gone—I didn't think I could bear to have myself explained again.

"So, what's this job in Columbus?" Pop asked, the way he had used to ask me about school.

"Cincinnati," I said, but though he had asked the same question, with the same error, at lunch, I was relieved to hear it. It's the sort of thing fathers and daughters talk about, and I had, for once, a good answer.

"Assistant professor," I told him, "I mean, it's mainly teaching composition, but—"

"But it's a job," he said. "You won't be on the dole anymore."

"A teaching fellowship isn't quite the dole."

"It's all Greek to me, sweetie," he said with a laugh. "I'm sure it's very important. Nothing wrong with a little work, though."

If he saw the irony in this, it didn't show in his face. These were phrases he'd heard, 'Greek to me,' and 'Nothing wrong with a little work'. He repeated them just to have something to say. He hadn't gone to college—his mother thought it extravagant, so he'd never quite understood what I'd been doing studying all the time. To deal him a sharp reply would have been like striking a child.

"It'll be a lot of work," I said, careful to keep the eager, Horatio Alger note in my voice. "But it's great just to get an interview. You wouldn't believe it, but they said almost two hundred people applied. And now it's just between me and two others. And they've been so nice, you should have heard what they said about my articles. . . . Considering the market," I said, thinking now that in fact I hadn't done so terribly badly, had accomplished a little and had time to accomplish more, that I could really give him something to be proud of, that he might even see that if there was promise in my life, his, too, could be redeemed, "I'm doing pretty well."

"You can go pretty far with a nice set of tits these days," he said.

He was smiling as if he had just gotten off a wonderful mot, and I wanted to smile, too, because if I smiled we could go on as if he hadn't said this, and soon it would really seem he had not. I couldn't manage it, but I carefully avoided looking down to see if my sweater was too tight, or crossing my arms over my chest, or cringing or shrinking in any way. I looked past him for a minute, at a Kudu, lithe and proud in its glass enclosure, looking out over a glittering lake.

You're all he's got, I said to myself. *Be kind.*

"Do you suppose that's real water?" I asked, hoping to lead him back to safety. He likes a mechanical question, and can spend hours explaining about pistons and spark plugs, how the keystone holds the arch and the moon pulls the tide. Now he began on the properties of chlorine, but a morose fog settled into his voice and he stared a long time into the scene.

"No," he said suddenly, rousing himself. "By God, I *wouldn't* mind marrying again, not one little bit." His voice rang against the marble walls. "I'd like to find a woman who loves to cook, and loves to talk, and loves to hike, and loves to *fuck*—"

He paused, darting a glance toward me, worrying I might be offended? Hoping so? Testing, to see if I might be the woman described?

"And then I'd like to buy a piece of property on the sunny side of a good, serious hill, and we'd start building a house there."

He drained his drink and looked around for the waiter.

"I was right," he told me, "I *knew* T-bills were going to turn around this week. If only I'd been able to get a solid position, we could be having this drink . . . on Antigua! Or, how would you like Positano? Looking out over the Bay of Naples? Bougainvillea cascading down the hillsides? What would you think about that?

"I've *been* making money," he said again. "This time next year, who knows?" He lifted the empty glass to his lips again.

"*Where is* he?" I asked, but the waiter was gone.

Then came the Girl Scouts, two by two, swinging their clasped hands, unable to quite keep themselves from skipping until they stood before the woolly mammoth, whereupon a hush seized them as if they were in the presence of a god or a living dream. Daneesha, the one with the red and yellow beads, greeted my father now as an old friend, shaking off her partner and running to him to show off a new gyroscope from the souvenir shop.

He woke up. For a minute he was in the thrall not of the past or the future but of Daneesha and her gyroscope, which he spun for her on his fingertip, then along its string. Soon he was writing out his phone number, inviting her to dinner the next time she came into town.

"Your whole family," he told her. "Do you like spaghetti?"

It was just her mother and herself, she said, and they loved spaghetti. She was hungry, as I'd been: she wanted to draw her hand along a man's scratchy cheek, to be lifted in a pair of arms that could carry her anywhere. As she took the business card with his number, her clear smile faded into an expression of secret greed. She pocketed it quickly, and, as if afraid he would snatch it back from her, ran back to the troupe, whose leader turned a hard warning glance at him. I remembered that the mother of a little girl in his building had told him if she found her daughter at his place one more time she'd call the police. Nobody gets it, I thought—it's not that he wants sex with little girls, it's that he wants to live like they do, in a world before all that.

"It's hard to believe that you used to be that age," he said, as the Scouts went off toward the planetarium. He checked his watch.

"If we leave now," he began, "we can change at the World Trade Center before the crush . . ." Call Hunan Kitchen from the ferry terminal, catch the 5:40 boat, be on the island by 6:15, and pick up dinner on the way home. And he was off into the city with me only one step behind. The subway station felt just like always, comforting in its clangor, the crowd of preoccupied faces pressing onto the escalator, the couple of latecomers running edgewise down the stairs.

The doors of one train closed with hydraulic authority and it slid smoothly off as another slammed in around the bend. Pop put one token in the stile for me, wave me through and strode ahead of me again toward the first car. From here we could easily cross to the express at Grand Central. And it was waiting, already packed. I folded myself between two men in suits and swayed with them all the way downtown. *I do*, I thought, *I love it here*. At South Ferry we ran up the ramp, and though the boat was boarding Pop dialed Hunan Kitchen: he could see by the size of the crowd that there was plenty of time.

We were the last up the gangplank, and the first to disembark, running down the iron stairway down to the street, crossing with the light, turning up the street past the Hadassah Thrift Shop and Winnie's Bridal and Formal, and Island Cleaners, where suits and dresses moved in stately procession on their conveyor, and as we opened the door at Hunan Kitchen they were calling our number.

"Steaming!" Pop said, opening the little cartons and setting them in the center of the table, as proud as if we had ridden unscathed through the gears of a great machine.

"It's all in the timing," he told me, feeling paternal now, ready to share the wisdom of his lifetime with me. "It's an instinct—you have to have a sense for it. The crowd is going one direction, everyone's jumping on the bandwagon, and you have to be willing to stop and think, 'Maybe there's another way.' I'm always ready to take the risk, move against the prevailing winds, and it's paid off for me."

He gestured in the direction of the newspaper, still folded to the market tables. "What I would have done this week, if I'd had the money," he said, "nobody else even considered, but it would have been *very* profitable."

He shook his head. "But for a lack of cash, really, I'd be on top of the world today. I've just gotta back in there, sweetie, and with this kind of opportunity, you know, by November, the clouds are closing in here, and I can be thinking where I'd like to retire to."

He popped the beer top as if it were champagne, but in another minute he was lost to his thoughts again. The lamp over the table, all four hundred watts of it (he had hated my mother's dinners by candle) shone pitilessly down on his face. Everything in his apartment, the bare bulbs, the month's worth of newspapers piled by the couch, the box of sugar he plunked down defiantly before me as if to say, "I suppose you expected a bowl," still set itself against my mother. But on the wall facing his chair hung her engagement photograph, taken when she was twenty and secure in a luxuriant beauty. I had nothing of her in me, I thought—I was his daughter exactly and it made me want to rip at my skin.

"Curaçao is nice," Pop said suddenly. "Coves, inlets, nice private spots. I don't need a glittering nightlife, wide beaches, high-rise hotels . . ." His voice swelled. "Some people have to have that, the glamour—it makes them feel like they are somebody, I guess . . . I never felt that way. That's one thing I like about Beverly Dill" (this was the news anchor he admired) "—she's down to earth. She's smart, but not so smart you wouldn't trust her. She's not looking for fame or money, not the kind of gal who would turn up her nose at—"

"I have found you ridiculous since the time I was old enough to laugh." I could taste these words on my tongue, and they were delicious. To have nothing to be proud of but the fact that you didn't like high-rise hotels! To be cooped in your deathly apartment beneath a photograph of your former wife, sketching, sketching on the blueprints for the next one as if anyone at all could bear to love you!

But it was valor, almost, his relentless optimism, the way, though his life had eroded beneath him, he refused to feel the loss, counting his blessings, keeping his eye on the future even if by now he could see no more in the future than these worn old fantasies, the escape to the island, the beautiful woman's love. To despise him was to remember, suddenly, a time when I was twelve and he had driven me to the dentist for an extraction that went awry. An hour of bloody probing and wrenching ended in an operation with scant anesthesia, but the worst part was seeing Pop stand by helpless, one minute trying to make light of it, the next turning away, aghast. If I'd ever dreamed he could take care of me I had to admit myself wrong that day. On the way home we passed a Kmart and suddenly he was doubling back, determined to buy me a gift. Dazed and aching, I waded in behind him among racks of too-blue jeans and stacks of lawn furniture poised to fall. In the music department I grabbed the first thing on the rack, just to get it over with. It was *Yellow Submarine*, and I still can't hear it without thinking of everything I wanted that purchase to assuage: he was failing, at marriage, at work, at fatherhood, and he had one hope left, the hope that I was too young to see.

Now I continued to pretend. "—at the simpler things in life," I said. This was a phrase of his, and to speak it was a way to say, covertly, "It's okay, it's only money you've lost, nothing important."

"The *simpler things in life*. Exactly," he said. "*Exactly*. There are so few people, sweetie, who really understand. . . ." He turned to me with a true smile, even a loving smile, and I felt, and despised myself for feeling, overjoyed. His discourse on simplicity carried us to bedtime, when he cleared the newspapers off the sofa, pulled it out for me, and gave me sheets, the same ones Grammy had ripped up their worn middles and restitched for him before she died. As I made up the bed I heard him brush his teeth while the bathroom radio gave the financial news. A cold rain pricked at the window, and under the marquee of the defunct movie house across the street a tired prostitute looked up and down the empty street. I went to pull the curtain, but of course there wasn't any.

"You know, the way you're standing, you could almost have been your mother for a minute there."

I jumped. I hadn't heard him come out of the bathroom.

"Sweetie," he said, coming toward me, "it's only me."

I was afraid for a minute he was going to put his arms around me, but instead he took off his shirt.

"Would you mind just looking at my back for me? This—boil, or whatever it is—I . . ." He trailed off—I could see he didn't like to ask.

"Oh, Pop, I don't know anything about boils," I said, but after all he was alone, while I had Louis to look at any boils of mine, so I sat him down to examine him. His skin was coarse and oily—I remembered all I knew about skin, how it's the body's largest organ and full of various glands. How heavy a skin is, like a wetsuit: I pictured his folded over the back of a chair. The sore was a round raw center in a nimbus of pus, and I saw he'd been picking at it, like a child who can't leave a scab alone.

"Press it and see what's in it, sweetie," he said. "I thought something crawled out of it yesterday."

He looked up at me and some ancient, familiar shadow crossed his face. Was he cut so absolutely free of his moorings, so adrift in fantasy, that his night-terrors were as alive to him as his island dreams? I felt frightened myself, suddenly—he seemed a mire that might any minute pull me in, and I tried to remind myself that he was only a man, a lost, confused man who had no one to care for him but me.

I set my finger to the edge of the inflammation, and the pain pleased him. "It's doesn't sting," he said, "more like a burn . . ."

"It just needs to be disinfected," I said. "There's only a little swelling here, nothing to worry about." Truly, I thought it might want lancing, but I knew if I suggested that he'd ask me to do it, and dabbing it with a bit of cotton soaked in witch hazel was almost more than I could bear.

"That's good," he said with a little shudder. "That's so good."

"There," I said. Blood poison was unlikely, and no one would count me responsible if his blood was poisoned, or neglectful if he died. I probably wouldn't feel more than the occasional prick of guilt myself—nothing compared to the way I felt for hating him so. "I think it's going to heal up fine."

"It's wonderful to have family, isn't it sweetie?" he said, standing up, relieved, it seemed, of every fear and sorrow by my little ministration. "So few people understand that, that it's family, not glamour, or money, or fame, that's the important thing."

He turned, glowing with good feeling, to hug me.

I knew it would be insane to scream. I leaned stiffly toward him, patting his back above the sore, concentrating on my breath so as not to panic, doubly gentle because I felt as if my fingers might sprout claws.

"Is there a sheet or something I could tack up over the window?" I asked when he released me.

He looked puzzled. "Nobody can see in here, sweetie," he said. "We're on the sixth floor."

He was right, of course. Still I felt exposed.

"If you're nervous," he said, "you can come in and sleep with me."

His voice was studiedly casual, but his eyes had the angry gleam of a man who has bet everything on a single number and is watching the wheel spin. It was a proposition, and I felt the room swinging around me like a nauseating carnival ride, in the center of which I— my heart, breath, mind, and most of all my eyes, must keep fixed absolutely still.

"I'm okay," I said. Very lightly, hoping I could somehow back away from him without moving. It was the first such suggestion I had ever declined. Professors were so magnificently arrogant, they'd leave the marks of their grip on my arm, asking me to bed as if they were challenging me to a duel—it would have been cowardice to refuse. And the others, the timid boys who tried a little ruse, like my father— I could never bear to turn them down. Men—you can feel their sadness—but how to assuage it? You have to do it through sex, they can't take nourishment any other way. And I was always so grateful to be wanted, to feel them drinking their strength from my beauty, drinking and drinking until they seemed powerful as gods.

Pop shrugged. "We used to do it, when you were two years old," he said.

"So, Columbus tomorrow!" he said when I didn't answer. "Teaching, you say?"

I nodded.

"What would you teach?" he asked, sounding baffled.

"Comparative literature."

"You don't need some kind of certificate for that?"

"No," I said, knowing he didn't count the Ph.D.

"Amazing. Hey, you don't think there might be a something out there for me, do you? I've got a real soft spot for the Midwest. Good people, salt of the earth. Nothing keeping me here—you might say I'm footloose and fancy free. We could get a nicer place if there were two of us. I've *been* making money. . . ."

To invite him would be suicide. To say no was more of a homicide. I settled for silence: cowardice seemed a bloodless crime.

"Well, just something to think about . . ." he said. "It's just great to have you here, sweetie."

He spoke so sincerely that I was afraid he was going to hug me again, but no, he went into his bedroom and closed the door, and a few minutes later I saw the light blink out beneath.

I curled against the far arm of the couch, pulling my knees to my chest, keeping the blanket tight around me, the way I used to sleep as a child. I had a recurring dream then that some awful force had come to suck me out the window, and I'd hold my breath, playing dead until it went away. I was always looking for a charm, something to wrap myself in for safety, the image of Zeus or Louis or whoever— everyone needs something like that, something to grab hold of in the dark. Now I tried to think of Cincinnati—a sleepy river town, sun on the factories, the pleasure of getting to know a new city, any city— but all I could feel was that I didn't dare leave Louis, I needed him to keep my father at bay. After a long time I fell not asleep but into a kind of purgatorial consciousness, full of specters but still at one remove from that room.

"There's no one else," a voice said, so clear it seemed to rouse me, "*you'll* have to marry him."

Then I heard my father's bedsprings and his feet as they touched the floor. Soon he would pad past me on his way to the bathroom. I held myself tighter, trying to take the deep, slow breaths of a sleeper. He might be only inches away from me, but he wouldn't guess I'd awakened, and I'd never let him know.

An Early Death

The morning of his ninth birthday Stevie awoke with a sense of great promise and looked out the window toward Brooklyn as if he'd see the ship of his future coming in through the Narrows, guided by one of his father's tugs. It was May, he could smell the sea, not the oil and salt of the harbor but a brilliant astringency that belonged to the open water beyond, and he heard a ship sounding: one sharp blast, another long lowing, a moan. "I yearn, I *must* go!" Then the doorbell—already! And it wasn't even nine. Lottie got it, of course, and came into the parlor bewildered, carrying a bamboo cage with two very large spotted kittens in it. Ocelots, from Señor Villanueva, whose bananas and sugarcane Stevie's father imported: *they grow to about three feet in length, eat raw meat, make faithful pets.*

"Sweetie—no—," his mother said, smiling uncomfortably. He was an impossible child; his every move disarranged things, she'd have to follow him through life with a soapy cloth. Yesterday, while she went over the week's menus with Lottie, he had disassembled the toaster; now he was poking his fingers into a cage of wild animals. And his father seemed to be living another childhood, all mystery and tenderness, with this younger son—having been so stern and exacting with the other. When she'd sent Big Stephen in to speak to Stevie about the toaster, father and son sat down on the floor and put it back together, emerging proud as if it were their own creation. Who knew why they should be so close? The name, or a coincidence of temperament, or the fact that the boy, conceived by accident when his brother was nearly grown, had come when the man had established himself and could turn his heart back to his family . . .

"Oh, Señor Villanueva!" Big Steve said, shaking his head and laughing. "Señor Villanueva, time and again I tell you gifts will not be necessary, and time and again . . ."

"Sweetie, you'll really have to speak to him more firmly," Mama said, "We can't—"

"Well, we *can't* send them back," Stevie broke in. He was so thin, still in his drop-seat sleeping suit, you could imagine the wind wafting him up like a seed. The cats tussled in the cage, one knocking the other down with a wide, clumsy paw, then commencing to wash it, while the other, the one who'd given in, had a luxurious stretch. "Isn't that true, Papa? It's an insult, in the South American cultures, to return a gift."

"We were going to open presents *after* breakfast," Papa said. "But as we *will* have to call the zoo about these fine fellows, perhaps . . ."

And he led Stevie out through the garden and threw open the toolshed door. It had been transformed into a laboratory, whitewashed, with a new sink and a Bunsen burner, a rack of test tubes, clamp stands and beakers, a microscope and a shelf of chemistry books. It was 1945, the war was won, all things seemed possible. The basic elements were for sale at the pharmacy. Papa filled a flask with silver nitrate, and gave Stevie a length of copper wire.

"Go ahead," he said. "Drop it in; it won't explode." Stevie did, jumping back in spite of the reassurance, and saw silver quills whoosh down the length of the wire.

"Papa!" So, there *was* such a thing as magic! It went by the name of science, that was all.

"There's one rule," his father said. "You must never come in here unless I'm with you. Do you understand?" Big Steve's rules were more like promises: Stevie would do as he was told, and his father would stay beside him. Stevie nodded, meeting and holding his father's gaze, seeing in it the proud authority that would one day be his.

His other gift was a guide to the North American butterflies, Papa having planted butterfly bushes along the garden walk. "We had them in the backyard, when I was little," Big Steve said. "The most beautiful thing I've ever seen." His voice caught in his throat, and Stevie thought that if butterfly bushes could so move his father they must be the most beautiful things in the world.

"You don't often find them in the U.S." Big Stephen said. His spade sliced sharply into the soil, and he rubbed his shoulder: "This bursitis, it's the cold fog. Hot damp is good for the joints."

In fact it was cancer, of the stomach—the pain thrown from its source so for months they thought bursitis, then arthritis, then—an ulcer, maybe? By the time they knew what it was, there was nothing to be done. On Stevie's next birthday Papa lay wasting in his bed. From which he'd have seen the butterfly bushes, if only they had bloomed. Papa squeezed Stevie's hand: sometimes, he said, things come in late the first year. It might only be a few weeks before the bushes flowered—they might be cloaked in monarchs by July. Even now he was an optimist—it was Ellis Island confidence, the sense that, having come anonymous and empty-handed, learned a new language at night by reading two editions of *War and Peace* side-by-side, begun as a messenger and built a fleet of messengers, then trucks, ships, and now planes, the sense that, having done all this, you might be able to do anything. This confidence gave onto courage, and patience. One had been surprised many, many times. Plants may not bloom by the book, illness may go dormant and pass into memory. . . .

"Another few weeks may well make the difference," he said.

But there were no buds, which Stevie couldn't bear to tell him. How fitting, that spring should come without flowers that year, when all plans were given up and all hopes revealed to be foolish, impossible.

The rules fell by the wayside, too. Dinner, once served on the dot of six, was often forgotten entirely on Lottie's days off. Stevie had believed his father had some kind of infrared vision and always knew what his sons were doing, could guess their transgressions by looking into their eyes. Now he skipped school; spent a whole day in the movies. It was a kind of test, and Big Steve failed it—smiling painfully from his sickbed, pretending to listen to his son's fabrications. The pact was broken, and the next day Stevie walked boldly into the laboratory and repeated the copper and silver nitrate experiment unsupervised—there was no explosion, no thunderbolt, the sky remained cloudless overhead.

He was set on a new course: which, of all the laws he'd been taught to live by, had meaning? One by one he began to flout them. At dinner he pushed his smelts and lima beans through the hot air register under his chair. They were either consumed in the furnace or dried in the duct—whichever, they didn't stink and no one was the wiser. He skipped school again, and this time walked home from the movies along the waterfront, where the bums, as his father called them, drank from bottles wrapped in paper bags—they looked dirty and rough but nothing like the menace he'd been warned of, and the only one who spoke to him said kindly, "Hello, son."

That afternoon he took the yellow phosphorus out of the freezer. It ignites at room temperature, Big Steve had said; they'd wait to use it until he could learn more about it himself. Stevie set a small lump out in an ashtray and after an hour of warming, it burst obligingly, quite safely, into flame.

He packed some in ice with a strip of caps from his cap pistol, took it to the Saturday matinee and left it under the back row of seats. The ice had melted by the end of *Rocky and Bullwinkle*—there was a hissing sound, then the caps shot off and smoke filled the mezzanine. "Get out, fire!" a man shouted. People began to file out of their rows, orderly at first, but fear hardened their faces; when a woman with a little girl pushed at the man in front of her saying, "I have a baby," he put up his shoulder to block her. Now a terror shot through Stevie, too, seeing the adults confused and afraid. It was the awful underlayer of life that he'd glimpsed in his father's face as Big Steve folded the newspaper and set it high out of his reach, the chill that crept over the grownups when they spoke of the war. There was something he hadn't known about life; his father had shielded him. Now he was going to be alone with it.

He ran home. He had to confess and be punished, get free. Just to push open the heavy front door with its leaded window, see the afternoon sun spilling into the dining room, was to know that the safety and order of his father's kingdom was still in place. It was Sunday, so a chicken was roasting; the smell rose reassuringly from the kitchen. His father would banish Stevie's terrors back to the world of nightmare, put the laboratory off limits, draw a lesson from his son's misbehavior, set everything right. Stevie ran up the stairs, cupping his palm over the head of the marble elephant on the landing, a habit that had become a superstition so that if he forgot, he'd turn back to correct the oversight lest he accidentally set off some disaster. At the bedroom door he hesitated for a second, but took himself in hand, ready to admit his transgressions and face the consequences, and tapped. The shades were drawn, the room smelled of illness and medicaments, and his father was gone to the hospital, where no children were allowed.

Steve saw his father next at his wake. Big Steve lay emaciated on his bier, his skin fallen in webs, cheeks rouged like a music hall dancer's over the gray cast beneath. It was the first anniversary of Hiroshima. For the rest of Stevie's life he'd recall the day suddenly at moments of happiness or pride, and feel his joy sour as he thought of what lay in store. A weakness his father would have despised: he fought it with all his strength, keeping up an indomitable good cheer, an absolute outward refusal of despair. He *would* be happy, in memory of his father. His brother followed the more conventional path, studying medicine, then oncology.

Next summer the butterfly bushes bloomed in profusion, making up for the lost year. Swallowtails floated over the lavender arches whose beauty seemed a rebuke, as if Big Steve's longing to see the flowers of his childhood again had been a weakness that led to his death. How vital he had been, taking the helm of a tugboat some days so his men could know and trust him! How carefully he'd packed the roots of the butterfly bushes with sopping peat, to nourish them for a long life. The life *he* should have had. But nothing is just. Steve never crossed the laboratory threshold again—he had promised never to go there without his father. He began to avoid the flowery path, too, and his studies, and almost everything.

He'd also promised to "take care" of his mother, though it was hard to know what this could mean. Edith was less grief-stricken than bewildered. Her parents had chosen Stephen as her husband and so, of course, she'd married him. She counted love among childish fancies, with magic potions and royal toads. When, on their wedding night, Stephen had explained to her what was expected of a wife, she'd been appalled. He said it was natural; she said that if it was natural she would surely have heard of it before. But as she didn't have the courage, let alone the language, to speak of it to anyone else, she allowed him into her bed at night and did her best to forget in the morning. She was "a new soul," on her first visit to earth—this fact had been divined by a carnival palm reader, who had then folded Edith's sister Lucy's hand silently back into itself and bowed her head. Lucy's dress caught fire at a dance that winter and she lived only a few days more. So Edith took her own ignorance as fate, and a lucky fate at that. She obeyed her parents, then her husband . . . now . . .

It was frightening to see her, to realize all she didn't know. She deeded the household management over to Lottie and sat down once a week with Big Steve's office manager to sign the checks. She played bridge. When she didn't have a task she became agitated, but as long as she was counting stitches or pennies her fears let her alone. It became Stevie's duty to protect her from the world's confusions. He ate his dinner, smelts and all, never took things apart anymore, kept his room neat and his grades reasonable, and checked every night to be sure all the windows were locked, the way his father had used to banish the monsters from his closet when he was six years old.

The explosive elements, cobwebbed now in the garden shed, must be got rid of, and one day he gathered them up and took them down to the harbor, meaning to pour them in. Kneeling on the bank where the waves lapped under a crust of foam, he felt suddenly as if he were trying to rid himself of a terrible secret, and with it must give up his father's memory, too. He turned back up Victory Boulevard hugging the stoppered tubes to his chest, as if they contained a precious essence, and thought of people turned back from suicide to life, with all its dangers and disappointments. That night he dreamed Big Steve was showing him how to steer a boat: he heard his father's voice, felt his presence as if he were standing right beside him again. Awakened, he cried in gulps like a child, which so shamed him—he was in his last year of high school, played varsity basketball, almost a man himself—that he forgot all of it, even his father's qualities that he'd been so grateful to see again in the dream.

When he went away to school (a two-year business course, inexpensive and, as his mother said, "appropriate"—she'd been afraid his fiddling, as she called it, would lead him into the trades, nor did she care to throw good money and time away on a university education), he took the mercury and the phosphorus with him, reasoning that this was the best way to protect his mother. He was a poor student—he'd always learned through his hands, or by studying how one part fit another, and he shrank from abstractions like price/earnings ratios. And his father had ridden so magnificently astride the world of business that the son hardly dared imagine such a mount for himself. Sealed in plastic, immersed in the dormitory toilet tank, the phosphorus lived as a secret energy source in Stevie's mind. He always checked it before an exam and the little surge of confidence he felt, just knowing it was there, would sometimes dispel the inner fog so he'd discover as he ticked down the rows of questions that he knew more answers than he'd dreamed.

Smoldering in the darkened doorway of the cafeteria, surrounded by the pert girls from St. Elizabeth's who'd been bussed in for a dance, stood one Theresa Lester. Would Steve light her cigarette? A funny question, as clearly she could ignite anything with a glance. He struck the match and felt something in himself catch, too; from that instant his life was refocused, on her. Could she really long for him as she seemed to, or was he the butt of some terrible joke? If he gave in and admitted his feelings, would she taunt him, who was so gullible he'd imagined she could love such a timid boy? He could never really own the man's broad-shouldered body he saw in the mirror—it bore no relation to the quavering heart inside.

But Theresa was desperate—thank God! She had no choice but to love him. Her father had walked out, and poverty, or loneliness, had driven her mother into an alcoholic daze. It was easy for Steve to forgive Theresa's tempests, when he knew their origins—she screamed, she threw whatever came to hand, because she guessed he was about to be cruel to her. Cruelty was all she knew—of course it was what she expected. When he forgave her she threw herself against him and sighed as if she could sigh a life's unhappiness out now she was safe in his arms, and made love to him ravenously, without a qualm. This while his friends were exultant over getting a finger under a date's brassiere strap—but Theresa wasn't like the others; she belonged to nature, to the genuine heart of the world. Her narrow cat's eyes—even golden like a cat's—looked out of the wilderness at him, begging him to take her in.

Sex itself upset him: the pitch of his own feeling, the way she lay back and flowered around him while he rose over her as if she were prey. He wanted to apologize for his rude intrusion into her body, make amends to her somehow. So, he would marry her, take care of her. His father had left enough money so that really Steve had no need to work, though his mother would have gasped at this idea. But this life reduced to figures—inventories held, sales expected—with no meaning, no purpose but money, numbed him, and he was determined to escape. *She*, Theresa, held the meaning. When he was deep inside her it seemed he had almost touched it.

She was such a creature as his mother could not imagine. "Sweetie, no . . . ," Edith said, smiling in puzzlement: surely he couldn't be serious? A poor Catholic girl from a broken family, a girl who glowed less with beauty than ambition? Anyone who saw them together would know her son a fool. "We don't want to disappoint Evelyn," she said quietly. Evelyn's father was also in shipping, and for the last few years his mother had lost no opportunity of mentioning Evelyn's travels in Europe, her excellence as a golfer, her efforts with the Junior League. . . . Steve looked at his mother more with pity than defiance; the poor woman had been sheltered until she was nearly blind.

"I don't think it will come as a big disappointment to Evelyn, Mom," he said.

Though the tilt of Theresa's chin, as she walked down the aisle toward him, gave him a momentary chill. She looked more proud than happy, as if she'd made a brilliant acquisition and was planning her next move. Her mother, a dithery creature in a feathery hat, did not look capable of unkindness, and having downed several vodka martinis at the reception recited "The Owl and the Pussycat" so tenderly Steve's eyes filled with tears.

They were moving upstate, into the country. He'd found a house that fit them; it had begun as someone's folly, a pile of fieldstones mortared together, used as a hunting lodge with only the fireplaces for heat. It lay in a hollow—a brook wove along beside it and a long meadow spread out in front with a big old sugar maple blazing in the middle. It was a place such as a child might draw in crayon, the yellow rays of the sun touching the blue water and green grass—happiness on a page. And soon there were children, four in quick succession: Katherine; Stephen III and Michael, the twins; and finally Stella, who was somehow most clearly his own. He stood on the porch watching them catch fireflies in a June dusk, trying to take pleasure though he felt only foreboding: if he died, like his father, at fifty, he had only twenty years to go.

Not to mention the nuclear clock on the cover of *Harper's*: four minutes to Armageddon now. Seize the day, there may not come another. Steve had his real estate license, worked—when he could make himself—out of an office in Tiverton Center beside the feed store. He loved the old farmhouses, the torn curtains at broken windows, overgrown orchards, root cellars opening out of grassy hills, rusty harrows abandoned in the fields. Whole lives billowed inside those houses, like the willow growing through the floor and out the windows at the old Atwater place. Once he found a shelf of spiced peaches in mason jars, glowing in the basement of a ruined cottage, fresh and delicious though their maker had long ago died.

The few souls who might bother to look at such places quickly lost heart, and sales were rare, but he accepted this with peculiar good cheer, as a chance to affirm again that money was a small thing to him. Was success more important, after all, than family? He'd leave the office early, go home and build the kids a dollhouse or a child-size dory with a red sail. Once he saw a ragtag circus in a parking lot and convinced the manager to sell him a pony foal that was tied up at ringside while its mother gave rides. He got it halfway into the back of the Buick by piling sugar cubes on the seat, then held its back legs to keep it from kicking him and pushed it the rest of the way. It nipped at his shoulder all the way home, but that was nothing next to the looks on the kids' faces.

Scarecrow as they named him, for his manginess, fit Steve's two major purposes: he astonished the children and infuriated Theresa at once. She was disappointed, bitterly, in marriage, in life, in him. Whatever it was she had wanted he had not been able to provide it, and now she turned her anger on him. The more she tore at him, though, the stonier he became. "A *pony*," she said, disgusted. "*I'll* have to take care of it, of course." Little Stella rested her head against the pony's shoulder, with a shy, cozy smile. "It's not enough the sheep and the chickens and the dogs, we have to have a *pony*! The kids don't give a damn about ponies—they want a *father*, that's what!"

But what father had ever loved his children more? It was intoxicating to see his own reflection in their eyes: the conjurer of Tootsie Pops and ponies, the master of this world. And the phosphorus waited in the basement freezer for the moment when Steve could pass along his knowledge of the earthly miracles. Though the children were growing impatient with his tricks and games. He found himself posturing, trying to act the part of father, talking with put-on sophistication about things he didn't understand. Stella and the boys played along, listening with earnest interest, trying to respond as he would want, but there was always a shadow of suspicion on Katherine's wary face, as if she were keeping watch on the false thread that ran between them and would pull it out one day. Stella had nightmares—a monster came, Daddy couldn't save her. The kind of dream Steve used to have after his father died.

Work cluttered his life. His days off turned to weeks off, until he had stopped going in to the office altogether—his secretary could handle most of it anyway. The old farmsteads were in demand, suddenly, as second homes, though he detested the type of man who was buying in—cocksure, more likely to demolish than rebuild. They reminded him of his brother, his big successful brother, and sensing their condescension, he found himself defensively explaining that he didn't care for money and prestige, it was his kids that mattered, after all. One morning his secretary called to say someone had come in wanting to look at places "in the million-dollar range." "A million dollars, and he was *so nice*, so thoughtful!" she sighed. As if no one had ever been nice to her before. Like all women, she looked at a man and imagined his bank account naked. "You take him," he said, and drove north into the mountains, caught six sleek trout for dinner. Ralph Lauren bought the Atwater place, willow and all, and the boom began in earnest, but Steve had lost interest in real estate. They lived by borrowing against his inheritance, Theresa in a black boil of fury that turned to pure seduction when she was near a stronger man.

"Sweetie, I don't know. . . ." His mother was always dubious about the loans, though it was she, he thought, who was wasteful, a wealthy woman throwing away her life on measures of thrift, molding the last bits of soap together into one bar, going from bank to bank every week to deposit a few hundred dollars and get a "free gift" until her attic was piled with boxed clock radios and toasters. She understood money no better than physics or philosophy, and she had long forgotten that her husband had amassed that fortune *for his children*. Well, Steve would have every mote, every cent that was left of his father. And, of course, his mother gave in and lent him another fifty thousand, chiding him, a few minutes later, for throwing away a perfectly good paper bag.

This time it was winter, there was a blizzard swirling upstate, no trains and even the Thruway was closed. He'd have to stay with his mother another day, and was surprised to realize how glad this made him, as if he was getting to stay home from school. He called Theresa, who said they were all fine—there was no power, but they were playing pioneers, had a fire in the woodstove, and the twins had braved it up to the barn to feed the animals. . . . It was romantic, really, with the winds battering the house and the five of them inside. Then she sent the kids out of the room and her voice turned to ice. "Alone here, with four little children in the snow, but then what do you care about us? You're home with your *mommy*."

"Treesa . . ." he said, but he recognized the blind, lost rage he'd heard in her voice when he first knew her, the feeling he'd been certain he could cure. She had turned toward him with eyes wide with grateful amazement, had taken him so deeply into herself he'd felt immersed, tangled undersea, until he gave in and breathed water, was drowned and transformed. Now he'd become the thing despised. She slept at the edge of the bed. If he brushed against her in his sleep, she curled into herself all the tighter.

"Treess it's the snow, it's not that I don't want to . . ." This was the deepest truth. Even when he was there at home he wanted to be with them. He watched his children like a man looking in through a lighted window—he'd have reached in to touch them but he didn't know how.

Theresa was silent, and he looked out to the wide double strand of lights over the Narrows—the Verrazano Bridge. If Big Steve could have seen that bridge! A steel garland, spanning an incredible distance in one exuberant sweep—just what he'd expected of the future, and here it was, right here now.

Steve slept, that night, in his childhood bed, as he hadn't slept since he left home. In the middle of the night it was no different—*he* was no different—from twenty-five years ago when the future was still before him. It seemed he could still smell his father's cigars.

At four A.M., though, he sat bolt upright, out of a nightmare. The test tube of phosphorus was still in the basement freezer, and the power was out, it would thaw. Five children had died Christmas night, trying to hide under a bed from a fire. He'd seen it in the paper and couldn't stop thinking of them, so soft and trusting, certain of safety under their parents' wing. He tiptoed into the living room, not to wake his mother, and dialed Theresa—he'd tell her just to throw the phosphorus out into the snow—but before it could ring he hung up. She was looking for a good reason to despise him; it would not be wise to tell her he'd hidden a bomb in her larder. He took a deep breath—without electricity there would be no heat: the phosphorus might thaw, but it was hardly likely to reach room temperature. He would let it lie, and as soon as he got home would dispose of it once and for all.

But carrying the stoppered test tube out to the brook, he thought better. You couldn't buy yellow phosphorus anymore. He ought to save it for the boys. And if Theresa left him—no, he might need it; he couldn't bear to throw it away. So he took it across the log bridge into the woods and suspended it in between two stones in one of the old stone walls there. He never walked this way without thinking of the men who'd cleared this land, wrenched enough stones out of the soil to build these miles of walls, tilled it and worked it and nevertheless nature had overtaken it all. The fields were grown into forests now—oaks and maples and cherries whose new leaves and blossoms, deep red, translucent green, were stippled together in a pale haze in spring. Standing here now, he looked down over the house and saw the roof sagging on the western side where the weather hit it. . . . Rain leaked into the wall there, and the paper was peeling off: the bedroom smelled of mildew. The place was a morass of half-accomplished projects, things he couldn't lift his heart to finish. . . . The bills were so overwhelming he'd stopped opening the mail. What did such things matter, anyway, in a transitory world? He still felt like a naughty child when he took out his toolbox, and when he saw men working in the open air his heart sank as if they were gods on a mountaintop and he only mortal. His father—but his mind flinched back from the thought of his father, and a plan sprang up instead: he'd dig a moat around the playground . . . the kids could swing across on a knotted rope . . .

Yes, he'd failed, failed and what of it? How many lives are misspent succeeding . . . amassing a useless pot of gold? *He* had lived for his children . . . in the anguish of his impotent love for them, watching them tuck their bears into bed at night, fluffy as chicks themselves in their sleepsuits, their downy heads on the pillow, their little starfish hands holding tight to his. His throat closed, he couldn't think of such fragile creatures subject to life, fear, pain.

Katherine was thirteen; picking her up from school he switched to public radio: "Listen, a polonaise!" he said. "A polonaise is like . . . like dessert!" Her glance flicked away; she knew his favorite songs were "Bewitched, Bothered, and Bewildered," "Don't Fence Me In," tunes his father used to hum. Katherine had arrived at adolescence ungainly, cringing one minute and grandiose the next, embarrassed and, supremely, embarrassing, rushing from the room crying in gulps and snorts after the smallest criticism, her face covered with pimples, clothing so tight it seemed a plea for sex. She was taking after her mother, he thought, too sharp and aggressive, all claws and no womanly softness. He could hardly look at her, he was so disappointed—and she ignored him in kind. She sat down to her algebra problems and he saw over her shoulder that she had written *Isaiah* over and over in the margin. The name of a wretched boy who lived in a trailer in the valley, with whom she imagined herself in love.

"Why is it so foggy, out back?" she asked, looking up. "I mean, why out back and not in the front at all?"

Theresa sat across from her—she was taking a correspondence course, aiming toward a law degree. Steve had only discovered this when the first lesson came in the mail. Theresa took it from him with a look of defiance. She was figuring a way to escape him. This would be no mean feat, as she'd become a wraith, haunting her own house, her hair in tangles, her bathrobe cinched at her waist so tightly you could see she'd done it as she did everything—in a rage. And why? He had never been unfaithful, she had this house, these children, everything she'd wanted so long ago. What could be wrong, here in the sunlight, on a brilliant autumn day? A ripple of shame ran through him—it was his lack that left her longing. She would leave him: he thought of his father—he could not bear such a loss a second time.

"I think of fog as a spring thing," Katherine went on, in her overserious, teacher's pet voice, meaning, "I don't have to admire you, I see further than you do already; I'll find my own way." She took an encyclopedia volume into bed with her at night—she intended to figure everything out, to surpass him. Theresa looked toward the window, but blindly. Steve refused, as always, to look where Katherine was pointing.

"It—it can't be smoke, can it?" she asked then, in a voice so uncertain—unlike her—that it cut, finally, through the spell they lived under, and everyone looked suddenly and saw an orange flame licking out of the woods.

"Fire," Theresa said—with shocked certainty as if she had always expected such a thing.

It was a drought year: the dry trees flamed over like torches one by one, passing the fire up the hill.

"Fire," Katherine whispered, with a quiet thrill.

"It's not a show," Steve said curtly, dialing 911.

"We ought to get out of here," Katherine said a minute later, though she was still entranced by the flames and didn't move. She was right, Steve saw. If the wind shifted it would come right at them . . . and he took the boys by their hands while Theresa grabbed Stella up in her arms.

"We're together, that's all that matters," he said as they drove away down the hill. He felt a strange lightness, a spring of hope . . . the past would burn away now, it would finally, really, be over, and hardship would bind them together so they could take strength from each other again.

"We're safe," Theresa corrected him. Later she would say they'd never been together, that he'd kept in his own bubble and imagined a happy family life because he couldn't have made one for real. He pulled over and the fire trucks roared by, shifting gears for the hillcrest with a low growl that made Stella shriek as if they would eat her. The others knelt in the backseat, looking out the window. It smelled so good, of autumn and burning leaves.

Next day the smoke still curled up from the charred tree trunks and the stone fences stood out again on the hillside. The stone walls of the house looked more massive with the roof burned away. The devastation seemed fitting—it suited Steve's sense that everything ends in dust, and he felt strangely lighthearted, because what really mattered, if so? "It'll be good blueberrying," he said, and saw his wife smile, tenderly, one last time. A relief to her, too—nothing to pack, nothing to fight over. The insurance renewal had been on his desk, among the other things he couldn't bear to attend to. He heard a catch of sympathy in the Aetna woman's voice, when she said, "That policy has lapsed . . ." as if it hurt her, too.

He awoke on his fiftieth birthday in his childhood bed, with the fresh scent of the sea blowing in. Fifty—he had feared—and expected— an early death, had never imagined himself living so long. Where his father's footsteps had ended, so, he was sure, must his. It was ten years since he'd seen Theresa. He'd returned to his mother's—he'd promised to care for her; though at seventy-five she was stubborn and vigorous, and the best he could do for her was to pretend she was taking care of him.

"Good morning, sweetie!" she said. She'd been to the bakery already, there were warm brioche and soft butter, and FedEx rang the doorbell and left two packages—a book on the life of the Amazon rain forest from conscientious Stella—he would add it to the high pile by his bed—and a nautical chart of the Narrows, from Stephen the third. This was how it had turned out; they knew him by his minor obsessions, the places his father still lived in his mind. He needed to keep his hand set on these things or he'd have floated away into space. To awake from the anesthetic of memory was intolerable; in the evenings, when the day had worn through it, he drank until it seemed to return.

"How nice, Mom. Thank you," he said, sitting down with the *Times.*

"This came yesterday," she said, indicating a small package in brown paper, with Katherine's return address.

"I remembered you liked chemistry," the card read. A book called *The Periodic Table.* Yes, it was all memory. Katherine would call later, and put the grandkids on the phone; she never said anything of substance and somehow he was afraid to ask a question for fear of putting a foot wrong and losing what little he had of her. He set the book aside with a small laugh, or sigh—it was years since the periodic table had meant anything to him.

It was only then that he remembered the phosphorus, the test tube he'd hidden in the woods. The winter, the freezing and melting, would have cracked it, the dry leaves sifted over, and one warm day . . .

They'd never known what caused the fire. A hunter, careless with a cigarette? A broken bottle magnifying the sunlight on the leaves? No, he'd set it himself. *He* was the danger. Unwitting, of course, always unwitting. To see, to know, was more than he could bear.

"Schuler's has fallen off," his mother said. "Carl doesn't do the baking anymore."

Stephen looked out over the tangle that had once been the garden, where the butterfly bushes struggled now for lack of sun. The laboratory roof had collapsed under a snarl of bittersweet and Virginia creeper. The world he'd been born into—where explosive chemicals were sold from glass pharmaceutical jars, exotic animals sent between continents in crates—that world with all its possibilities was gone. The mercury was here, in his mother's basement, with the few other possessions left after the fire. Stephen kept meaning to take it in on hazardous waste disposal days, but month after month some inconvenience prevented him.

"You can tell by the texture, they use a machine," his mother said. Her voice went on, and on, and on. If only his father could have had her longevity! It seemed to Stephen there was only one precious thing left on earth: that teaspoon of quicksilver. He had seen himself in the bathroom mirror that morning—the big, lost eyes of a child in a weary face, and likely to live another thirty years.

Out of Purmort

"Now, His Honor is a very *short* man," the bailiff said, holding his hand out hip-high, which, even given that the bailiff was a very *tall* man (and he stood with his feet apart, thumbs at the belt, looking out over us jurors with . . . well, discomfort, as if he wanted to apologize for the lack of judicial stature) would have meant the judge was at best a dwarf. I glanced around, but no one else seemed to find this declaration unusual—the rest of the jury pool was listening earnestly and several people appeared to be taking notes. Not wanting to be conspicuous, I opened my notebook and wrote *short* at the top of the first page. I'd never been on a jury, but I'm an excellent schoolgirl.

"And he speaks very softly. . . . ," the bailiff continued, with me hurriedly copying. "He doesn't speak from his diaphragm, but from his throat, so it can be hard to hear him. If you have trouble, please don't hesitate to raise your hand. Are there any questions?"

"Any impotence?" I imagined asking, but supposed the matter had been addressed. I wondered if we could hear his quirks—which offenses he found particularly loathsome, which he might condone. I'd have been soft on kids, I knew—my high school boyfriend asked his father for money one morning and, being told to "rob a bank," obediently went across the street to brandish a pistol in Purmort Savings and Loan. He got three years and when he was released he came straight to my college dorm room and found me in bed with *Madame Bovary*. We looked at each other across a horrible chasm, me trying frantically to locate the well of tenderness I'd used to feel for him, he squinting in an effort to see the girl he'd known (jeans dragging, head hung) through the new veneer. By the time I collected myself and offered him a glass of the sherry I'd taken to keeping on my dressertop, he was backing out the door, and the next time I saw him he was pumping gas at Purmort Texaco. I started using the Shell station when I was home. I couldn't bear to think of the little flicks of fate that had sent my life up while his went down, and I had a foreboding that if his hand so much as brushed mine, I'd lose my footing and slip back into Purmort forever.

"Please rise," said the bailiff (from his diaphragm), and we did, eyes trained on the door to the judge's chambers, at about the height of its knob.

He emerged to disappoint us—slight, yes, and fair, engulfed in his robes, but not the white mouse I'd begun to look forward to, though he did show a mouselike curiosity, eyes lighting quickly on each of us, thoughts ticking until he nodded in minor satisfaction and began:

"Jury, you have been called here to do one of the most deeply serious things that will ever be asked of you." His voice did lack resonance, but this suited the modern courtroom with its metal desks and polyester satin flag. I'd gone to the state courthouse first by mistake, and climbing the steps between the great columns there had the sense that American justice would protect me absolutely, for all my days. As I was ducking in under one of the velvet ropes though, a constable came out and directed me to the county court across the way: a box covered in steel links, like those vests made of beer-can pop-tops in the seventies.

Here I passed through the metal detector and joined the ranks, who—attorneys and defendants both—looked as if life had pressed down on them until they were slightly misshapen. Their mouths were crumpled, their eyes half closed, and every one of them was smoking with rapt concentration. The whole town of Purmort smoked like that when I was a kid; most of them still do. My mother is a virtual chimney, and after she visits us, my husband pointedly washes the curtains and beats the rugs. "We came to Cape Cod for the air!" he says, but really I think he's afraid our lives will be tainted by some nebulous, ineradicable Purmort stain. He's thoughtful and deliberate and he can't imagine the tempest that rages constantly in some people, abating only for that one sacred moment when the lungs are wholly, deeply, filled with nicotine.

I've given up smoking, needless to say, and I sat, like the other jurors, poker-faced and looking neither right nor left, as if fearing squalor by association.

"You—people of all cultures and experiences, each of whom will see the defendant through different eyes—are the backbone of the American system of justice," the judge said, "and flawed though this system may be, it's still the greatest in the world." His tone was tender, dignified, and very slightly patronizing, and I felt tears pricking, a great swelling in my breast, as if by sitting on this jury I was at long last being given the chance to come to the aid of my country as I'd wanted to do since third grade. The notion that we random souls might be able to balance the scales of justice together seemed so cheerfully quixotic that I was proud to be a member of the society that had dreamed it up.

"We have ten cases on the docket, and by noon most of them will be resolved, because *you* are in this building. Defendants are searching their souls . . . wondering if they really believe a jury of *people like themselves* will agree that they are not guilty. . . ."

Might there be people like oneself? In my experience, no. Sent to wait in the jury room, the thirty of us sat wedged together with nothing in common but the deep inhibition that prevented us from speaking or even shifting in our seats. The others looked numbingly ordinary: secretaries locked into tiny, windowless lives whose furniture they daily rearranged; businessmen plodding through like dray horses; a guy in canvas coveralls and a woman whose sweater had two fuzzy cats knitted in. I forget that everyone lives as the hero of his own drama, and I'm vain of my life, the way hardship has formed me; in the bottom of my mind I'm always thinking how the scramble out of Purmort made me tougher and smarter than everyone else. My mother's a bartender—she named me Brandy, I think in hopes I'd appeal to a wealthy man. She didn't realize she was marking me as a raggie from the valley, who was supposed to get drunk, knocked up, onto AFDC, and no more. Instead I became a dogged student, or really a wolfish student—I'd have torn out the throats of my competitors before I let them get the better of me, and no surprise, I was high school valedictorian, got a regents scholarship, got away.

Only to find, at Vassar, that my "sleazy life," as my roommate dreamily called it, had slicked me over with the exact glamour the others aspired to. They were shedding their bourgeois manners as quickly as they could, and I can always make something of other people's castoffs. Pretty soon I had the aspect of a Vassar girl while they looked at risk for head lice, and now people think I'm "well brought up"—it's a riot. Not that I've succeeded by Seven Sister standards: I'm director of the Department of Tourism in Spinnaker, Massachusetts, in charge of making a dead fishing village seem like a wonderful, exciting place. My envious roommate is Moscow correspondent for the *Atlanta Constitution*. But for a person named

Brandy, *Director* is a heady title, and my husband is the high school principal. I drive a Volvo. We live on Main Street. Our daughter is named Victoria.

Squeezed between an old man whose suit smelled of mothballs and the guy in coveralls, I pushed my elbows out and laid my work on the table. It was my report on the Pilgrim Festival, at which the mayor, having coined the town's new motto ("They Landed Here First!"—the *Mayflower* ran aground briefly at Spinnaker on its way to Plymouth) and coordinated the celebrations including the fireworks and the parade of direct descendants, suffered a last-minute change of heart after listening to some Native American protesters and changed his speech to compare the Pilgrims' landing with the Nazi march on Poland. I was supposed to put a positive spin on this, and an air of suspense built in the room as I racked my mind, to be released with a sigh every time my pencil hit the page. I was working while they sat avoiding one another's eyes, and out of such things an authority can grow. When we were called back to the courtroom, I automatically led them, and they sat when I sat, waited for me to rise before they stood to greet the little judge with his flying robes.

There was one case left, a DWI, for which a jury of six persons was needed; everyone else would be allowed to leave.

"Now if there is *any reason*," the judge said, "that you feel you may not be an impartial juror—if you or anyone you care for has been involved in a motor vehicle accident which may have involved alcohol, and certainly if you are a member of Mothers against Drunk Driving, or Students against Drunk Driving—any of these organizations—please see me and you will be excused."

Nearly everyone in the room stood up: the woman whose face was puffy as if she'd cried all night, the environmentally conscious man in corduroy and a beard, the lady with the kitty cat sweater, and the beauty whose hair fell so softly at her shoulders that she'd become an object of contemplation—so her departure caused a kind of awakening as we all looked around for something else to rest our eyes on. Finally six of us were left: the drunks, I supposed, myself the only woman.

"Juror number thirty-two, you will act as foreman. This does not mean you are more important than the other jurors, but that you have additional responsibilities. . . ."

I wasn't fooled—they thought he was better than me, or they'd have put me in charge. No one will trust real responsibility to a person named for an alcoholic beverage. I'd have been a great foreman—by the time I was sixteen my eye was so steady that when my stepbrother threatened to stab me, I just held his gaze unwavering until he dropped the knife. Juror thirty-two looked so utterly flaccid I could hardly imagine anyone pulling a knife on him in the first place. He also looked extremely uncomfortable, and as he went up to take his tally sheet from the judge he kept one hand on his windbreaker pocket like he had something hidden there.

"Jury," the judge said in his patient, paternal way. "Today you and you alone will decide the guilt or innocence of one of your fellow men . . ."

And here she came, our fellow man: one Dawn LaRue, blowsy, fortyish, wearing jeans and a jacket that wouldn't quite close across her bosom, her hair pinned up hastily as if dishevelment was her natural state and she'd worried that a quick comb might make her seem false and suspicious. She looked worn out, not so much by life as by love: you could guess that her heart went out everywhere, she'd take in stray animals and men, that she was always a little hurt and full of wistful hopes and ready to have a good time while she waited for those hopes to come true. That is, she was the kind of person I'd have become, in a very slightly different world, and therefore almost certainly guilty of whatever she'd been accused of—and much, much more. I imagined bumping into her in the ladies' room and telling her she looked beautiful, so she wouldn't feel so bad when she got convicted.

The prosecutor, a skinny woman with lips pressed tight together in case something might try to crawl in between them, laid out the case with righteous disdain: Ms. LaRue had been discovered in the driver's seat of her boyfriend's car, parked half in the road at 1:30 A.M., with traffic (and *what* traffic—the bars close at one) snarled behind it, while she performed an operation described by her own lawyer as removing lint from between her toes. When the cop asked her to recite the alphabet, she gave up a hash of letters and then retrieved her sandals from the pile of empty Budweiser bottles in the hatchback—

—and walked what she insisted was a straight line, though the cop fiercely disagreed, which led to a long and unresolved debate about the reliability of those machines that paint lines on the road. Told to touch her right forefinger to her nose, Ms. LaRue instantly complied—with her left, and at this point her boyfriend, who was either obnoxious (cop's testimony) or boisterous (boyfriend's testimony), began either bellowing, or merely singing, an alternative version of *La Marseillaise*. Both Dawn and the boyfriend were taken in to the station to be booked, including mug shots, which—

"Objection, Your Honor. Exhibit A would be prejudicial to the defendant." Dawn's attorney jumped up and approached the bench, followed by the prosecutor, between whose toes no lint could ever have accumulated. She whispered vigorously to the judge, who patted his robe for his reading glasses, withdrew the photograph from a manila envelope, and, with a dry glance at the defendant, said he would sustain the objection.

Wounded, the prosecutor began her cross examination: "So, Ms. LaRue, you spent the afternoon at this barbecue..."

"At my daughter's place."

"And your daughter's place is . . . number 28 Forsythia Lane, in the Pilgrim Spring Trailer Colony?" She cast a significant glance toward the jury, as if the address alone were reason to convict. The police blotter would pretty much have confirmed this, which only inflamed me: I thought of barbecues back in Purmort, the way they, like everything there, had to do with our pride in our own hardihood and ingenuity, our ability to make a good time out of nearly nothing. Bluefish, burgers, tomatoes from the garden, a pitcher of Ma's special Bloody Marys . . . what else did you need? In Purmort you were always thinking about the things you didn't need. What you never thought about was the future—age, illness, hard poverty. It just hung over you, a vague dread to be answered with a shrug. You might win the lottery; you might die tomorrow. . . .

"That's right, Pilgrim Spring," Dawn said, defiant.

"And you admit to having had a—a couple of old-fashioneds there, correct?"

. . . So, have a couple old-fashioneds, turn up the stereo, throw something on the grill . . .

"Yes."

"You were . . . unsettled . . . by something. There'd been an argument . . ."

"Yeah," Dawn said, "Brad—this guy my daughter's with—he came back. He hadn't been around for months, and then he was outside screaming at five o'clock in the morning, waking up the baby . . . and Sherry locked the screen door and he tore it off the hinge and then he came in and lay down in the recliner and cried himself to sleep."

"And . . ."

"Well they couldn't close the door, see, and we made a run to the . . . We had to do some shopping, and a snake got in the trailer . . . into the bird cage, and ate my granddaughter's parakeet."

"What became of the snake?"

"Once it swallowed the bird it couldn't get out of the cage." Dawn said.

"So? . . ."

"So I cut it in half with the garden shears." This with a gesture of Purmortese insouciance—*I took care of it.*

"Actually, you cut it into six or eight pieces, am I correct?"

"Your Honor?" Dawn's lawyer said, and the judge nodded, and the prosecutor desisted.

"Tiffany loved that bird," Dawn said.

"And on the way home, at about—?"

"We left about eight. . . . Brad woke up and we wanted to give them some time alone."

"You passed the Myles Standish Tap, and there you stopped in for . . . a beer, two . . . more?"

"I used to wait tables there," the defendant explained. "All's I had was two beers."

"Two beers over four hours? . . ."

"For old times' sake. And then Brad came in, to say he was sorry, and he bought us another round, and we couldn't just go . . ."

"No, no. And you'd taken codeine for a back injury some time earlier . . ." Waiting tables is hell on the back, and bartending can be worse, if you have to drag the kegs up from the basement like my mother.

"Yes, six hours before, at three P.M."

"Six hours? In *fact* it was nine hours earlier," said the prosecutor, swooping in. One short step, apparently, between losing track of the hours and vehicular homicide, but I wondered how much effect a codeine tablet could have nine hours after it was swallowed. They hadn't mentioned the Breathalyzer—had they forgotten?

"And the keys were in the ignition."

"No ma'am," Dawn's boyfriend boomed out from the side. "The keys were on the dash."

"I was questioning the defendant," the prosecutor said.

"She doesn't remember, but I do," he said.

The judge shook his head and the boyfriend sat back in his chair.

"Your memory on this point is not clear?"

"No," Dawn said meekly. She was guilty, that was the problem. She'd been drunk, she was old enough to know better, she was sitting in the driver's seat because she had been and would be (if she could only find the keys and get them back in the ignition) driving the car—plus the codeine, flagrant misuse of garden shears, a daughter living in the Pilgrim Spring Trailers with a no-account guy like Brad, serving old-fashioneds at a barbecue—and this boyfriend with his belligerent belly and long ponytail . . .

She was guilty, but the prosecutor was mean.

And I myself, as it happens, can't tell left from right, so could easily have made the same mistake with the nose test . . . and be found out and sentenced to return to Purmort where I belong. I felt dizzy and nauseated and wondered if I should have asked to be excused.

The foreman's watch said two-thirty, and the arresting cop got on the stand. He was only a year on the force and looked so natty for his court appearance he seemed like a waxen statue.

"Did the defendant seem to you intoxicated, when you first saw her?" the prosecutor asked.

"I could not make a determination," he said with a note of professional pride. The prosecutor's eyes met mine for an instant, as if she recognized in me a fellow traveler. I always forget how Vassared up I am—how utterly incognito.

"When *did* you make a determination?"

"After the sobriety tests, ma'am."

"I see."

The defense lawyer had only one question: Had the cop discussed the case with his lieutenant as they drove to court that morning? No, he said—no, certainly not. But he squirmed a little, and with reason, because the lieutenant, interviewed earlier, had looked mystified by the same question and answered that of course they'd talked it over, it was part of their job.

"The police have no reason to lie," the prosecutor said, opening her summation. She looked so terribly stingy, hardened from the kind of unhappiness that draws pity without sympathy, as if, having done without comfort and pleasure in her life, she was now dedicated to making sure others suffered the same. "The police are doing a job. Look into your hearts, jurors, ask yourselves—this woman was sitting in the driver's seat, with her feet out the window, while her car blocked the southbound lane of Route 38, the Pilgrims Highway; she failed every test she was given. You have it by her own admission that she'd had a great deal of alcohol as well as codeine that afternoon, that her speech was slurred and her companion here taunted the police with a ribald song. I ask you to find her guilty of driving under the influence, a crime which took thousands of lives across this country in the last year and which often goes unprosecuted and unpunished."

She was right, but she was mean.

"Jury," the judge said quietly, "you must work until you reach a verdict, considering all the testimony *without* adding your own speculation. You may come back with any questions pertaining to the law, but I cannot answer questions about the facts." And the bailiff escorted us to the jury room, with an air of respect and deference— our stature had risen now that the case was in our hands.

. . .

There was plenty of space in the jury room now that we were only six, and we ranged ourselves around the table, keeping as far from each other as we could and continuing silent, as if it would be embarrassing now to admit we knew how to talk. The foreman sat across from me, making notes on a legal pad, his arm curled protectively around it like it was a test and he was afraid I'd cheat. When had any of us ever held a serious discussion with a bunch of strangers? They say it happens all the time on Israeli public transportation, but this was Cape Cod in winter, a land where almost everyone is either comfortably retired (and therefore conservative Republican) or desperately unemployed (and therefore liberal Democrat). It works out fine as long as you only talk about the weather. Now we were supposed to talk about something with consequences—and we hadn't yet summoned the courage to say hello to each other. The old man in mothballs was still there, and the man with the coveralls and a couple of others who looked to be carpenters or electricians. So the jury was a representative sample—three out of every six people on Cape Cod *are* builders, and they work all day every day squeezing "distinctive homes" where you wouldn't think you could fit a chicken coop. They seemed too big for the room, and restive, like they needed to get out and tear off a roof or something to clear their heads.

At first we all looked at the foreman, but as he kept scribbling the gazes turned back to me until I felt responsible to do something.

"How should we go about this?" I asked finally, and he looked up with irritation as if I'd made a breach of etiquette.

"I just have a few questions before I make up my mind," he said.

"What are they?"

"Well, I *don't* think I should say," he said with some severity. "We're not supposed to talk."

"No, that was on the lunch break. Now we can talk. We're supposed to." I meant this kindly—I knew I was wrong to despise him
just because they'd set him above me. I should have been foreman—*I*
won the scholarships, *my* glance has caused a knife-wielding hand to
spring open, and I'm a *Director*, I've taken a sodden little village and
made it pass as an Essential Historical Site. If it weren't for jury duty
I'd have been back in my office pacifying all the groups the mayor
had offended: Wampanoag Nation, the Mayflower Society, and the
B'nai B'rith, to name a few. But no, rather than a woman named
Brandy, they'd put a guy who "didn't think he should say," a feature-
less representative of the great homogenous middle class, in charge.
In charge of what?—I might have asked, but I didn't care. It's sur-
vivor's bossiness, a Purmort thing—it starts when you're eight or nine
and you take over for your parents, realize you're better at life than
they. And ends when you become a ridiculous popinjay of self-
sufficiency, someone like me.

"That's what *deliberations* means—talking," I said primly.

"He *told* us *not* to discuss the case," the foreman snapped and
looked back at his page.

"How are we going to come to a verdict without discussing the case?"

"She's right—I, I think she's right—," said the guy in the coveralls.
How had I just lumped him in with the others? Looking again I got
my eyes full of his, which were dark and sparkling, as if he'd spied
out all my weaknesses and found them endearing.

Hearing his deep voice the foreman looked up finally—gratefully—
and turned, with the rest of them, to me.

"Maybe we should start with your questions," I said. Foreman
looked miserable again and I felt sympathy for a minute—suppose
his opinions made everyone hate him? Would it be stodgy of him to
think her guilty? Weak to acquit her? Better to just lie low.

"Well . . . like, what about the Breathalyzer? Why didn't they give her one?" he asked. "And . . . why did it take so long to have the trial? I mean this happened almost two months ago. . . ."

It was January; the "crime" had taken place in August.

"Five months ago!" I said, relieved to find myself on his side, but he took it as disagreement.

"I don't know, two whole months," he said. "I don't feel comfortable with this, I think I'm going to have to substain."

"Me, too, I'm going to . . . substain . . . too," said the guy on my other side, who had the sparse mustache and goatee of a consumptive poet and earnest, piercing eyes—he reminded me of a man I'd known who was "born again" suddenly in the middle of his motocross racing career and so radiated a strange blend of pious sincerity and full-throttled aggression. "I mean . . . she says she had a couple beers . . . The police quote her saying it was a six-pack and some old-fashioneds—who you gonna believe?"

"*Nobody* has *a couple of beers* at the Myles Standish. I mean, give me a break," said the smart one—the one who'd told them to listen to me. "I mean, does anyone else here recall the size of the glasses at the Myles Standish?"

Born Again gave an obscene whinny, and the old man, who looked as if he'd been dozing so long that he now resided at some indefinite point on the continuum between sleep and death, came alive suddenly and chuckled to himself.

Foreman looked forlorn, as if we'd gone out partying without him. "Could somebody write down the questions?" he asked me. "My handwriting—"

My own handwriting is cramped and jerky—it's obvious a pen is a weapon to me—but how would he have known? He saw a woman, an overspreading tree, who bends down to whisper truths into a child's ear and then writes them out in a clear, round hand—and who hates to disappoint people and would naturally do as he said.

I did. "Why didn't they give her the Breathalyzer?" he dictated, his voice sharp and confident now that he was telling me what to do. "How much had she really had to drink? Why did it take two months to bring to trial?"

"We're not supposed to ask about the facts, only the law," I said, thinking he'd wanted me to do the writing so he wouldn't be blamed for his own stupidity.

"Well, these *are* about law," Foreman said. "Aren't they?" He looked sad and confused and I wondered what on earth he might do for a living—he wasn't confident enough to be a real estate agent, or toughened like a fisherman. . . . His hands looked soft and white and useless—maybe he was a clerk at the Motor Vehicle Registry. "I mean, I'm just not comfortable about this—in the first place I *don't* think we're supposed to be talking to each other . . ."

I sighed, and when I called the bailiff he sighed, but carried the questions soberly out to the judge and returned to gather us up and lead us into the courtroom.

"Get back in the order you were seated in," he told us, and we circled each other in a complicated do-si-do, trying to figure out which of us was who. I was aggrieved to find neither of the men who'd sat beside me recalled this, as if my femininity gave me no distinction. Finally I had to push the foreman to the front—he seemed to be trying to hide behind me.

"Try to stay in line, okay?" the bailiff asked—plaintive, wishing for at least a semblance of order, a few clear outlines or an impartial understanding or *something* of the sort one might have expected from a tall, authoritative deep-voiced judge and a group of jurors who knew men from women and were able to form a straight line.

"Jury," the judge said, once we were settled. "I instructed you *not* to speculate and *not* to ask questions of fact. Yet I have received from you one speculative question and two questions about the facts. Jury, I am disappointed in you. Please return to your deliberations and do as you have been charged."

He was looking straight at me, as if he knew the others were hopeless, but had expected I would do better. Even the bailiff, as he marched us back to our chamber, seemed to blame me. Well, they should have made me foreman. . . .

But no. We sat sheepishly around the table. "I'm just going to have to substain," Foreman said again.

"It's *abstain*!" I snapped, "and you can't abstain, we have to be unanimous."

"It's the defendant who should have abstained," opined the smart one, sadly.

"We have to know if she was really driving," Foreman said, with his hand on his pocket again and a strange sound in his voice as if he was guilty of something, too. "The police say the car was running, her boyfriend says the keys were on the dash. I mean, it's a big question!"

"Those cops in Brewster, they'll take you into custody for a bent license plate," said Born Again, adding, "but the boyfriend, what about that belly? He's a drunk. They're both drunks, it's pretty clear. And *Brad*—"

"We're not supposed to speculate," I said, though without speculation our hands would be tied. But this roused the old man.

"Speaking of which," he said, a little color rising in his face. "The question *I'd* like an answer to is about the Dow Jones. . . . Wasn't that *absolutely glorious* yesterday?" He sighed with a deep and sensual pleasure so that I pictured him stepping into a hot tub full of money. The others peered at him—to them the stock market was a notion on the order of intergalactic travel or the Follies Bergere. One had heard of it, had an image of some sort—a silver phallus speeding through the dark, a frothy pink centipede, a board with flickering numbers and orders to buy and sell—but no more. It was years before I'd realized that my friends' trust funds made more money every year than my mother did working—we never spoke of such things, for fear we'd all have to despise each other. (My own shrink, who pouts when I won't tell her my masturbation fantasies, said, "Oh, no, I don't want to pry," when I started talking about money one day.) So how could this man go on about the stock market in a room full of working people? He must be suffering from Alzheimer's. I smiled at him, and he looked deeply comforted and closed his eyes again.

"Maybe we ought to take a poll," I said. I wanted to get the thing accomplished, go home.

"Are we allowed to take a poll?" Foreman asked.

"Yes, yes," I said. "We're allowed to take a poll."

"How *can* we take a poll?" he asked then, in despair. "We don't know what happened!"

"The cop himself said he couldn't make a determination of drunkenness right away," Born Again said, and Dow Jones was suddenly wreathed in smiles.

"Could *not* make a determination," he affirmed. "That's what sticks in my mind." The two of them gazed across at each other with delight, as if posing for a UNICEF Christmas card.

"I daresay he was trying to establish impartiality," I said. "He was saying he didn't jump to a conclusion just because this woman was giggling and wiggling her toes out the driver's side window in the middle of the Pilgrims Highway at one A.M. in the morning."

"How do *you* know what the cop was thinking?" Born Again asked. "I mean, do you know him? What I remember is that he said he could *not* make a determination."

"So how can *we*?" asked the foreman. "We weren't even there!"

"Let's all go to the Myles Standish and hash it out over a couple beers," the smart one said, laughing, and I felt cozy suddenly, back in Purmort with my friends, those guys who could fix anything, do anything, except find the road out of Purmort—they're there fixing things now.

"I'll go first," I said, to set an example. "I would have to say not guilty, as things stand now."

Smart One nodded.

"You can count me in," Dow Jones said with great good fellowship.

Foreman shook his head. "I'm abstaining," he said. He was right, too: it's terrible to have decisive power, even in a matter as minor as this. Probably someone was being killed by a drunk driver even as we sat there, and somewhere else a woman was getting ten years without parole for carrying her boyfriend's cocaine in her purse. And here was Dawn LaRue, a tired woman who'd done the best she could with her life, getting by on her miserable salary with a little help from codeine and beer . . . and she'd managed to get out of the dump for a week to see her family, dragging along the boyfriend, who she knew was no good for her but couldn't help loving, bravely avenging the death of her granddaughter's pet, had a few too many trying to get into the holiday mood and then Brad came in, and as the situation stood there was just no way to refuse, and when she finally got to feel the warm air on her toes here came some martinet cop . . .

"What if we let her off, and next year she smashes herself up and somebody else, too?" Smart One asked. "I mean, I feel for her." He looked around the table, and catching my eye took a quick breath for courage and said, "I'm a recovering alcoholic myself," with a great lightness, as if it was a privilege to be intimately acquainted with one's own desolation, an active member of the great, striving, desperate world. My heart reeled: could it be, that someone else got out of Purmort alive? "But, she's a grown-up, she's got responsibilities," he said.

Born Again was the last man in the circle, and as the question came around to him he put his hands over his face.

My heart went out. "I know it's stressful," I said. "But this isn't the final vote after all. It's only to get an idea, see how we're leaning."

He didn't move. "We'll have more discussions," I said. "You don't have to worry, we can all change our minds. . . ."

He looked up. "I'm having a dosebleed," he said, and blood coursed down over his lip on cue, so that he covered his face again.

"I guess we're a hung jury," Foreman said happily.

"We are *not* a hung jury," I retorted, while Born Again gazed upward and pinched the bridge of his nose. "We're an undecided jury . . . and one of us is having a nosebleed . . . but we have a job and we're going to do it. Now it *does* sound as if we all have some doubt—"

"Not me!" Foreman declared. "I just have to abstain, that's all."

"What about the Breathalyzer?" Born Again asked the ceiling.

"She wasn't *driving*, the car was *parked*!" Smart One said suddenly.

"Someone was going to drive that car somewhere," I said. They didn't want to deal with it and would do whatever I said, so I wanted to think it through.

"Why did it take so long for the trial?" asked the foreman. "Two months, it's inexcusable."

"Five months, *five months* it was!" I said. "From August to January is *five months*! Ever heard the phrase 'the wheels of Justice turn slowly'? For God's sake, read the paper once in a while!"

"No, I never *have* heard that phrase," Foreman said stiffly, but under the table he was counting on his fingers.

"And why couldn't the cop form an opinion about her drunkenness?" Dow Jones asked for the fifth time.

"He was saying he didn't *jump to a conclusion*," my smart darling explained.

"Didn't form an opinion," said Dow Jones. "And didn't use the Breathalyzer. I just keep coming back to that."

"Any of us could be in her place," I said.

"You can say that again," said Smart One, and I laughed happily. We'd lived through it, we understood.

"What if she's got three drunk driving convictions on her record? What if she goes out and runs over some kid tonight?" he asked, and relief poured over me. There were two of us, it wasn't all up to me. I thought of the day the police finally came for my stepbrother; my mother said she couldn't bear to see it and left me there to look in his eyes while they put the handcuffs on. I wondered if Smart would like me to bear him some children—he was so solid and unadorned— so deeply, beautifully familiar; I felt I knew exactly what it would be like to kiss him, how in him my whole life of longing would be turned to sex and assuaged.

"You're so right," I said. "It's a serious thing."

Everyone made a long face, and Born Again said, "You gotta take the snake into account—I mean, I can't condone animal cruelty. If she did that, what else is she capable of?"

"It's not a charge of animal cruelty," Smart One pointed out.

"Humans can fight back, but a poor defenseless bunny . . ."

"It was a *snake*!" I said, feeling like a racist.

"Is it two-thirty yet?" Foreman asked. "I really gotta go."

It was 4:45. My husband would be picking Victoria up from Girl Scouts and going home to set up his telescope (he's an amateur astronomer and something was about to happen in the Orion Nebulae) and start dinner—chicken breasts and mesclun; he's got a state pension coming, so he's very conscious of his health.

I polled the group again and we acquitted—against the pain conviction would have caused us, the evidence was not enough. That, apparently, is the definition of reasonable doubt. I wrote a note to the bailiff and gave it to the foreman to sign, and we scrambled into our places—in the right order now.

"Foreman, how say you?"

"Not guilty," the foreman boomed.

"How say you all?"

"Not guilty."

Dawn LaRue directed a shy smile to Smart One, then a quick sharp glance at me, as if she imagined, with the prosecutor, that I'd been against her. But the prosecutor looked at me with what seemed to be contempt—why had I given in and betrayed her? The bailiff stood stoically still, as if he himself had been convicted, sentenced to stand there day after day up to his neck in the American muddle. Sitting at the side now was a woman who must have been Dawn's daughter Sherry, with Tiffany, clutching a stuffed parrot, on her lap. The little girl was wreathed in pink ruffles, which did nothing to mitigate her watchful expression and I thought that years from now when all this was forgotten, she'd hear metal tearing or a man's anguished voice, and feel a fearful anxiousness so deeply familiar it was almost a comfort, the way the things of childhood always are.

Oh I wanted a cigarette, all of a sudden.

"Great job, Foreman," said the Smart One as soon as we were back in our quarters. I glared at him and he winked.

The door opened and the judge blew in, saying, "Don't get up, don't get up, please."

"You had an incomplete case," he said. "You did the right thing. She doesn't have any other DWI's. She was polluted, it's true—she refused the Breathalyzer, but we can't tell you that."

He started laughing—"I do wish you could have seen the mug shot," he said. "But she's suffered plenty, her daughter's got boyfriend trouble, the family pet passed away, she got lost on Cape Cod in the tourist season, spent the night in jail, she had to hire a lawyer—those Breathalyzers don't tell the whole story. A real drunk can drive fine with a stratospheric blood level, it's only the amateurs who get impaired. That touch-your-nose test, I can't do it either. These cops get a little overenthusiastic sometimes—you know how it is."

"But why did it take so long?" Foreman asked. "I mean it's two months since it happened. . . ."

"Four months, actually," the judge said, though it was five, five! Foreman gave me a spiteful glance, which I returned in kind. "You did good, jury. You can sleep well tonight. By the way, does anyone have jumper cables?"

Foreman, looking stricken, admitted he did.

"Would you mind?"

"No, no, of course not," he said, looking terrified, so that I wondered what else he had in his trunk. Probably *Hustler* magazine, or a Mars Bar—people don't need to do much to feel desperately ashamed, God knows.

"Let's be candid, it was a matter of the lint between a woman's toes," the judge said, but I was thinking—suppose it had been a matter of life and death? Juries just like us decide those all the time. "I shouldn't laugh," he went on as he left. "I know I shouldn't, but if *you'd seen* the mug shot!" And he was overcome, wheezing as he tried to get his breath, while the foreman walked stiff as a puppet behind him.

Out we went into the frigid evening, calling good-byes across the parking lot as if we'd come from a choir rehearsal. "Sometimes you have to go with the flow," the foreman was explaining to the judge.

"Cigarette?" Smart asked, tapping two out of a pack and holding one out to me. The thrill that ran through me was wildly out of proportion to the offer, but I managed to shake to my head.

"Did that seem at all . . . *odd* . . . to you?" I asked him as the others drove away.

"I have to admit," he said, "that since I got sober *everything* seems kind of odd. It was nice meeting you, though."

"And you!" I said. We were standing beside his truck and I patted it tenderly, thinking he probably had another at home in the driveway, for parts. "Brandy," I said.

"Excuse me?" he said, looking puzzled, even embarrassed.

"My name . . . I mean, you said you were glad to meet me, so I—"

"Oh! That's your *name*! I thought . . . I . . ." A wide grin began to spread over him. "I'd figured you for an Elizabeth, or a Caroline."

"Fooled you," I thought of saying, but then I'm always thinking of saying that. "Afraid not," I said instead, giving him a complicit smile, with a memory of waiting for Butchy on the corner on a frozen winter night, watching the lighted tip of his cigarette swing up, glow, and fall as he came toward me. There were cornfields on one side of that road, and the roadhouse my mother worked at, on the other, and me named after a song on a jukebox . . . was it different, really, than being named Swift Water, or Lily, or Joy? It has the sound of real life in it—a woman weeping, a cash register ringing in back—to say "I'm Brandy" is to say "I've known things, taken part in the world."

"Frank," he said. "Frank Wills." *And that's it, I thought, the name, the truck, the hands, that's all he has—enough to build a solid life on, if you work at it day by day.* I slipped my car keys back into my purse—I didn't want him to know about the Volvo. The sun was nearly down and it blazed out for a minute between the heavy gray sky and the horizon, flushing the soft dry heads of the marsh grasses red all the way to the sea. It was one of those instants so beautiful that everything stops breathing to attend: in that perfect stillness you can feel the pulse of longing that's always there beneath the ordinary movement of life. Then it was over and I was standing there shaking Frank's hand.

"Hello, Frank Wills," I said, feeling a signal flash in my mind—*Alert! Family! Remember that family!* They were waiting for me—they needed me, at home, where nothing is ever as ardent, as arduous, as it ought to be. I'll never get used to it, I'll always feel there's something missing, something false in the simple good of my life. My husband calls me honey, as if the name Brandy is a little secret we needn't mention. All evening he'd be checking his telescope, to be sure it was focused exactly where his stars were going to be. It's his great source of astonishment—the way, if you keep steady night after night, watching, a galaxy begins to sort itself out in your eyes.

It's the kind of thing no one in Purmort would think of. You can't concentrate like that when necessity has a knife at your throat. I wanted to escape that place so badly I'd have run the hundred miles to Vassar in my bare feet—but now I thought of the way Butch used to hold me, like he wanted to tear me open and get his hands on my heart.

"And, good-bye," I said, and walked away without looking over my shoulder, because the natural thing, the right thing it seemed, would have been to swing myself up into Frank's passenger seat and say, "Take me home. I never meant to leave my own people behind."

Six Figures in Search of an Author

"He can't be ninety! My God, he just turned eighty!"

I was speaking of Moss Genthner, *the* Moss Genthner, who would be Auden's contemporary if only Auden were alive, whose other associates have long since committed their suicides, so that Moss is all that's left, now, of his time. He floats around like a Chagall figure, talking in a hallowed poetic voice about Halley's comet and the conversion of the gas streetlamps, already commanding a reverence no one is supposed to get until they're dead. His eightieth birthday celebrations had lasted most of a year, with parties in Boston and New York, interviews on PBS, and the conversion of his childhood home into a small museum.

And, of course, readings by his former students, who form the backbone of the poetry community, teaching each other's work in the universities until almost every creative writing student in this great nation of creative writing students has felt the thrill of knowing that he, or usually she, is studying under a poet who studied under Moss Genthner—it's as if one had visited Berryman in the asylum, or taken Marianne Moore to Ebbets Field. I felt certain we'd been given a guarantee, that having attended all the eightieth birthday parties, readings, testimonials, and dedications, we were excused from further celebrations. Now I wished I'd asked for it in writing.

"He's a marvel," Peregrine said, assuming I'd spoken in admiration—how else did one speak of Moss? "Still teaching . . . writing, and a three-book contract . . ." He swept his hand into a fist around some imaginary brass ring. "Inspiring, that's what it is," he said. Peregrine's forebears were Puritans, and like them he is sternly religious—difficult for him because he can find no God to believe in. He believes in Moss.

Who was already looking immortal in so many ways it seemed dangerous to encourage him with another party, but Peregrine was not to be swayed. He began to prepare as if he were bringing Zeus down from Olympus, which meant at least that the party could not be held at our house. Our house faces a seasonal parking lot and the most interesting natural phenomenon we've sighted there was a woman who assumed that since she was squatting behind her van she must be relieving herself in privacy. Zeus, and Moss, must look out over brimming seas toward the spouts of the leviathans.

Kit DeLoup's house is directly on the bay, and Kit is fond of Peregrine, although (or perhaps because) she has never slept with him. Times have changed, but while I was learning to diagram sentences, Peregrine was living in the dunes, drinking Bloody Marys poured from the slit throats of sheep, and sleeping with women. That's what art *was* then! When I married him I had to understand that almost every woman of roughly my mother's age in town had once had physical relations with my husband. They're all very sweet, solicitous of me when I bump into them in the post office and the pharmacy and the library and the liquor store and the A&P, grandmotherly toward the twins, but it can make for awkwardness, and I have to watch my tongue. Kit only likes black men, jazz guys, so her relationship with Peregrine is easy and calm and she said she'd be happy to let him use her place as long as a couple of friends who were staying with her could come.

Peregrine said no. Easy sociability is not a Puritan virtue. This would be the party of the year on the island, he said, and everyone would want an invitation. We would have to be ruthless if we were going to keep it an intimate gathering of Moss's dearest friends, and *nobody else at all*.

Did I really think, Kit asked when she found me evaluating sun-screens at the Wharf General Store, that it was a good idea to let Pere-grine do this party thing all on his own? She sounded offhand and confidential, but she always does; she has the voice of someone who sidles up and offers to sell you a pack of pornographic playing cards.

"I know you're stretched awfully thin," she said, nodding her gray dreadlocks toward Ruby and Jade, who were crawling toward a low shelf of jelly jars, turning every few seconds to be sure I gave their naughtiness its due. "But it might mean less work in the long run, if you . . ."

She knows what to leave unsaid, and I nodded. I'm officious by nature, but in any case my time of leaving Peregrine to his own de-vices would have ended the day I found him trying to "clean out" the electrical outlets with a screwdriver, and no one can hope to be an author, a Visiting Adjunct Lecturer in Creative Writing, and a mother, and still have the time and patience necessary to translate the basic rules of etiquette into language recognizable to a Puritan.

"It's not possible," I said, just as the jars came tumbling, and by the time I had gathered them, and the twins, up, Kit had gone her way.

So she had to act as Peregrine's helpmeet. I eavesdropped on his end of their conversations, careful to hold my tongue. It was going to be a magnificent spread, Peregrine said; everyone would want to bring their best dish in Moss's honor. Marsha Sewall (widow of Sewall the abstract impressionist, who'd planned to be buried beside Moss, but at the last minute, feeling Moss had given his work short shrift, took the plot by the Motherwells instead) was donating two cases of peach champagne. As for the cake, Kit knew a healer who did baking for special occasions. . . .

"Eddie makes a nice cake," I said, and wished I hadn't. Peregrine had not approved of the double replica of Scarlett O'Hara's hoop-skirted picnic dress—with layers of marzipan and vanilla cream—that Eddie made for the twins' birthday.

"I'm sure Kit knows best," Peregrine said stiffly. "People are still talking about the party she gave when she married Piero."

"We're not having electric Kool-Aid this time, are we?" I asked him. Kit and Piero have been divorced for twenty years, but certain decades have pancaked in Peregrine's memory, like so many floors of a high-rise in an earthquake. Bits of the sixties turn up fossilized— his rage at Richard Nixon is still fresh as the dew, and he is shocked, shocked at my shallow understanding of the Bay of Pigs and the Tet Offensive, no matter that I was five or ten years old at the time.

It's true that the great international movements have taken place outside my consciousness, but I feel a really good historian ought to try to understand the general nature of time and space, and maybe electricity. I know that if one once trysted with a woman who was suckling a babe, and one meets that babe twenty years later in a bar downtown, the babe, no matter how well-licensed, is still something like your own child and you should not try to drink it under the table or seduce it. I know that art has made a desperate leap out of the bars and into therapy—writers these days brag about all the drugs they *used* to take and which of their friends have AIDS. Peregrine's still drinking like Hemingway and talking like Mailer, which would be all very well if we were at war, but an epidemic demands a different vocabulary.

Which reminded me to ask if Cleome was coming. She was one of the stars Moss marked to join his constellation, and she gave up an excellent career as a nutritionist when he brought her out to the island to study and gave her the idea that the only place of honor on earth was his inner circle, that one was either a poet or a failure—but she flickered out somehow and now she cooks at the hospice and runs a hand-dipped candle shop on the wharf, while the other brilliant, sensitive women in his fold go on to fresh triumphs every week—they'd be stepping off the ferry the day of the party just across from her place.

"She's not on the list," Peregrine said.

"You've got to invite her . . . ," I insisted, and somehow we found ourselves arguing about grade inflation in the universities, the empty "self-esteem" that leaves students feeling proud, proud of themselves without all the bother of accomplishing anything. "There has to be a willingness, *somewhere*, to step on toes!" he inveighed.

"Cleome's toes?" I asked, but a Puritan has his responsibilities. I'd just put the twins down for their nap and was feeling as strong and honest and virtuous as only a woman who has just rocked two children to sleep in her arms can, when the phone rang. I put a finger to my lips when his voice began to rise, but when I saw his face I retreated—it had taken on the exact likeness of his grandfather, the Reverend Sawyer.

"Certainly not," he was saying. "This is a *private* party, not a society event." (Who could it have been, who would dare link Peregrine Whittington with a society event?) "No, no . . . no," he said, with the icy amusement he always turns on solicitors. "I do not think that would be appropriate, and I have no way to help you." He hung up, looking very deeply satisfied.

"Who *was* that?"

"The New Yorker."

I sat down on the landing. "What do you mean?"

"They want someone to write up the party."

He found the idea revolting, but not surprising; I thought it was utterly incredible.

"Is nothing happening in New York?"

"Well, I told them absolutely not."

"Because they're not old friends of Moss?"

"Because I'm not in the business of that kind of procurement."

"But Peregrine . . ." My life was passing before my eyes, and what a sorry procession—the book, the "promise," the students who in their search for anything consequential read wisdom into my every word, the sense that as a teacher of creative writing I was part of a metaphysical Ponzi scheme that created comfortable employment for those of us at the top by milking the benighted souls at the bottom, who were no more than boat people fleeing the poststructuralists in the literature departments where they would otherwise have been happily, obliviously at work. The guilt! The shame! The desperate need for further publications . . .

"Peregrine, I would have written the party up for *The New Yorker,"* I said.

He looked at me as if I'd offered to jump out of Moss's cake.

"I'd do a great job of it, Peregrine," I said. "I really *know* Moss, I could show why people love him, what his example has meant . . ."

Because suddenly I couldn't help thinking how beautiful the world would look from Kit's deck as it sagged under the weight of all the greatest living poets . . . the terns diving, the light in the crystal glasses, the bay full of sails . . . I knew exactly how I'd describe it, Moss as a legend among his successors, looking out to the far horizon, standing amidst the abundance of life on the threshold of the unknown . . . how inspiring he was and how selfless, nourishing all these young poets . . . Why, I *loved* Moss, and a shudder passed over me as I remembered asking him, when he was only seventy-eight, whether he thought he'd ever win a Nobel Prize, and hearing him explain and explain and explain the way my college boyfriend used to patiently enumerate for me all the reasons he was only wait-listed at Yale.

"They don't want you; they want Mullins," Peregrine said.

"Mullins?" Park Mullins was *the* poet, just then. His poems were intelligent, deeply felt, tinged with the kind of self-satisfaction a white Anglo-Saxon Protestant male can only feel when he has been purified of the colonialist/genocidal taint by virtue of his homosexuality. He lived up the street from us with his boyfriend—I'd asked them over for dinner once and he'd said they'd love to come if nothing better turned up, but apparently something had. "Was he invited?"

"Why would he be invited?" Peregrine asked me.

"Peregrine Whittington hung up on *The New Yorker*?" We were at the beach, and my friend Sinead she was laughing so hard the woman beside us peered over her sunglasses in furious disapproval, which caused Sinead to laugh louder, at which the woman lifted her book over her face like a shield. It was *Under the Table*, Patsy Grue's memoir of her childhood sexual abuse and the adult substance abuse it led to, with the giant words *"Gripping! Darkly, disturbingly erotic!— The New York Times Book Review"* splashed in neon orange across the jacket.

"And, of course, we have to invite *her*," I said. "I *loathe* Patsy Grue."

"For God's sake, be quiet!" Sinead beseeched, snorting horribly as she tried to rein herself in. "You don't think she'd be reading that if she wasn't a friend of Patsy's, do you?"

This sobered me.

"We won't say Patsy," Sinead said. "Call her Georgina."

"I *loathe* Georgina!" I cried. "It's not that I oppose pretension per se, but to be haughty because your father raped you—more-victimized-than-thou! That's where I draw the line!"

"Well, the advance . . . ," Sinead said. "For a poem they'll give you six copies; for a memoir six figures . . ."

"It's not the money, I don't care about the money . . ."

"With me, it's always the money," Sinead said.

"With me, it's the goddamned zinnias!"

"Don't say zinnias!" she hissed, as everyone knows Patsy takes absurd pride in her zinnias while mine mildew and die every year. "Say *hydrangeas,"* she suggested kindly.

"Georgina's hydrangeas! And then to complain about censorship when the publisher wouldn't have a big throbbing penis on the jacket—"

"—as if representations of big throbbing penises weren't common as potted rubber plants these days—"

"Exactly! Fortunately I don't think she can come to the party— she's on tour in Australia."

"Australia!" Sinead said. "I mean, it's an awful book, but exile . . ."

"The wanton murder of defenseless trees . . ."

"All sins can be forgiven," she replied. "Look, Peregrine hung up on *The New Yorker*, and you're not mad at him."

"Of course I'm mad at him," I said. "He's my husband."

At Moss's eightieth birthday I'd been Peregrine's child bride. I wore a crimson sundress, a William Morris print, and I remember drifting across a wide lawn toward the Hudson feeling, like a blossom carried along by the breeze. Upstairs in this mansion, whose owner was shaving a truffle over the risotto on the buffet, I opened one door after another, to see paintings that would have amazed me in a museum: a Rembrandt, a Corot, two Picassos glaring at each other across a double bed . . . Here it was, the House of Art, exactly as I had imagined—an immense solid structure with an infinite number of rooms, large enough to encompass the great contradictions, so bright as to illuminate the finest distinctions, resting on a foundation neither history nor geology could shake. The oriental carpet lay thick as new-fallen snow in the hallway, and when I reached the library I saw shelves that rose two dizzying stories, with an oak ladder on which it seemed one might glide straight to the Truth. I remember wanting to kneel down there and thank the gods for Peregrine, who had ushered me out of the dark, into the knowledgeable world.

What possessed me to think I might ever do more than sneak around in that mansion, I don't know. As I was about to leave the library I met a woman entering, whose still, spare beauty was more perfect than the paintings—she was like a stone you'd pick up on the beach. It was clear she belonged to the house somehow, and I began to make excuses for myself—I was looking for a bathroom, had taken a wrong turn . . . She looked at me wonderingly and said that she was just trying to escape—she was Cal Lowell's daughter and so had sat on Moss's lap as a child, but she had to get out of this party. Of course, she was fleeing—it was her world, only a daydream to me. And Peregrine? He was comfortable there as Ahab would have been if he'd landed in *The Golden Bowl*.

The day before Moss's ninetieth dawned a deep aquarium green. Two oil tankers and a cruise ship had taken refuge in the harbor. The halyards rang against the masts—Peregrine looked fit to lash himself to one.

"A gale," he said, through his teeth. "Moss flying in through a gale. And what if it's still raining tomorrow?"

"Aren't we supposed to go over and help Kit clean house?" I asked him.

"Yes," he said, "but I talked to her last night and she said she'd take care of it—it's not a big job, she lives by herself. . . ."

"But the cats—" Kit is philosophically opposed to neutering cats and owns five, all male, who follow each other around staking claim to the furniture all day.

"This is a party of intellectuals," he told me with infinite condescension. "They are not going to be checking for perfect cleanliness and criticizing the décor."

I came very near informing him that the Pottery Barn catalog shows Park Mullins's books scattered artfully around the Mendocino bedroom collection, but I didn't want to break his heart, and I had to reserve my strength to argue for tablecloths and cocktail napkins and other bourgeois indulgences that a party of intellectuals would necessarily disdain.

"We do have to think about parking," I said.

"We don't need *parking*," he said. "Francis Drake walked two miles through the dunes every night after the bars closed, his whole life! He lived by foraging for years! He has a mushroom named after him!"

"I'm not questioning his manliness, but he just had a stroke!"

"He would be appalled to hear we were making special arrangements just for him."

The subject was as closed as the airport. Cleome was dispatched to pick Moss up in Boston. They didn't get back until ten, but Moss was twinkling all over and took the porch steps like a mountain goat, joyful to see us, shocked the twins were already in bed. He knows nothing of children—what would be the point? Do they give prizes, or write reviews? No, they can't even read! I'd assumed he'd want some rest himself, but he was famished and thought we should go straight to Les Sables. Les Sables used to be a cod-salting shed, then a kind of flophouse in the sixties—Peregrine got kicked out of an orgy there—but now it's got three Michelin stars: it's the only place in town to get really decent bouillabaisse (though it costs the earth, of course, because the fish have to be flown in from Maine—it's a long time since anything worth eating swam in this bay). I begged Sinead to baby-sit and put on a black dress, but we had no reservations, and to Peregrine's stupefaction the name Moss Genthner had no effect on the maître d'. So we tried Porcini, the Sea Street Café, and Barbarella's, but there was no room even at the bar. Finally I told Moss to come back to our house for an omelette.

"Hmmmm," he said, in his old man's oracular warble. "Do you have any salad?"

"It's iceberg," said Peregrine, as if this were illegal. Moss turned to Cleome.

"I think I have some mâche, but it's kind of old," she said.

"Let's go over and take a look," Moss answered, with the patience of a man who's willing to search months for a right word. "We can take it back to Peregrine's." Cleome lives in Spinnaker, four miles away. "Now, what about bread?" Moss asked happily. "And wine?"

"I've got some white," Cleome said, though Moss looked alarmed. Cleome of the jasmine and *frangipani* candles could not be trusted on wine. "And rolls," she added, glad to be a part of things. "Whole wheat!"

"What kind of seeds?" Moss asked. "Sesame, or—"

"No seeds," she admitted. Like her poems, the rolls were missing something.

But Moss's inspiration never fails: "You must have some poppy seeds, eh, Jane?" he asked me.

"Which are poppy seeds?" Peregrine asked, "those little black ones? I think Kit has some."

"Kit is sitting in on drums at the Clamshell!" I said.

"Well, that's just down the block," Moss said. "You can run in and ask her, Jane—"

"*No!*"

"I have soup," Cleome said in a small voice. "I mean, it's not Les Sables, but I have soup and rolls and the mâche" (she glanced over at me: her lettuce had surpassed mine) "and wine. . . ."

"And all in one place. Perfect, Cleome," I said. "West, Peregrine!" There came a muffled grunt as if Moss had been punched in the gut, but I ignored it.

"The Lundgrens have sniffed out the party," he said, when we had climbed the steps up the hillside and were settled at Cleome's table. Spinnaker hasn't been papered over with money like the rest of the island, not yet—the houses are still crooked and peculiar, angled to take in the north light for painting or catch the odd glimpse of the bay. The winds had switched around, and we heard the tankers sound their horns as they left the harbor—maybe there was hope for the party.

"What party?" Cleome asked.

"Communist," I said, and diverted her attention to *Under the Table*, which was sitting on her sideboard, while Moss and Peregrine got off on Kissinger. "Well, it's . . . gripping?" she said. ". . . It's . . . erotic? It's kind of disturbing. But some of her adjective-noun combinations are just so good. . . ."

"The Lundgrens don't have to come if you don't want them," I heard Peregrine say.

"Yes, they do," Moss said, shaking his head over the immutable laws of the universe. The Lundgrens teach at Harvard; even Peregrine can't cross them. "They do. This must be very healthful, Cleome," he said sorrowfully, tasting the soup.

"It's good, don't you think?" she asked. "It's a California minestrone."

"It's very nutritious, I can tell," he replied.

It was nearly time for the party, but Peregrine had pressed the wrong key on his computer, and his poem came out in columns like an account book. At first I pretended not to hear him, but as his sighs increased my heart softened.

"When you have a minute . . . ," he said sheepishly, and I went over to press REVEAL CODES. As I scanned for his error my eye caught on the text: his poem was about women, many, many women, and not one of them was me. I skimmed to the bottom and onto the next page. . . . Every shopgirl in town was seen to turn up her pretty behind.

"Peregrine, what is this?" I asked.

"It's just about—it's about—well, the narrator—"

"The narrator?" I said, "the *narrator*! I have never once seen you write anything that wasn't absolutely something that happened to you the day before! And now we have a narrator? How dare you? . . . How could you *write* this, and having done both those things you have the nerve to ask me to come *fix your columns*? You hypocrite! You *wolf* in narrator's clothing! I'll fix your goddamned columns, you . . . you *narrator*."

Whereupon he turned into the Reverend Sawyer and informed me that I was making him late for the party.

Now the curious thing about the young women whose talent Moss has fostered is that their great insight, their gripping and disturbing eroticism, their very unique and original spirits have somehow caused them all to look very much alike. I don't know why this should be, but it's just true that poets now are willowy and soulful and have thick hair growing like ivy out of their extremely fertile heads. There's none of this Emily Dickinson homeliness, nothing raw and clutching, no Sylvia Plath sea-urchin spininess or Elizabeth Bishop scraggle— no, when you look at them you can tell instantly you're seeing a lovely soft poet, someone you can plunge both arms into right up to the elbows. And they greet you with such warmth and generosity—it is amazing how kind they are, how careless of their prestige, willing to embrace you almost as if you were one of them.

"Jane! Oh, Jane, it's been *years!*" cried Marietta Brunelle (formerly Mary Brown). She leaned in to embrace me in a great swirl of perfume. "I got your book, by the way, thanks, I mean I haven't read it, but what a great jacket, and wow, the blurbs!" And seeing Park Mullins over my shoulder she sang, "*There* you are!" and tried to step through me.

"Your new *poems,*" he said, in a sacred hush, and their gazes (very intense gazes, his contacts being blue, hers green) locked—it frightened me to know they weren't acting on sexual attraction. The day was hot; the bay and sky turned their brilliances to each other to make just the dazzling backdrop we'd always imagined for ourselves. Moss had chosen us, *The New Yorker* was covering us; we would be studied, anthologized, and in the afterlife Moss would introduce us to Lowell. Here I was—I, whose father owned a Midas muffler franchise—among the grand old literary and artistic world of Milliken Island: Francis Drake, Trotskyite and discoverer of a mushroom; Rann Slivka, patterned after Monet down to the girth and hat, an ebullient lecher who made women writhe and glow; Celine someone, whose translations of Akhmatova would not easily be surpassed, who had married one of the lesser Nabokovs *and* one of the lesser Rothschilds, whose beauty Moss and Peregrine swore they could still see flashes of, even now, though, of course, her generation was nearly forgotten, overtaken by Peregrine's and then by Park's and Marietta's and mine.

I had the perfect dress, simple as a Greek column, printed with entymologically correct tomato hornworms and boll weevils, and Jade and Ruby looked like Victorian babies in their embroidered smocks and frilled panties: I supposed they might be discovered here, by a painter who'd want to base a show on them or a poet who'd find inspiration for his next cycle. Park Mullins himself might notice that the energetic curiosity that would propel them through the rest of their lives was already in place. Oh, it was perfect for *The New Yorker*—these radiant children, illuminating the melancholy passion of age. . . .

"It was a *poem*," Peregrine said angrily, coming up behind me. "It was not journalism. If you'd seen the last page, you wouldn't be upset at all."

"Well it's too bad you didn't ask me to *fix your columns* when you were on the last page," I said, wondering if it might possibly be true that he'd started to write from his imagination suddenly after all these years. . . .

"I'm a poet," he said. "I take poetic license."

"You are an anachronism. If you were a poet, you'd be dead." At the very least he'd have joined Sexaholics Anonymous and written a memoir.

"I'm too busy for this," he said. "There's not going to be enough to drink."

"There will *be* enough to drink, O narrator. There are two cases of champagne. There is every kind of liquor on the bar. There are *ten gallons* of wine. And there are fifty people coming, half of whom are recovering alcoholics and the other half so old and frail they can hardly take a little glass of Dubonnet!"

"I've seen Moss drink all night and at three A.M. he can still give you the source and probably the year of any line you quote him, no matter how obscure."

"That was thirty years ago! He was only sixty then!"

Kit came in from the deck to ask where the ice was.

"Ice!" Peregrine said, and ran out the front door.

"He isn't a natural host," I admitted.

"No," she said, with only the mildest note of reproof. "Want some blow?"

"Excuse me?" The twins were standing! It was the first time they'd both pulled themselves up at once, and now they were edging along the coffee table toward a great branch of pink coral on an ebony stand.

"Some *blow*," Kit said again. "You know." She was offering me cocaine, and dosing herself as she awaited my answer, with something homeopathic from a brown bottle. "Shingles," she said with a shrug, and the coral crashed to the floor, and the twins started howling, and in the midst of it all Moss appeared at the doorway, bent into a slight bow as if in eternal, humble acceptance of adulation, silent, ancient, and mysterious as a stone Buddha in the corner of a temple garden. Everything ceased, poets broke from their conversations and began to drift in his direction like dandelion fluff. He embraced them in turn: "Marietta, Liliane," he said, giving each syllable a benedictive weight so that I thought of Linnaeus naming the flowers, "and, *Giselle* . . ."

"Jane," of course, does not have the same effect. I felt his irritation even as his arms went around me—I'm so unethereal, unyielding . . . entirely unsatisfactory, a stone in his bowl of sweet cherries.

"Ninety !" I said, "and you don't look a day over seventy!" The others had called him immortal. He smiled and escaped. The room was filled and would have emptied again if not for the strange pilgrimage one had to make to get out to the deck—a winding pathway between a pile of cardboard boxes on one side and a forest of drums and cymbals on the other. Standing in the middle of that narrow aisle was Tim Grue, Patsy's estranged husband, a big, very handsome man, so well aware of his body that he seemed almost like a woman in spite of his strength and size. He was so fixed on his divorce he hardly knew where he was—fitted like a bottle stopper between the party and the sea.

"She—Patsy's a very—dark—even disturbing, sensibility," he was saying to Liliane, who nodded with grave concern. "I mean, the in-vitro was a very intimate time for us, but now . . ." Liliane had not blinked, and taking account of this suddenly he leaned in and stretched his arm over her shoulder to the door frame. "I like pleasing difficult women," he said. "I'm fine, I've never been better. I just need someone to love in my life, that's all." Liliane gazed up at him in pure calculation—he would adore her; she probably wouldn't even have to bother sleeping with him.

Out on the deck a gust had blown the tablecloth off the bar and the bartender was scrounging lemon pieces from the floor. Standing up, he caught sight of me and made an interrogative gesture—where was Peregrine? Where was anyone? Why was he out there all alone? I went out by the front door and around on the path, but as I did I heard an all-too-recognizable voice, a loud flat yaw like a siren, saying "*lovable eccentrics*—I'm *glad to say* I've never met anyone like that. I don't why she bothered to write that insipid little book."

It was Patsy Grue, talking to Park Mullins, and all too likely the subject was me. I felt dizzy for a moment, struck broadside by an appalling thought: Suppose everyone at this party was as spiteful as I was?

"Jane!" Patsy said as I came toward them. "Here you go," she said, lifting two heavy pans into my arms. "*This* will feed the millions.

Crabcakes, and that's kugel, and here—" having piled these on me she bent down for a loaf pan, "—is the *vegetable terrine*."

"You went to so much trouble," Park said. "It's much too hot to cook."

"I just save the ends of the soups until I have enough, press it into the mold, maybe a little curry, and everyone loves it," Patsy said.

And one must make a compliment, and the compliment would elicit further helpings—it was the same with her books.... "Patsy, how good to see you," I said. "I thought you were in Australia." I'd rehearsed it, and took a deep breath to try and say it: "A real achievement, so dark, so..." But the words stuck in my throat.

"Congratulations, by the way," Park said.

"On what?" I asked, thinking here was my chance to be nice.

"On her new job!" Park told me, "She's going to chair the Recovery Studies Program at Brown! Salary in the six figures, I hear."

I did not exactly gasp. Still, "The—the—excuse me?"

A shudder of revulsion, barely concealed, passed over Patsy's face. Of course, I wouldn't understand it—what had *I* ever had to recover from? My life had been so simple and easy I'd never even written a memoir. "Recovery Studies," she enunciated. "It's new."

"Oh! I ... my goodness ... Well, that's wonderful—"

"I can see you're thrilled," she said, turning away just as Peregrine came up the walk—with two bags of ice sagging in his arms like a corpse. To my own profound vexation, I was glad to see him. We've been married too long: when I look at him now I remember seeing his face over me during my caesarian—he'd kept hopping up to peer into my guts, though the doctors tried to push him back behind the screen. What could the rest of it matter? Probably his poem was only a flight of fancy and instead of criticizing I ought to have praised its verisimilitude. "Where were you?" I asked him.

He shook his head. "I had to park on the highway. At least a mile away."

"Slit, slash, gash, slice, twat, that's what it all comes down to, that's the bottom line," Patsy was saying, and Park agreed with a burst of very, very loud laughter. As author, as cook, as *enfant terrible*, Patsy works very hard. Peregrine helped me carry her dishes inside, and setting them on the table we saw that otherwise there were only some chips and a bowl of poached green beans. The cake, somber and healthy looking, was on a box behind Tim Grue, who was taking his turn as grave listener to Liliane. You'd have to be mad to walk between them. Someone had opened a window in the kitchen, and tiny old people on canes were helping each other through it onto the deck.

"I'll never have a popular success," Liliane was saying, and somehow the way she pronounced *popular* raised the image of maggots teeming, though she was not disdainful at all—no, she felt only kindness toward Patsy and other, more accessible, authors. For her, though, reality was a broken thing, and if some pages were blank, or half their words sifted into a pile at the bottom, then, of course, certain less cognizant readers were bound to be left behind.

"People don't often mention how really *funny* your books are," Tim said, leaning back.

"No!" Kit cried, but too late. Tim's elbow was deep in the cake.

"Oh," he said. "Oh, that's all right . . . This is an old shirt . . ." and Liliane looked up into his eyes and said, "Funny?"

"You'll have to go out through the window," I told Peregrine. "There's no other way."

Park Mullins was at the bar trying to pour himself some seltzer, but the bottle was empty. I don't suppose suicide has ever even crossed his mind—what poet has time to consider such things nowadays, with all the benefits to read at and competitions to judge, and the students lining up after class to find out whether you use a computer or a pen? The bartender filled a cup with ice and ducked in through the window.

"Where's the seltzer?" he asked, but it was long gone. The foghorn on the back shore started, and a minute later the one at Wood End joined it, though the day looked perfectly clear. Moss stood alone, looking over the water—his toes were gnarled and cracked like roots, his hands trembled, but his gaze was fierce and acquisitive, as if the beautiful world was a woman he was determined to possess before he died. Everyone steered around him—it would be embarrassing to repeat last decade's tributes, and what else was there to say? It was too hot, we'd been close on each other all summer, all decade, most of the century . . . A lavender sail flicked by—Cleome's boat, *The Gift of the Magi*—how I wished I were on it. Behind me Guinness Potzer was roaming with his camera, taking those pictures of his that show everyone's fatuity—who invited him? And Park, having stood at the bar for a moment, ironically dripping the last of the seltzer into his cup, shook Moss's hand and set out for the street—he'd seen enough. I guess his piece was for "Talk of the Town."

"Can the champagne have been stolen?" Kit asked me. "There were two whole cases."

"Peregrine brought it over last night, right?" I asked her.

"I meant to," Peregrine said.

There came a little crash from inside, almost inaudible now the place was so full. Ruby and Jade had knocked over a nest of tables, breaking one leg off each. If you're going to have such flimsy furniture, what's the point of having furniture at all?

"Come, my jewels," I said, and called a cab, and waved good-bye to Peregrine, who looked to be in mortal pain, with Guinness dogging every step of his search. *Snap*, Peregrine peers into the dumbwaiter; *Snap*, he lifts the tablecloth gingerly as a woman's skirt. Guinness was not, I thought, looking entirely dignified himself. Leaving, we passed

Lundgren, the only person who had actually wanted an invitation—he had his new book on the ethical fallout of nuclear war under his arm, and he looked like Leonard Bernstein at Carnegie Hall—I worried he'd be crushed if there was no ovation.

I turned back, overtaken by a lofty impulse: no matter how mad I was at Peregrine, the twins must kiss their father good night. Their father, whose illusions were some of the finest on earth, such a far sight above the banal illusions people live by today. And there he was, looking somewhere between perplexity and rage, like Ahab rudely awakened to find himself in *Under the Table*. I kissed his cheek—an act of historic preservation.

"The *champagne . . .*" he moaned.

It was in our basement, keeping nice and cool. I called Kit, but no one answered, and Jade and Ruby were asleep, and I didn't have the car . . . so I gave up, I just forgot it all. I put on Peregrine's pajamas, the real linen ones that had been his father's, and got an ice cream sandwich out of the freezer. The phone rang—it was Sinead.

"Tell all!" she said. I began with Peregrine's poem. . . .

"Don't get mad," she said after half an hour, as I was trying and discarding phrases to describe the infinite pervasiveness of the reek of cat, "but I have to wonder if Peregrine wasn't right. . . ."

I got mad immediately. "What do you mean?"

"You might not have been just the person to write it up for *The New Yorker.*"

"Why?" I heard the foghorn and saw tufts blowing in off the water like cotton wool. There they all were, on Kit's deck without champagne, being gently enveloped, as if to be stored away like glass ornaments for use this time next year. "I've got the true essence! That even the cake showed civic responsibility, that the only real gift was a book about Hiroshima . . ."

"Mom's bomb!" said Sinead, whose mother had been a mathematician on the Manhattan Project—honest employment, I mean, and a place in history, too.

And the foghorns, each on its own interval so the calls come to meet each other, and diverge, in a slow, irregular rhythm. "Oh, my God, I have to go," I said: Park Mullins was walking his Shitzu down the street, and if he saw me, he'd know the party had gone wrong. I hung up the phone and slid down onto the floor so he wouldn't be able to see me. There was no paper at hand, so I smoothed out the ice cream wrapper: I thought I should take a note. I've almost never felt as happy, as surrounded by beauty and hope, as I did just then. Myself—spiteful, jealous, always in a rage—ceased to beat her fists against my skull, and for a minute or two I felt a great benevolent heart beating: I was an author and I loved everything human.

The Funeral Party

They, who now made all decisions, called Warren back from the city to his father in Spinnaker-by-the-Sea. His mother was there, too, but she was on the night shift, and they didn't dare leave Warren alone at night. The whole bus ride he wondered how he'd recognize his father—he'd only seen Emerson once in the last fifteen years. And he hadn't been to Spinnaker for so long he'd forgotten what winter was like there; no one would be left except the people who couldn't get away.

The bus station was closed and Emerson was standing under the streetlight, looking tall and gaunt and impassive, the same figure as in Warren's dreams.

" 'lo," he said, picking up Warren's bag and turning down the street, away from the harbor and the driving wind, walking so quickly Warren felt he was trying shake him.

"I can carry that," Warren said to his back. Should he address him as *Dad*? "I'm not sick, you know." Only weak, and foolish, unable to bear the ordinary blows of life. "A disgrace," as Emerson had said after Warren's childish attempt to slash his wrists in high school—

a disgrace that he'd tried to kill himself, or that he'd hardly broken the skin.

" 'S only two blocks," Emerson said. All the storefronts were boarded over except for the Pilgrim Tap, where a lone man sat with his head down over his beer, maybe avoiding the sight of the Weather Channel on the television over the bar. They turned up Sea Street past the neat little houses, each sheltering an old woman who was hooking a rug and watching television until the time came for her to join her neighbors in the graveyard. Warren's grandmother had already passed; in her place, resting her cigarette in the same ashtray, sat his stepmother, Noreen. "Warren!" she said, her voice constricted, her smile immense in a face entirely gray. "I've heard so much about you."

He flinched and turned away. His thoughts were viscous, his tongue had grown thick and slow. He saw a hideous greedy emptiness in every face and imagined the same in his own—of course people recoiled from him. He'd been wrong, he thought, ever to go back to school, to leave his place in Maine, where isolation was natural and the bleak landscape—the ranks of spruce stretching infinitely north, the log trains slamming down from Canada—had fit his deep sense of things. In Maine, leaving Beth for the city had seemed an act of romantic courage, a casting away from safe harbor toward art and adventure, destiny. Now he realized how easily she'd let him go. She wanted marriage, a child, and, finding these were beyond him, she had pushed him out of her nest. Fooled him the way women do, tempting him into love so as to see him vanquished in the end. Three months in New York and he'd forgotten it was he who left her and not the other way around.

Brooklyn had been bleak in human terms: dirty, unseeing, unkind. His apartment windows looked into two airshafts, both gated as if thieves might get in somehow where no sunlight could. There'd been new women, of course—a design major who told him she was attracted to his desperation, and Sabra, a painter like himself, though unlike him she was able. When she spoke in class, the professors nodded grave agreement or argued as with an equal. The day Ned Fisk had "critiqued" Warren's entire semester of canvases, calling them derivative and dated, singling out certain paintings with contempt, he'd asked Sabra's opinion, and she'd tried to speak up for Warren, but without, he thought, real conviction. She was sure, she said, that he was "on his way somewhere"—though it was clear he had yet to arrive.

It became awful to look at the world: every glimpse of beauty was a rebuke, to a man who couldn't create it. Ned Fisk now seemed to Warren nearly visionary, the only one of his professors who had seen through to the empty heart of his ambition—he'd have turned himself inside out to please the man if he'd only understood what he wanted. But no—and he gave up, spent days playing solitaire on the computer and calling Beth far too often; watching his hand punch her number into the phone, he thought of an alcoholic reflexively pouring a drink. The ground went out from under him the minute she answered, and his voice would go soft and needful like a child's; it filled him with shame.

So, like a child, he had to come home. He told himself he wouldn't call Beth anymore, but as soon as he heard his father get into the shower, he went to the phone. Her voice was quiet and soothing; he'd have preferred bitterness, anger, *something* that showed she missed him too. He heard himself telling her how much he wanted to give up, to die. Carefully, implacably, she kept him on the line, and hearing her familiar exhortations, the things she'd memorized for his sake— Van Gogh *never* sold a painting, the very nature of originality meant it was hard to recognize—he felt a calm come over him. As they talked he heard the church bell across her street ring three and four and five, then the 5:47 train from Presque Isle that had always acted as their alarm. He thought of her, moaning, pulling up the quilt to turn over, the warm luxury of her smell . . . "Beth," he said, but he couldn't bring himself to it, the admission that he loved her.

It was his thirtieth birthday, two weeks until the new semester. By then, his mother insisted, the pills would be working, he'd be fine. Yes, he owed a term paper—he'd sit down and write it out, one sentence at a time. She took his hand. "I'm a nurse, honey, I know," she said, the way she used to cajole him when he was in second grade. He might have been listening underwater for all he understood, but that afternoon he sat down and to his own amazement began to draw, in deep, rich pastels, feeling he was pulling the far-flung pieces of himself together stroke by stroke. Yes, art was still there, and at night-fall when the usual terror descended, he imagined he saw a path through it, beyond.

His mother had invited the family for dinner. Warren marveled at Martha's capacity to forgive, to let go. Here was Emerson, who'd abandoned her, with Noreen; and on her other side, Drew, who'd lived with them for years after Emerson left, with Cecile, the young woman he'd left her for. Martha smiled over them all, matriarchally proud. Across the table, Warren's older brother, Tim, put a hand to his wife's flushed cheek as if to cool it—she was pregnant, a living talisman: it was hard to keep from touching her.

Warren smiled until his face ached, to repay them for coming, for pretending all was well. Cecile tried to draw him out, earnest as if she belonged here, though Warren thought with irritation that, since Drew had never married Martha, never officially been his stepfather, even he was an interloper. And Cecile was barely older than Warren: when she came to dinner that first night, years ago, he'd thought to walk her home and see what might follow, but Drew volunteered first.

That was that, Drew was gone, Martha and her sons were left alone. Now, with her hair falling smooth over her shoulders, Cecile fixed on Warren, asked who he liked among the moderns, with a smile of quiet condescension, he thought, as if she was saying, "See, I've joined the adults, you're still just a boy."

It was true—he'd waited for one of these fathers to reach out, pull him up into manhood, but they had all averted their eyes.

"What's the year-round population of Spinnaker these days?" he asked Emerson, feeling pleased with himself for once—this evaded Cecile and had a real, conversational ring.

" 'Bout thirty-five," Emerson said. His voice was so deep it seemed only to express ironies or matters of fact, and this seemed to be the former so Warren laughed.

"Hundred. Thirty-five hundred," his father corrected, with irritation. "Though they never get the full count," he said to himself, and Warren thought of the basement Emerson had lived in when he was drinking. Martha used to bring the boys to visit there until Tim, who knew when to cut his losses, refused to go anymore.

"The past is past," Martha was saying, with a little wave of her hand. Her eyes shone—Warren's life was reconstituted here, and that was what mattered, she insisted: the whole. "Isn't this delicious!" she said, of the flounder, and everyone agreed, almost tearily.

"Is it lemon, in the sauce?" Warren asked.

They leapt at it, all talking at once. Fascinated, they were, giddy with the mysterious resonance of lemon in a sauce. . . . What *was* it about lemon—? Because, if he'd noticed the lemon, noticed it and spoken of it, and in a perfectly ordinary, conversational way, then he must be getting well! Circumstances bound them together, they were no less than kin, a frail band rappelling down a cliff together: if Warren fell, he would take them with him, so they must go carefully, help him set each foot. This, more than the wine, took hold of them . . . and here came the cake with its thick soft frosting, the candle flames blowing into each other. Someone held the phone out, saying, Warren thought, "It's Beth," but as he reached up, Tim took it.

"Dr. Betts!" It was their obstetrician, with the results of the amnio: a healthy, perfect boy.

"I'll call you, and we'll go do something, eh?—a movie?" Drew said, slipping Cecile's coat over her arms, and Warren recognized suddenly how false it all was. His mother might smile now, but he remembered how she'd wept, until he thought she would dissolve. And Drew, asking him to the movies! Drew had only contempt for movies, their empty prettiness, the liberties they take with the truth. It reminded him somehow of Ned Fisk, and the humiliation went through him again like poison.

"A movie," he said. "Great."

When Warren got back to his father's, he took one look at the afternoon's drawings and decided Ned Fisk had been kind. He stuffed them into the trash, but fearing Noreen would see them there, tied up the bag and carried it out to the shed. There, leaning against the wall with the broom, was Emerson's rifle. A household implement, ordinary, reassuring. He kept it with him through the night, and in the morning, as soon as he heard his father in the shower, braced the butt against the mattress and took the barrel in his mouth. He only meant to remind himself there was a sure way out, but the iron tasted of blood, hope, and he felt himself drifting toward death as toward love or sleep, giving himself up to it, letting it have him. A little wan sunlight came in through Noreen's curtains, over the braided rug. There was no beauty, no refuge here. He put his thumb to the trigger, just to see if he could work it: it turned out to be the easiest thing in the world.

. . .

The force of the bullet knocked him back into the corner, so Emerson found his body propped against the bureau. He took him under the arms, thinking to maneuver him toward the bed, but the full weight fell against him and pinned him to the wall. It took all Emerson's strength to push him up onto his feet, and then immediately Warren flopped sideways and Emerson had to struggle fiercely to right him. In the chaos of the moment he thought only how shameful it would be if he let his boy fall, so he stood there swaying under his son's weight, thinking of nothing so much as the dance in the dark auditorium the night Warren was conceived. He had come into the world as the mother's lever, to pry open the father's heart—and failed. Now Emerson felt a well of pity as if he had been not only the stony father but also the pursuing son, and unthinking went to stroke the boy's head and put his hand in the mess of the brain.

"I've got some—sort of bad news," he began. Cecile had answered the phone at Drew's, and hearing her voice Emerson felt suddenly relieved. Men's instincts seem always to lead in the wrong direction, while women are naturally decisive—feeling wells up in them and becomes action before the thoughts and counterthoughts take hold. In the awful times, that stream of feeling can be relied on, to carry a man through.

"No," she said, with such certainty that for a minute Emerson questioned the thing himself. "No, that can't be."

Because what could be *sort of* bad about that? If Warren had shot himself, Emerson would certainly have said *ghastly* or *sickening*, not *sort of bad*. Therefore, Warren was alive. In fact the day before Cecile and Drew had gone into Boston, because Martha had wanted Drew to speak to the psychiatrist with her. She never missed a chance to drag Drew back into the family circle, Cecile thought, skimming the magazines in the waiting room. And they came out of the consulting room arm in arm.

The doctor had shaken Martha's hand, smiling with tender amusement, patting her shoulder. Lost loves, failed ambitions: these are the materials of life! If only he were still young enough to partake of such things. A few weeks for the antidepressant to take effect, and they'd see, it would all turn around.

Therefore, *Warren was alive*! Driving home Drew and Cecile had talked about him as if he was their own son, playing at parenthood, safe together in the overheated car and united by a common purpose—really married, Cecile had felt, as they'd never been before.

"He's so young," Drew said. "This will pass and be forgotten. Martha's a brilliant mother, she won't let those kids go down. She worries too much, that's all."

Cecile bristled—he praised Martha for her motherhood while refusing Cecile her own child.

"They're hardly kids," she said. "Warren's just my age."

He looked startled for a minute—Tim and Warren were still children in his mind's eye, and Cecile, she was his wife, if anything she seemed older than he was. "Apples and oranges," he said.

"He's not a kid who's doing badly in school," Cecile said. "He's a man in despair."

"Despair is probably the central feature of life," Drew said. "Everyone has to struggle with it alone."

"Why?" she asked. "Why can't people struggle with it together?" He was as old as her father, he ought to have answers, a firmament of knowledge against which she could brace herself and build.

"Because that's not the way it works . . . ," he said, irritated. Why didn't she understand even the most basic things?

"But *why* not?" she asked. They drove on in silence until she felt she'd won, and she reached over to stroke his hair: it reminded her how they'd loved each other, before they came to hate each other so.

"Don't you see, Drew, how it would be if we had a baby?" The conversational equivalent of pulling the pin on a grenade, but instead of flashing angry for once he'd looked only sad, and they left the subject, grateful that it hadn't come between them, and talked back and forth about Warren, Cecile imagining a child, lulled by their voices, asleep in the back.

"We could struggle together, you and Warren and me," she'd said. But all the time they were talking, and earlier, while they sat with Dr. Schiffenhaus, while he explained it with such patience and optimism . . . Warren had been dead all that time.

They found Martha in the eye of it, unearthly peaceful, greeting the dumbfounded visitors who climbed the narrow stairway to her apartment with a kind of devastated élan.

"Cecile," she said, with great emphasis and open arms, embracing her as a sister. She was small, plump, and cozy-looking—pretty, one might have said—but now a fierce beauty had come over her. All the trouble we go to, Cecile thought, to keep from looking death in the eye—so the first true sight of it, the leviathan bursting up through the old imaginings, is almost an exhilaration. She felt something like envy toward Martha, who was standing so close. To be childless was to spend one's life jostling and peering over people's shoulders for a glimpse of the essential things.

When Drew came in, though, she saw an awful hope rise and burst in Martha's eyes: no, Warren wasn't with him, and her face collapsed, and she became an old woman.

"Drew," she said, "Drew, he. . . ." Her arms went around Drew's neck and she hung there, though he held her without conviction.

Cecile stood behind her, trying to gesture to him, mouthing *tighter*, but he never really saw the point in an embrace.

"Did he . . . did he *say* anything, to you, Drew?" Martha asked. Cecile sat down—she couldn't bear to hear the answer—and found herself beside Emerson.

"I, I'm so sorry . . . ," she began—how on earth could one encompass this? It seemed that even to mention it would harm them. And the words that sprang to her mind were not condolence but reproach. They were his parents—they ought to have saved him.

"It's done," Emerson said, waving the thing away, his jaw set, eyes focused straight ahead.

Martha was still holding tight to Drew, saying, "I didn't think . . ."; "I didn't believe . . ." The door downstairs banged and there were more voices and steps on the stairs. Nathan Polchikov, proprietor of L'Hermitage Café down the street, came in carrying a platter of tarts heaped with raspberries, and gave a slight bow as if it was his privilege to be among them.

"I came the minute I heard," he said. "It's like I have a sixth sense. Just today I thought—as I was walking down this street—I had the feeling . . . My father killed himself, you know."

Martha sat him on the couch and listened carefully, with a pride Cecile understood—it was a gift, this womanly endurance; to bend toward someone else with a tender expression, when your own son was . . . was . . .

"Dress shirts. Dress shirts my father made," Polchikov said, shaking his head slowly and looking past Martha as if his father stood behind her. "It's one thing to get the phone call, another to really see . . . ," he continued, ". . . as I did . . ."

"I told him to give the gun away, throw it off the wharf . . . ," Tim said when his father left the room. "He *knew* how Warren was." To hear him speak, you'd think Warren was a five-year-old who'd broken something Emerson left on a low shelf. There was always a shrug in Tim's voice, when they talked about Emerson's disappearance or Drew's leaving the family for Cecile. These things happen, one has to take them lightly. But the effort had seemed to bleed him pale.

"To kill yourself," Emerson said, returning. "It's not in my lexicon." To give away the gun, in the belief his son wanted to die? No. He went home to Noreen—the paramedics had given her a shot so she could sleep, while downstairs the neighbors pulled up the blood-soaked rug and steamed off the wallpaper. Warren had left no note.

"It seems like his wedding," Drew said. Last spring they'd been here for Tim's wedding, and his wife, Fiona, had aimed her bouquet straight at Beth: they'd wanted her with them—she could keep Warren afloat. Though some old dragon had said, "Her? Marry Martha Rookery's crazy son? I think she has more sense than that." And looked straight at Cecile as if to drive it home to her, just how senseless a marriage could be.

Which had been right, Cecile thought—her marriage was clearly a mistake. She'd come to Spinnaker, found this man sitting at the head of the table, and thought, "Why shouldn't *I* have a father like this?" It was hardly unusual—twenty-year-old women are out shopping for fathers this way all the time. His face was sharp, his eyes narrow as if scanning the horizon, relentlessly searching. So, he was like her; they were kin. He'd been reading *Doctor Faustus*, had scowled when Warren asked if she liked science fiction. The vehemence frightened and seduced her: she wanted philosophy thrust into her, and hard—in this way she would prevail over him, draw him away from this table, into her bed. Now here she was, married, alone. Drew loved her, but what did that matter? He was more austere every day, intent on his work, on proving out his life's ambition, so that distractions enraged him, and fatherhood would, he was sure, be his death.

And it would be her fault, it already was. She was all earthly appetites, the things he'd intended to renounce made real. Every time he put his hand out, she yanked him further away from his ideals. She tugged at her hem, which was far too short: she had good legs, she was praying some man would follow them up to her heart and save her.

A sturdy blond woman—one of the neighbors who'd gone over to help with the cleaning—planted herself in front of Martha as soon as she hung up, saying in a careful teacher's voice: "Now, there's always a time when the spirit hovers, before it's really gone." She closed her eyes and swayed, transformed from pedant to mystic. "He's over us now, he can hear us, *now is the time* to speak to him and be heard." Drew looked up at her with something between incredulity and revulsion, but Polchikov was listening, and Martha's gaze snapped around, betrayed her: she was waiting for Warren—she knew he wouldn't leave her without a word this way.

"It was a family decision," Tim said. "It seemed to make sense. He hates the hospital, he said he couldn't bear it—I mean this guy Schiffenhaus never knew Warren—he met him once and he wanted to lock him up. . . ."

"It was school, I think, that weighed on him," Cecile said, meaning: *It's not your fault.* As she blamed them absolutely she had to say this again and again. After all they'd loved him, meant no harm. Drew who hated driving, took him up to the hospital, talking all the time about how shameful it was to need professional assistance with life, while Cecile reasoned she'd be tampering in their relationship if she interrupted. Emerson left the gun in plain sight because he couldn't bear to acknowledge the risk. Martha let Warren decide whether to go to the hospital: he was a grown man; she was a civil libertarian . . .

Cecile might have walked home with him that first night, years ago, might have taken him to herself, instead of taking Drew, the best he had for a father, away. After all, they were the same generation, they had a whole world in common—a world she'd turned up her nose at when she married Drew. At the birthday dinner she'd told herself she'd call Warren and invite him for the walk she owed him— even try to act the father in Drew's stead. But what with the history of walks in that family it was bound to be taken wrong, or this was how she'd put it to herself, deciding to keep away.

Drew was going through the canvases, stacked against the wall. "I had no idea," he said, looking closely at one with veils of scarlet and chartreuse cascading over each other like layers of a waterfall. "If I'd known he was so talented, I'd have been able to talk to him."

"You might have looked, if you wanted to know," she said, too quietly, she hoped, to be heard.

"Where will we have the funeral, where can we fit them all?" Martha was asking.

"This is nothing," Polchikov reassured her. "My father, everyone loved him—he wasn't just . . ." He caught himself, but the message was clear enough. To lose a father is the worst thing—you discover in an instant that there's no ground beneath you, never was. To lose a crazy son . . . The drop of scorn in his voice woke Cecile up, she despised him for a moment. Here he was, this little man with a beret over his bald spot, coming here in the guise of sympathy when all he wanted was comfort. But Martha looked at him more kindly than ever—guessing, probably, that she'd soon be in his position, knocking on strange doors and offering sweets in hope of finding someone whose grief could match her own.

Cecile had wolfed down a tart on the sly—she was famished, greedy for food and love and beauty—everyone else seemed to have better management of self. In fact the rest of the tarts were untouched, and she wondered if she dared have another. The younger people, Tim and Fiona and some of Warren's friends who'd just gotten in from New York, were hugging each other, laughing and crying, talking with an earnest intensity she never felt anymore, while Polchikov held out the terrible crystal of his life for Martha's contemplation and Drew quizzed the pedant-mystic who had helped clean the room.

"He didn't suffer," she said, taking his hand in both of hers. "He just set his spirit free."

Drew gave her a look of boiling contempt. "What did his body look like, after he set his spirit free?" he asked.

Her gaze dropped. "Well, if you're just *curious*—"

"Call it that," he said, chin jutting, challenging her. He was always determined to batter through to some hard truth, until he seemed like a man hammering at a peach to get the stone. Cecile felt her eyes closing and caught herself just as she fell asleep, and Martha touched Drew's arm:

"Take her home, sweetie, look how tired she is. Tim's here, and Fiona . . . Which reminds me, when are *you* two going to have a baby?" She looked happy all of a sudden, flashing a conspiratorial glance at Cecile—they were women together; they overruled, enlivened the men. Drew looked cornered, likely to strike, but she paid no attention. Circumstance had given her license to say what she pleased.

"You'd be a wonderful father," she said. "The boys got so much from you—they *did*, Drew. And we *need* children in this family . . . *especially* now."

This family? Had Drew, leaving his position as Martha's lover, taken on the role of her son—since there was a vacancy at the moment?

"She's *not* going to be my baby's grandmother," Cecile told him as soon as they were back outside.

"It's too early to leave," he said.

"It's two A.M.!" Snow blanketed the narrow street so the town looked as it must have a hundred years ago: proud and lonely, face to the sea. Down by the dark church a gray figure stopped still under a streetlight, waiting for a skunk to nose across the road.

"Which is when things really happen," Drew said, pointing up to Martha's window, where the candleflame belled in a brandy glass, and three figures swayed in an embrace.

"Drew, it's a wake, not a party," she said. "And Martha is not your mother. Tim is your stepson, not your friend. They need a father, those kids," she said, remembering suddenly not to use the plural, ". . . not a drinking companion." In fact, she needed a father herself—or two, really, one for herself and one for her child.

"I could strangle you," he said, between his teeth—and she thought how, years ago, seeing her slip her dress off over her head, he'd said ". . . like vellum," with awe. Smooth and white, ready to have a history scrawled over—she had loved to see herself that way—an erotic angel who could magically erase decades of a man's life and earn herself a soft bed thereby. With this image she, who had wanted the most tender and encompassing love, had distracted herself, as he bent her over the back of the sofa, to have her—the first time—from behind.

"Another death, then, for you," she said now, in the hard voice of the woman she'd become. To think, she was asking him to father another child.

The day of the funeral. The gathering afterward would be at Drew and Cecile's, Martha's place being too small and Emerson's too macabre. In the mirror Cecile saw her black dress was all wrong—even in the shop she'd known she'd have nowhere to wear it, but seeing herself in the mirror had imagined herself happy with a man who loved her, so couldn't resist buying it. She tied a dull scarf at the neck, listening to Tim, who was dressing in the next room with Warren's friends, as they chided each other over their clothing—who had the proper stuff for a funeral at this age?

"Yeah, Eli," Tim said. "When was the last time you put on a matched pair of socks anyway?"

"Your wedding, bub," Eli replied. Cecile had danced with him there—his shirt had come untucked, his tie askew, his hair sprang comically off his head, and he'd clutched at her waist, holding on for dear life. "You dance divinely!" she'd said, and he spun her out and they crashed back together and bumped their heads, laughed, tried again. Then, of course, she'd had to sit back down with the grown-ups, who were still talking about Vietnam.

"The way people *danced* then," Drew was saying. "The sexual frenzy!" Cecile and Warren and Tim had been children, of course, with only the barest understanding. Now Cecile took a pair of Drew's socks across the hall to Eli and found him bent double as over a wound, with Tim kneeling at his side. They didn't see her, and she slipped down the stairs as he started to cry in great retching masculine sobs.

Drew grinned, a dizzying anomaly, and went for the liquor cabinet.

"Hair of the dog that bit him," he said.

"He's not hung over, he's crying," she said. "It's a funeral. A funeral. Someone has died. Your son."

"He wasn't my son," he said. "They were never mine. It wasn't like that. You weren't there." He looked surprised, as if he'd just remembered. It was true, of course—she'd been home with her own parents, those waifs lost in the phantasmagoria of the seventies. When she saw Drew she'd wanted him just because he *was* solitary, harsh. She'd chosen her husband the way men choose their mountains; now she was tired and cold and the air was too thin to breathe.

"He was someone who needed you," she said, wondering if she

was arguing for Warren or herself, and thinking that now it was Drew who needed her. "I'm sorry," she said. "It's a hard time, that's all."

"But you're right," he said, stern. "You're quite right." And looked straight into her eyes. "I failed him, as I would fail a child of yours."

Her eyes filled, but where she would cry, Drew seemed to parch, until a fissure split him down the center. Marrying him, she had contracted to do his weeping for him: she might weep all the rest of her years.

On the way to the church he drove slower and slower as if he hoped they would never arrive. She tried to think of summer light on the water, the dusky seaweed gardens and the green shallows paling with the tide. Now the bay looked hard as steel, too bright—the air had that frozen clarity; she could see the morning shadows across the dunes in Wellfleet fifteen miles away. It was high tide, and waves slapped against the seawall, spraying the pallbearers as they carried the coffin in.

"The black hearse, come for Warren," Drew said with cold dread. Yes, it was real. Cecile set a hand on his arm but he pulled back— Martha would see them. Ten years now and he was still guilty, still protecting them from her. Father a child now, when Martha had lost one of hers? Never—it wouldn't be fair.

But Martha must have realized this, that was why she'd brought it up last night. She'd been giving them her blessing.

The hearse driver, standing at military ease at the curb, glanced quickly over at Cecile—it was Wizz Mancini, dope dealer and sometime taxidermist whose moonlight job at the funeral home had been the source of some hilarity. He smiled at her with sorrowful tenderness now, not a spark of the usual lechery—in his suit, with his long, thinning hair carefully braided, he seemed entirely dignified and respectful, someone who'd seen enough of death that he could meet it on natural terms.

Inside, Drew stood for a moment with Emerson—they looked alike, weathered to silver like thousand-year-old olive trees.

"Woe betide," Drew said after a while, and Emerson nodded, and another long silence was broken by Emerson's asking Drew what he thought about the Serbo-Croatian situation. Cecile's interest fell away, and when she listened again Drew was describing a story he'd read, about a father and son blown off course during an afternoon sail. "Finally they're standing on a rock, while the tide rises—he puts the boy up on his shoulders . . . there's nothing else he can do."

Unbearable, to be responsible for another life. They looked off past each other, and Cecile imagined taking them into herself, healing them. The feminine fallacy, that sense that a man might complete himself, cure himself, by sacred immersion in her. Had she learned nothing, seeing that for all her warmth Drew had never thawed? In fact the kindest thing she could do for him might be to spare him from becoming a father.

Warren was dead, they could have their way with him, assigning him this or that role in their stories, each one using him as he or she liked. The church was full, everyone in town had come, humbled, washed through by it all. Last week they'd gone back and forth on their errands, never quite sure whether it was all right to be reading on the sofa when the dust was thick underneath, whether the baby ought to be comforted or left to cry . . . whether to send Warren to the hospital though he said he'd rather die. Last week their opinions had been quite definite: some acts were despicable, some could be forgiven. Now there was nothing to do but stand here and bear this together—and everything else fell into shadow—they remembered how little they knew. Bill Friedrich, whom Drew had punched in the jaw years ago when he made some crack about Martha, came in and pulled Drew into his arms.

"Depression killed him," he said, "same as cancer, or stroke."

"Let the family through, please," said Polchikov, having assumed the role of usher, and set a hand on Cecile's shoulder, guiding her down the aisle toward the second pew.

"We're not family," Drew said, but Cecile had seen Tim standing up front all alone.

"Actually we are family," she said, suffering Drew's murderous glance and feeling for him. He'd been so resolute in solitude, fathering no children, keeping even his lovers at arm's length, and still he found himself enmeshed, every flinch and shrug pulling at the human web . . .

"Because Tim *needs* you," she answered the unspoken question.

"Needs . . . ," he said—was there no end to the modern bathos? Martha was just behind them, the organ had begun. He was caught; he sat down, and Polchikov edged in beside him. "Of course, my father's coffin was draped in the flag," Polchikov said as Martha ascended the altar with her eulogy.

She might have been addressing Warren's commencement. He was "a hunter, fisherman, artist, an individualist who preferred bear meat to steak, who knew his way in the wilderness . . ."

. . . and only lost it, Cecile thought, among men. Martha ought to write for *GQ*, she thought—could she not say one true thing?

"It was Warren's life, and he lived it, and ended it, as *he* chose," she went on, so Cecile wanted to jump up and object. Though she supposed a mother might be forgiven for suffering a failure of honesty while eulogizing her son. She'd have liked to blame Martha, despise her, and forget her—and forget Warren's death from despair.

Tim went to the altar—to say how he'd looked up to his younger brother—and Cecile started to cry. That was the absurd truth of it: Tim who was steady and capable, a lawyer with a marriage and soon a child, had admired Warren, who fumbled through in terror, collecting women and unemployment, taking on the glamour that always fills a vacuum. Yes, we die after long lives during which the brave admire the fearful and the strong envy the weak! Amazing, when she thought of it, all the hours and days one spends *without* weeping, considering that none of us really knows the other, mothers are blind to their own children, eulogies sound like press releases and . . . Polchikov gave her a Kleenex; she blew her wretched nose.

Martha, who had turned around to face the congregation, glanced back with fond sympathy at the sight of Cecile weeping openly for her son.

Anyone who wished might speak. "I'm . . . I *was* Warren's girlfriend," a girl in a leopard-print coat said, and another jumped up and fled out the back door. Beth sat across the aisle, holding an old lumpy jacket around herself as if she was freezing. Every few minutes she'd sigh and her face would go more numbly haunted as she stared intensely at the floor. A man in a tweed coat stood up and read from a typed sheet: "I'm Ned Fisk, a professor of Warren's, and I speak for all of us at Ramsey when I say what a promising artist we've lost. His work was *juicy*, you could really *feel* its effect, and at the same time it had an intelligence, a . . . *walking interiority* that we at Ramsey are always searching for and *very* rarely find." A bubble in Cecile's throat broke from giggle to sob—no wonder Warren had fled. But Martha crossed the aisle and took Fisk in her arms.

"I'm not as eloquent as the professor," the next man said, "but I've done some hunting in the north country and I can tell you that I have only respect for a man who can bring the mighty bruin down. . . ."

They were, all of them, reminded of the shape of their own lives. Everyone spoke from his own grief or pride, Polchikov telling about his father, and Nita Schorb whose son had bullied Warren all through school and was in the county House of Corrections now, describing the deep bond she and Martha would always share. "There are *so many* ways to lose a child . . . ," she said.

"I'm an artist myself," someone else was saying, "and even though I've been much more successful . . . acclaimed . . . than Warren, I . . ." Cecile wanted to jump up and shriek at them, that they were supposed to be talking about Warren, raising him as a real, whole man one last time. But it was too late, he would live only as an actor in other people's dramas now. If she'd walked home with him, kissed him instead of Drew . . . but who could know?

A man in the back pew stood and laced his fingers under his gut. "I never had the pleasure of meeting Warren," he began. Cecile sank into her seat. "But he sounds very courageous, and his exploits seem to have meant a lot to his family and friends. Maybe he suffered something out for all of them . . . us . . . He looked straight at something the rest of us turned away from. . . ."

Wizz stood and motioned to the reverend for the benediction. The pallbearers came silently up the aisle. The ground was frozen; Warren would have to go into the vault.

The rest of them crowded into Drew and Cecile's little house. They'd taken the paintings down: the storm at sea, the glimpse along the grass alley were replaced with Warren's wild sweeps of color. It was as if they'd turned inward from the narrow windows they were used to peeping out of and realized they'd had their backs to a great vista all this time. The room was full as a rush hour subway so they had to brush against each other, absorb each other's warmth, and Cecile felt herself passed embrace by embrace through the crowd, hardly knowing whether they held each other for consolation or only because death had given them license.

Whatever, she accepted it—she wanted to take every man and

woman in her arms, feel them, smell them, kiss their mouths, make love to them . . . they were alive, all of them, and each with his own allure, the vision that arises from a glimpse . . . the woman whose fat braid fell against a heavy sweater, who no doubt had a soup simmering on her woodstove at home; the two ancient bohemians with their Gauloises; the kids, as Drew called them: Tim and Fiona and the others Cecile's age, looking pale, sweet, and yes, so much younger than she.

Warren's friend Eli appeared, wearing Drew's socks and carrying a white lily.

"It's beautiful, Eli, thank you!" Cecile said, going to kiss him.

He drew back. "It's . . . it's for Martha."

Of course. Still, she was stung, and imagined suddenly that Warren had taken pleasure in the thought of these people scraping his brain out of the dresser drawers—he'd left no note because he wanted them to reckon with his flesh finally, with no veil of glamour, of language, between them. Well, she would take up his cause now, hate them in his stead.

"I'll put it in water," she said, but the stem was too long, and when she went to cut it the knife glanced off and sliced her finger. Blood spattered over the lily, dripped through the fist she held the finger tight in—she couldn't bear to look.

"What an idiot!" she said, laughing anxiously, looking across the room for Drew. Who returned her gaze with what she could only feel was hatred. To *bleed*, now, here? And then to laugh? He turned back to the woman he'd been talking to, lecturing her with angry animation while Eli led Cecile through to the bathroom, keeping her hand in the air. As they passed Drew, she heard him say something about Thomas Hardy, loudly, as if he was talking over a rude distraction. Better to have married a fat man, she thought, who would try to stuff the inner void with cream puffs, than this one, who took only bread, water and knowledge in order to remain above the ordinary longings of men.

"Thank God you're a doctor," she said as Eli taped the wound.

"It's research," he said. "I never actually touch a human being." In the mirror behind him she saw herself smile joyfully because he was touching her, and looked away ashamed.

"Go, give Martha her lily," she said. "I'm fine."

A thin gray man came in and tapped her shoulder with timid urgency, like a child tugging at its mother's dress. His wine, had she seen it? He'd brought a whole case. . . .

"Maybe someone put it in the basement," she said, and seeing he needed company descended the stairs with him, imagining for some reason that he'd embrace her there. Warren had shattered the boundaries, anything was possible—but the man sank on the bottom step with his head in his hands.

"A whole case," he said, nearly crying. "Where can it be?" They were face-to-face with a painting of Warren's—a leering face with slashes of red and blue—that they'd decided not to hang, and behind it, the peaches Cecile had put up last summer. An advertisement, to say *"Here, I am fruitful."* And stored them in the dark here so as not to show off.

"I lost a son myself," he said, so lightly she took it first for aimless conversation; then she remembered it from the paper: he'd fallen from a highway overpass. Fallen or jumped, they couldn't be sure.

"When was that?" she asked, to pretend she hadn't known.

"1961," he said, which would in fact have been the year the boy was born. It was true, she thought, some people *are* lost from the start. What to say? It reminded her of the time she met the author Haldor Laxness: he knew so much, had thought so deeply and lived so long, she hadn't really believed he'd be able to see something so small as herself. Grief might have the same effect as wisdom: this man lived in another country, a place she didn't know.

"Where can it be?" he asked, peering into the darkness with anger and disappointment as if this were only the latest of the series of thefts and losses that made up his life.

"Who brought it in?" she asked.

"Oh, my God, of course," he said, and ran up the stairs two at a time. "I left it in the car."

Coming up behind him she could hear that the party had passed some milestone and abandoned restraint. Polchikov had claimed the sturdiest chair and was attacking an immense plate on which a filet of smoked mackerel trembled atop a molded salad. Behind him two men were discussing the largest of Warren's paintings, wherein several bright buoyant shapes bobbed in a thick atmosphere.

"You can see," one man said, "there's a breast, an ass, and these are like two legs spread wa-a-ay out over everything."

"It's a terrific piece," the other said.

"If I'd *known* he could paint this way . . . ," Drew was saying, and Cecile remembered she'd discouraged him from going to see Warren in Maine. He might have seen the paintings then, might have gotten closer to Warren, but she'd wanted to wrest him free of the other family.

Someone fitted candles into wine bottles and lit them; afternoon darkness was closing, and Martha sat on the couch, mistily drunken, while the timid man rubbed her feet.

"He's here," Martha said as Cecile filled her glass again, and leaned back with a drowsy, beatified smile. "Everyone feels it. They want to stay here, with Warren." She gazed at Cecile fondly, a mother opening her heart to the new daughter-in-law.

"You loved him, too," she said. "I know. I could see." Cecile shifted uncomfortably. "And he's here, Cecile, he'll always be here with us now."

"Drew, these people have to go," she said, as soon as she could get him alone. "They've been here since noon."

He looked at her with amazed contempt. *That's right*, she thought, *I'm a shrew. Mean and hungry, all teeth. I don't care.*

"I want to go to bed," she pleaded.

"Then *go to bed.*"

"Eli's asleep there."

"Eli?"

"Warren's friend."

A vague consternation crossed his face until he placed Eli—among the kids.

"Push him over," he said, and turned away.

There was a soup bowl of cigarette butts on the bedside table. Cecile took it into the hallway, but the stink would last for days. Eli was sound asleep, his hair a mass of dark, contrary waves. She pushed a pile of coats onto the floor, turned down the quilt, and got in.

Sometime later she awoke in his embrace. He seemed asleep still, but his arm was around her, pulling her tight against him. The room was pitch-black, and she could hear Jethro Tull playing downstairs—songs she'd used to get stoned to when she was fourteen and mad to smash her way into the gorgeous, terrifying world. It would have been the same for Warren—the same music, same rolling paper, same sense that all want would be fulfilled in ecstasy now they were grown. She took Eli's hand, and an immense warmth came over—every cell changed so she was entirely soft, a thing in nature like an anemone pulsing in the tide. It occurred to her that she didn't know him, but of course they must have the essential things—despair and longing—in common. It seemed he could carry her back, accept her as a prodigal sister returned, finally, to her own generation; the generation Drew and Martha and their ilk had wronged. She lifted Eli's hand to her mouth and kissed his palm, and he turned her toward him as if a long and careful courtship had reached its culmination.

Pushing his curls back, she saw his features were so strong they were almost frightening. His mouth curved as if sculpted and without the glasses his eyes seemed immense and raw, open as if he wanted her to fall in. She tried to return the gaze in its intensity, but it overwhelmed her and she closed her eyes to kiss him, finding the image of Warren in the dark of her mind.

A few minutes later they heard steps on the staircase and by silent agreement feigned sleep again. Tim came in and shook Eli.

"Come on, old buddy, we've got to give these good people their bed," he said. Cecile lay waiting for him to go so she could lose herself in the kiss again, but Eli jumped up as if he was relieved.

"How long was I asleep?" he asked, and Tim said it had been hours. Cecile watched through half-closed eyes as they left, Eli looking quickly back at her. She'd frightened him, as she had others—her boundaries would dissolve suddenly so she spilled over, out of her life, her marriage. . . . She wasn't properly civilized; she frightened herself, too. Had she really dreamt she might have a love of innocent discovery, with a man her own age? When Drew finally came to bed, she made love to him in an anguish of longing, thinking how alike they were, wraiths who hardly knew a wake from a wedding, vandals poking their fingers through the membrane that contained them into the cold dark outside. She locked her legs around him to push him farther inside her; bit his shoulder to urge his thrust—if death was real, if it might really arrive any minute, then the old agreements were void: ambition must be deeper and she would need more love—much more.

Afterward he lay with his ear to her heart, and she stroked his hair—she'd found the stream of affection again. "It was because you were laughing," he said. "I didn't think you could really be hurt, when you were laughing so."

"I know," she said gently, thinking he'd seen her with Eli and been too proud to intervene. And generous: he'd been waiting all this time for someone to come for her, someone in whom the life force had yet to be overwhelmed by doubt, someone her own age. He was stoic, prepared to let her go, if unwilling to attach himself very deeply to someone he knew he'd lose.

"We have to have a child," she said. "You know that."

"I do." He closed his eyes, waiting, she thought, to feel it crush him.

The timid man, the one whose son had jumped or fallen, was named Duncan LaShay, and he and Martha were getting married.

"Very small," Martha said, "just the family, but after all that's what you are, my dear." And touched Cecile's belly, smiling. Her pictures of Tim's new son were laid out on the table.

"*Two* new babies! An embarrassment of riches," Martha said. In the months after the funeral she'd often call Drew at exactly five A.M., so they'd know she'd been up for hours and hadn't wanted to wake them. Drew would sit up to listen, and Cecile would drape the quilt over his shoulders, hearing him repeat, "We don't, we won't know," almost by rote. Then came spring, the red buds swelled and burst, and one evening they'd passed her on the street with Duncan, talking so intently she didn't see them. Life had pushed up through grief and was stubbornly blooming. In August came Tim's son, and Martha went down to help Fiona: task by task, she undertook, she went forward.

"What a darling," Cecile said, of the infant in the pictures, who looked but exactly like Warren. No one else seemed to notice, or perhaps they didn't say. One didn't speak the name *Warren* aloud anymore: it was like opening an airplane door midflight—all the air got sucked out of the room. Still, they'd all known him, and this made them like each other more. And his painting, that the men at the funeral party had understood as the parts of a woman, hung over the couch now, the flower of bliss, her own.

"Yup, it's a baby all right," Emerson said, passing through. He was building Drew and Cecile's addition: the nursery/playroom. He'd quit work and spent the months after the funeral transforming the room Warren died in—it was all cherry paneled now, with acanthus and laurel boughs carved over the lintels and at the side of the man-telpiece a hinged wall, which gave onto a maze of compartments which led finally to a sort of altar behind the chimney. Word got out, and people began coming to see it; then they wanted bureaus and bedsteads and sometimes a whole room in "Rookery paneling," as it came to be called. Other bereaved parents had come to the door, asking to stand a minute in the quiet dark there. Was it meant as a shrine? An act of contrition? Or forgetting? Emerson said it was hap-penstance: a wild idea he'd gotten one night. When Cecile saw it, she found herself in tears: Emerson had worked until he made something beautiful out of the bloody room.

It made her love him . . . but then she loved everyone these days. Who'd have guessed it after all the talk, but having a baby had turned out to be a simple, carnal thing, and estrogen was a euphoric—since her third month she'd been blissed-out, slow and fat and pliant like one of those life-size inflatable sex dolls that flop woozily into any position. Sex being the only way Drew really knew how to absorb warmth, it made him love her more. Yes, it had been a mistake to marry him, but what marriage is not in some way mistaken, after all?

". . . 'nother goddamned rugrat nose to wipe," Emerson grumbled, grinning—a nod to cynicism, purely ceremonial.

"Oh, Emerson, honestly," Martha said, hand on Duncan's knee, and to Cecile: "Have you felt it move?" Cecile laughed and told them it felt like a badminton birdie going back and forth in there, though languid, "like a match between Oscar Wilde and James McNeill Whistler," she said. They laughed and Cecile considered her own cleverness, leaning in the crook of her husband's arm, one hand stroking the arc of her belly. The world seemed safer lately; the child was a new center of gravity, pulling everything into order around it, so she seemed to know, suddenly, what was essential, what to let fall away.

"It must be a girl," Drew said.

"I always wanted a girl," Martha said, ". . . to dress up, I'm afraid."

"Well, and never mind fashion," Cecile said. "They walk sooner, talk sooner, they understand life *a couple decades* before boys do! No, with a boy you're just lucky if it doesn't slam itself into a bridge abutment or shoot itself in the goddamned head!"

There it was, the appalling jack-in-the-box, springing out with no warning, and from Cecile's own mouth. Only one beat though before Martha's light laughter washed over them. "Look," she said gently, "it's snowing."

"We'd better get on," Duncan said, standing up, going to embrace Cecile while Martha congratulated Drew one more time. "How lucky, lucky for all of us, to be expecting a new life!" she said. "Now your little one will be playing with Tim's—maybe we should have Christmas Eve together next year."

"I'd love that," Cecile said, with her whole heart. Her child would need its tribe.

"Every foot goes in the mouth occasionally," Drew said to comfort her, when everyone had gone.

"Not all the way down the gullet like that."

"I doubt they even noticed," he assured her. She smiled: she knew they'd tell themselves they hadn't. They were bound and determined to like her.

"It's like the Red Sox," Drew said. "Why lose by a point when you can blow the whole season?"

They laughed, together. It was like their beginning, when she felt she'd found a man as fierce as she was, as curious, as likely to go wrong. After that, one act of her will, her calculation, or her hubris, had followed another—the wedding, the house, now the child. And if the first task of the child must be to seduce the father . . . well, perhaps a child of hers might succeed? Nothing was true, nothing whole, her deep sense of well-being now was no more credible than Warren's despair. But she felt it, she had no choice but to trust it. Dusk belled over them, a luxuriant purple, full of snow, and she went to the supermarket for a pot roast, in case the power went out . . . or rather, in case they wanted to bask in the comfort of their life, light a fire, stir the pot, make love with their child, their future, between them.

Everyone in Spinnaker seemed to have a similar vision: the one main street was crowded with cars, the snow falling over them like ticker tape on a parade, the physical manifestation of the abundance, the accidental grace of their lives. Polchikov waved Cecile in ahead of him, and "Natural Woman" came on WRLS, "Radio Lost at Sea," Spinnaker's only station. As the procession wound up through the cemetery toward the supermarket, Cecile saw blue lights flashing: Officer Manny had pulled over the hearse.

"Speeding, speeding in the hearse, I am shocked!" she said when Wizz got in the express line behind her.

" 'Natural Woman' came on," he said, and threw up his hands.

"You've got a radio in there?"

"My God, honey, I drive to the crematorium in Providence two and three times a month! Sometimes I have to pick up a stiff in Tewksbury, in Wrentham . . . What am I going to do without a radio?"

"I, I just never thought of it," she said.

"Well darlin', there's a lot people never think of, about driving a hearse," Wizz said. "Speaking of which, you know that guy who collapsed on the dance floor at Piggy's last week?"

Now everyone—the immensely fat man in front of her with a package of chocolate eclairs, the mother with an infant in a yellow snowsuit, which Cecile in her impatience had considered kidnapping—turned to listen. Here it was unbidden, in the grocery line—the sense of belonging to something if only to an odd, lonely town boarded up for the winter against the cold wind off the sea. Spinnaker wasn't much different now, Cecile thought, than in 1850: they were terribly alone here together, with only each other for comfort and a vast dark beyond.

"Well, you know they got his pants off and found he had a pepperoni strapped to his leg—for a codpiece—"

"Wizz!" Cecile said.

"I prefer a salami," the fat man said, and he laughed, and the woman with the baby laughed, and Cecile and Wizz laughed—together, brimming with the tender condescension the living so often feel, during the time of their great, brief, victory over the dead.

ACKNOWLEDGMENTS

I would like to thank Sarah Blake, Margaret Carroll, Christopher Hewat, Roxana Lehmann-Haupt, A. Thomas Lindsay, Maureen McCoy, Daniel Mueller, Camille Paglia, William S. Pollack, Candice Reffe, and especially my husband, Roger Skillings—colleagues whose thoughts and visions have added so much to this book, friends who have inspired, encouraged, and sustained me.

Jennifer Carlson's intelligence and advocacy have meant the world to me, especially in her finding the wonderful Reagan Arthur as my editor. And my abiding thanks to the Fine Arts Work Center in Provincetown, fertile ground for so many writers over the years.